Praise for

I'll Get Back to You

"Full of humor and tenderness, *I'll Get Back to You* inspires
readers to embrace the surprises life tosses our way. A cozy, sexy
romance."　　　　　　　　—Ashley Herring Blake, author of
Delilah Green Doesn't Care

"A festive and poignant romance about new adulthood, growing
pains in friendships, and embracing your hometown. You'll be
drawn in by the clever fake dating scheme, but Murphy's mean-
ingful journey of finding herself in her early twenties is the real
star. *I'll Get Back to You* is the Thanksgiving romance I've been
waiting for."　　　　　—Susie Dumond, author of *Queerly Beloved*

"With compassion and heart, Grischow masterfully touches on
the growing pains and self-discovery associated with those early
years of adulthood."　　　　　　—Iman Hariri-Kia, author of
A Hundred Other Girls

PENGUIN BOOKS

I'LL GET BACK TO YOU

Becca Grischow is a Chicago-based content creator, gossip, and ghostwriter for celebrity memoirs. She grew up in Geneva, Illinois, and the middle school rumors about her bisexuality were absolutely true. You can find her at your local coffee shop or sharing writing advice on TikTok and Instagram @BeeGriz.

I'll Get
Back to You

BECCA GRISCHOW

PENGUIN BOOKS

PENGUIN BOOKS
An imprint of Penguin Random House LLC
penguinrandomhouse.com

LIBRARY OF CONGRESS CATALOGING-IN-PUBLICATION DATA

Names: Grischow, Becca, author.
Title: I'll get back to you / Becca Grischow.
Description: [New York] : Penguin Books, 2024. | Identifiers: LCCN 2024011742 |
ISBN 9780143138419 (trade paperback) | ISBN 9780593512470 (ebook)
Subjects: LCGFT: Romance fiction. | Queer fiction. | Novels.
Classification: LCC PS3607.R5688 I45 2024 | DDC 813/.6—dc23/eng/20240322
LC record available at https://lccn.loc.gov/2024011742

Printed in the United States of America
1st Printing

Set in Tibere OT
Designed by *Christina Nguyen*

This one is for the people who raised me up—
Mom and Dad, but also Molly, Liz, Meaghan, and Connor.
And, of course, for the gays of Geneva High School.

I'll Get
Back to You

one

❄

The World Series of binge drinking."

That's how Kat first described tonight, like a cultural event we'd be stupid to miss. Blackout Wednesday, she insisted, wasn't just any night out; it was a tradition, a legacy, a rite of passage we were practically obligated to undergo. In fairness, no one has ever accused her of being *under*dramatic.

This was months ago, back before she packed up and transferred to the University of Illinois, leaving me behind for a surprise fifth semester at Weymouth Community College. We were crouched on her bedroom floor, shoving a semester's worth of going-out tops into too few suitcases and talking about our upcoming birthdays, the first in a decade we'd be celebrating apart. Not just any birthday, either—*the* birthday. Kat's twenty-first was just days before mine. I could drive down to visit her in Champaign-Urbana, or Kat could make a trip back for a weekend . . . or what about waiting until she was home on break? What about Blackout Wednesday?

Kat's eyes lit up as she described the drunken high school reunion hosted on Thanksgiving Eve in hometown bars nationwide. She painted the night with a sheen of sticky nostalgia— what better way to celebrate the retirement of our fake IDs than over two of our favorite hobbies: drinking and judging former classmates? Thus, the plan for Murphy and Kat's 21st Birthday Blowout was born: we'd meet at my house, walk to the bar, drink like it's the end of the world, and head back home to inhale Oreos and watch trash TV till we both konked out on my parents' air mattress, then head over to her parents' for Thanksgiving the next day. If you subtract the bar and the holiday, it's roughly how she and I have spent every weekend for the last ten years. My parents didn't *love* my pitch to hang back from our annual Thanksgiving Florida trip, but when I reminded Mom and Dad that I'd spent my actual twenty-first drinking a single Heineken and watching *Wheel of Fortune* with the two of them, they gave in.

Now, the night in question has arrived, and this usually divey bar is dressed for the occasion. A section of the sticky, beer-soaked floor has been designated for dancing, and the low ceilings are draped with Christmas lights that cast a red and green glow on the faces of townies and Geneva High School grads. The music is loud, but the crowd is louder, all of them shouting and slurring through their "how have you beens." Everything is just as Kat promised, except that we're short one critical element: Kat.

I sigh as I readjust the folded scrap of cardboard balancing the wobbly leg of this two-top table, then check my texts for the thousandth time. Still no word from our girl. I wasn't surprised when Kat said she was running behind and would meet me at the bar—it'll be a cold day in hell when she's on time for something—but I was . . . *annoyed*. Justifiably so, I think, considering this wasn't the first change to our weekend plans.

In a moment of self-pity, I scroll back through our text thread, hurting my own feelings all over again as I reread last week's breaking news: Kat's new boyfriend will be joining us for Thanksgiving dinner. Over the last three months, she's spared no detail about Hot Daniel from Music History, so I knew she was pretty serious about the guy. What I didn't know was that my Thanksgiving with the Flemings was being rewritten into a remake of *Meet the Parents*, and that I'd be playing the esteemed role of third wheel.

Not tonight though. We promised that tonight would be about me and Kat, endless *Drag Race* reruns, and a borderline-lethal amount of vodka. Or it will be, if she ever shows up.

"Hey, are you using this chair?"

A semifamiliar voice crackles across the table, and I look up from my phone, carefully placing the thick brows and crooked smile on my mental game board of *Guess Who? Geneva High School Edition*. Bryce Chandler, former Geneva Vikings point guard, frequent gay slur user, and, apparently, current spokesman for early-onset male pattern baldness. Bummer. He's gripping the back of the pleather stool across from me with meaty hands that probably haven't touched a basketball in years. A washed-up former athlete. We have more in common than he thinks.

"Sorry," I say, feeling not particularly sorry. "I have a friend coming." At least I hope I have a friend coming. I look like a loser sitting here alone.

"Cool, my bad." Bryce makes a clicking sound with the side of his mouth before wandering to the next table, leaving me to nurse what's left of my vodka soda and craft the perfect joke to text Kat about Bryce's receding hairline. Before I can decide on a punch line, my phone buzzes with a notification. One new text from Big Booty, aka Kat. Her contact name is a leftover joke from a long-forgotten Jason Derulo song, but I can't bring myself to change it.

walking in now!!!!!

Relief and excitement bubble beneath my tongue, and my eyes stay locked on the door as more already-tipsy twentysomethings trickle in, bringing the late-November chill with them. In a sea of black winter coats, Kat's deep-brown corkscrew curls and signature red puffer jacket stand out like a beacon of hope. My stomach trampolines up to my throat. There she is.

"Over here!" My arm rockets into the air, flagging her toward our table. She doesn't hear me over the noise; instead, she turns over her shoulder and stretches a hand behind her. "Kat!" I yell again. "Kat Fleming, over here!"

This time, her head snaps toward me, eyes wide and sparkling as she points repeatedly in my direction, like she's pressing an invisible elevator button. Her lips mouth the words, "That's her, oh my God, that's her!" and for a split second, I wonder when she started talking to herself, but as the crowd shifts, my stomach plummets, and all the pieces fall into place. On the other end of Kat's outstretched arm is an ultra-tall Asian guy buttoned into the same wool pea coat I recognize from dozens of text-thread photos. Hot Daniel from Music History. You've gotta be kidding me.

Even after the unforgiving mob of drunk twentysomethings spits them out, I'm still firmly stuck in denial. I haven't finished grieving the loss of what Thanksgiving was supposed to be; no way am I ready to mourn tonight too. I can't even scare up a smile when Kathryn half runs, half dances up to me, curls bouncing around her face with every step. "Holy shit, HI!" she squeals, launching herself at me in a hug so tight, I'm at risk of suffocating within the folds of her puffer coat.

"Welcome home," I say. Or at least try to say. My face is so smushed against her shoulder, the words barely leak out. By the time she lets go, Daniel has somehow already hunted down another barstool, an unwelcome addition to our two-top table. "This"—Kat gestures dramatically toward him—"is Daniel!"

Daniel ducks beneath a low-hanging strand of Christmas lights and extends a hand, which I take hesitantly, confirming that he's not some tragic hallucination. Unfortunately, Hot Daniel from Music History is actually here, in the flesh, ruining my night.

"I'm Murphy," I mutter. Hopefully he already knows that.

"I've heard so much about you," he assures me with a big dumb grin.

"Yeah. Same." I look down at my hand, which Daniel hasn't let go of for some reason, then back up at his kind, clueless eyes. "But I, uh, didn't know you were joining us tonight."

I glance in Kat's direction just in time to catch her smile slip. "I told you he was coming to Thanksgiving," she says.

"Yeah. Thanksgiving," I echo. "Which is tomorrow."

Her smile snaps back into place, but it's more indignant this time. "Same thing."

"No, not the same thing." I can hear my voice pitch up in that horrible, pre-yelling way. Daniel must hear it too, because he finally drops my hand and takes a seat, making himself as small as a six foot six man can in a bar with ceilings this low. "Tonight you're sleeping over, Kat. Remember?"

Kat's eyebrows huddle together like they're trying to strategize how to navigate this conversation. "I was going to, but when I told you like a week ago that Daniel was coming home with me for Thanksgiving, I said we'd have to rearrange some plans. *Remember?*"

I grit my teeth, holding back all the things I *remember*. For example, I *remember* that Daniel grew up in a suburb about ten miles from here, meaning he could've stayed with his own parents tonight. I *remember* that six blocks away there's an air mattress ready to be inflated and a stockpile of our favorite snacks that I used the last of my paycheck to buy. I *remember* that this whole night was supposed to be Murphy and Kat's 21st Birthday Blowout, and there was never any discussion of guest stars. But I guess Kat's memory isn't quite as airtight as mine.

"Plus, I thought it'd be good for you and Daniel to meet before tomorrow," Kat goes on, her voice as hopeful as it is desperate. "Since, you know, we'll have to tone it down in front of Bubby and my parents and all my little cousins. I'm sorry if I wasn't totally clear. I just wanted him to meet the *real* Murph."

Her gaze ricochets between me and Daniel, who is nodding along, silently affirming her like a good boyfriend should.

"Oh, of course." I pinch my tiny black cocktail straw and stab the wilted lime wedge floating in the bottom of my plastic cup. I pretend it's Daniel's head, then Kathryn's head, then settle on my own head, jabbing ferociously until I kebab the thing.

"So. Uh. Drinks?" Kat hoists herself up on the stool next to Daniel, who looks like he might turn and run any second. She unzips her puffer coat to reveal a black top with silver details that makes my oversize Cubs shirt look like pajamas by comparison. No one mentioned a dress code. Daniel hands Kat the drink list, and her big brown eyes flit over her options. "Do you think we could convince them to make me a blue guy?"

"What's a blue guy?" I ask, but I'm drowned out by Daniel's laugh.

"I don't think so, sweetheart." He kisses Kat on the cheek, peels off his pea coat, and cozies up to her to review the menu together.

"What the hell is a blue guy?" I ask again.

"It's a U of I thing," Kat says coolly, and I close my eyes to block my eye roll. I expected a heavy dose of University of Illinois–themed conversation tonight, but that doesn't stop me from being a little annoyed. And maybe a touch jealous. I'd never shut up about my college either if I went to a Big Ten school. Like I was supposed to this year.

Kathryn lowers the menu, her lips scrunching into a smirk. "Remember Sam's blue guy story from sylly week? After the darty?" She and Daniel exchange a quick look, just long enough to ignite an uproar of laughter between them. Blue guys. Sylly

7

week. Darty. I should drop out of accounting and start studying state school slang on Duolingo.

"So you guys drink Blue Man Group jizz down in Champaign or what?" My delivery comes out snarkier than I anticipated, and Kathryn shoots me a dead-eyed "knock it off" look that I probably deserve.

"It's this bright-blue, supersweet drink one of the bars in Champaign has," Daniel explains, seemingly unfazed by my jizz joke. "They're Kate's favorite."

"Who's Kate?"

"Oh, I go by Kate at school," Kat says offhandedly, sliding the menu across the laminate table. "Do you know what you want?"

I lob my empty plastic cup into the nearest trash can, a solid ten feet away. You can't say all those years of softball never did me any good. "Another vodka soda is fine, *Kate*."

Kat's brown eyes narrow to two suspicious little hamburger patties. "Our first time legally drinking together and you're drinking *vodka sodas*? I thought we were celebrating."

"And I want to celebrate with a vodka soda," I say flatly, more to my peeling cuticles than to her. *I will not blow up at Kat in front of her boyfriend. I will not blow up at Kat in front of her boyfriend. I will not blow up at Kat in front of her boyfriend.*

"All right, then I'll do the same," she says, either calling my bluff or honestly trying to adjust the downhill trajectory of this evening. "Would you mind grabbing those, babe?"

Daniel pushes back from the table, and his barstool stutters against the sticky floor. "Two vodka sodas. Gotcha." As he saunters off toward the bar, I make a silent wish on a blinking

Christmas light that he won't come back. It's not that I have anything against the guy. From what Kat's told me, we'd probably even get along. He's a music ed major, so I'm sure the three of us could swap high school band stories, and Kat swears that he's funny once he's comfortable enough to make jokes. I'd love to get to know him. Just not tonight.

The moment Daniel is out of earshot, Kat plants her elbows on the table, which wobbles a little as she rests her chin in the cradle of her palms. "Hi," she says. "Are you okay?"

I barely suppress a laugh. "No?"

"What's wrong?"

"What do you mean what's wrong?" The laugh sneaks out this time as I tip my head toward the bar, where Daniel has one hand half raised, trying to flag down the bartender without being rude.

"Oh, come on," Kat whines, and her lower lip slides out just enough to qualify as a pout, but not enough to suggest she's doing it on purpose. "Give him a chance, Murph."

"I am! He seems great! You guys are so cute together!" I'm really laying on the compliments thick, hoping it'll pad the back half of this statement, but Kat interrupts before I can get to the "but."

"I told you he's cuter in person," she says, sitting up a little straighter as her pout stretches into a smug little smile. "Don't you think?"

"Absolutely," I lie. Daniel is a far cry from ugly, but apart from his height, he's as ordinary looking as any other guy in this bar. One by one, I pop each of the knuckles in my left hand, watching as Kat's shoulders creep closer and closer to her ears.

As well as I know her, I cannot for the life of me figure out if she's playing dumb or if she actually thought I understood that Daniel coming to Thanksgiving meant he was coming tonight too. But I don't want to fight. I want to drink and laugh and catch up with my best friend who I haven't seen since the end of August. So I bite my tongue and pivot this conversation back toward the only thing—the only *person*—she wants to talk about. "What do your parents think of him?"

Kat's shoulders release back to a normal position as she stares off toward the bar, then back toward me, a hint of worry hanging on to the creases between her eyebrows. "They met super briefly, but they haven't *met him* met him yet. Do you think they'll like him?"

"You kidding me? A nice piano player from the suburbs? They'll be thrilled."

"He's not Jewish," she says, as if that's breaking news.

"It'll be great."

She crosses her fingers, twisting her wrist for emphasis. "Hope you're right."

"I'm always right," I remind her. "Can't remember a time I've been wrong." I pause for a laugh, but instead, Kat just stares off toward the bar again, a dreamy look clouding her eyes.

"I *really* like him, Murph. I mean, I know it's only been a few months. But something about him just feels right."

"That's great," I say, really trying. "I'm happy for you. For real."

"Thanks." Kat's sigh is heavy with relief. She sits up straight, and the table wobbles yet again, so I crouch down to readjust the cardboard. "So," she says, "what about you?"

"What about me?"

"Your love life." There's an implied *duh* at the end. "You've told me nothing the past three months."

I pop back up like a meerkat, pressing on either side of the table to test the balance. It's sort of better.

"Murph." Kat snaps her fingers for my attention. "You're ignoring my question."

My nose scrunches. "There's nothing to tell. The already microscopic gay scene out here dies when everyone's away at school."

Kat frowns, her eyes sweeping over the crowd of ordinary Daniel-types, plus some girls in sorority letters, and, of course, the locals. "What about tonight? I'm sure there are tons of girls from high school who are at least bi now."

"*At least bi*?" My laugh comes out as more of a giant fart noise.

"I'm doing my best here," she reminds me. Sometimes I forget just how straight Kat is. "There are easily, like, three or four girls from the trombone section alone who I bet are probably experimenting now, if you're interested."

"Sure, me and some girl who called me a dyke in high school and now wants to experiment," I joke. "Tale as old as time."

Her eye roll is strong enough to change the rotation of the earth, or at the very least, the vibe of the bar. The DJ, who is just some guy with his iPhone synced to a Bluetooth speaker, switches from annoying club beats to pop hits from our high school years, eliciting a "Woo!" from a gaggle of girls on the dance floor. Solid move. "I'm just trying to help," Kat pouts. "Just because you're stuck in the suburbs doesn't mean you can't date."

I absentmindedly check my phone. No notifications. Of

course not. Who else do I text besides Kat? "Hopefully I'll be out of here soon," I remind her.

"Yeah?" Kat's eyebrows jump an inch. "How's the U of I transfer app coming?"

"It should be good to go so long as I pull off a passing grade in accounting."

"And how's accounting?"

I trap a sigh behind my lips. "No comment." For the second semester in a row, the trajectory of my college career hinges on my ability to magically understand basic economic principles or schmooze my way into a passing grade. "Why do marketing majors have to take accounting anyway?" I argue, as if Kat could speak for the registrar at U of I. "I've been doing marketing stuff at work for two years and have never once needed to know any of that shit."

"You have Professor Meyers again, right? Do you want my notes from last semester?" She's being genuine, but we both know it won't help. We suck equally at this stuff, but while Kat is a verified *pleasure to have in class*, I'm more of a *needs improvement* type. If not for successfully sucking up to Professor Meyers for extra credit, Kat would be right where I am: stuck.

Before I can remind Kat of her teacher's pet status, Daniel returns, balancing three nearly identical drinks with the dexterity of a seasoned cocktail waitress. "I'm DD," he says, setting all three cups in front of his girlfriend. "So one of these is just water. Can't be hungover to meet the family tomorrow, right?"

"Plus Ubers are supposed to be, like, a jillion dollars tonight," Kat adds, sampling two out of three of the drinks and passing the outlier off to Daniel. "So, cheers to this guy for being our free ride."

"Cheers," I agree, but as we clunk our plastic cups together, I can't help but tack on, "not that we would've needed an Uber."

Daniel cocks his head as he sips his water. "Why not?"

"Because Kat was supposed to sleep over at my house," I explain, "which is walking distance from here." As I take my first sip of tonight's second drink, I can feel Kat's eyes burning into the top of my head. I'm being the worst and I know it.

"So is that your real name?" Daniel asks, a not-so-subtle attempt to steer the conversation anywhere smoother. "Murphy? Or do you go by your last name?"

I nod, swallowing a gulp of vodka soda that is more vodka than soda. I could be a royal pain in the ass and bring the conversation back to the plans I've sacrificed, or I could keep drinking and hope that it makes me nicer. I bravely go with option B. "It's my first name," I say. "My dad's a big Cubs fan, so he named me after the bar by Wrigley."

Daniel frowns, then leans across the table, cupping his ear. "The what?"

"The bar by Wrigley Field," I half shout, enunciating each syllable a little extra. "Y'know, Murphy's Bleachers?" Maybe we should've picked a quieter bar.

"Ah, gotcha." Daniel leans back, nodding at first, but then shaking his head. "Yeah, I've never been."

"To Murphy's Bleachers or to Wrigley?"

He shrugs. "To Chicago."

Vodka stings my nose, and I swallow hard, barely preventing a spit take. The cackle that comes after it, however, is unstoppable, and I can already feel the weight of the argument Kat and I will have about it later. "Sorry, I'm just surprised," I say, frantically backpedaling. "Didn't you grow up in a suburb close to here?"

"Daniel's parents are . . . protective." Kathryn squeezes her boyfriend's arm with one hand and tucks her curls behind her ear with the other. "Not really city people. But we're talking about going downtown during winter break for the Christkindlmarket." She takes a long sip of her vodka soda before throwing in, "You should come!"

And here we are, back to the feeling du jour: disappointment. I can perfectly envision how this Chicago trip will go. I'll play the role of designated photographer, following Kat and Daniel from booth to booth of the market and snapping photos of them by the Christmas tree, all in exchange for a five-minute one-on-one with Kat during a run to the train station bathroom. Same as I did when she was dating her one and only boyfriend in high school. I have no intention of accepting her halfhearted invite, but for now, I'll be polite. "Let me know the date and I'll see if I can get off work."

"Wait, hang on." Daniel holds up a finger, the proverbial gears shifting in his head. "Kate said you work at this really cool coffee shop, right?"

"It's called Sip, and she's the marketing manager," Kat brags on my behalf.

"I'm a barista," I remind her. "The marketing stuff is just part time."

Kat rolls her eyes and flicks her wrist to wave me off. "She's downplaying it. They just did this enormous renovation and

Murph did, like, a ton of the design work. She created all these cool videos to hype up the reopening."

"Which is Friday," I remind her. "Are you coming?"

"We wouldn't miss it," Kat says, speaking for both of them. "Plus I need my chaicoffski fix."

"Oh, that's that drink right? The one you invented?" Daniel asks me, then instantly turns to Kat for confirmation. "Am I making this up?"

"Yup, the one I'm obsessed with," Kat gushes. "It's, like, far and beyond the most popular thing on the menu. Murphy is brilliant about coffee. Tell him about it, Murph."

"I don't know about brilliant," I say, but Kat scoops her chin, urging me into a brag session. "It's mainly chai and coffee, so like, chai-coff-ski, Tchaikovsky. Get it? Like the composer?"

Daniel whistles through his teeth, nodding slowly, like a dying animatronic. "Damn, that's clever." He holds up a hand for a high five, and I accept, even though it's literally so awkward. My best friend's boyfriend, giving me the full fourth-grade softball coach treatment. "Kate's tried to get the campus coffee shop to recreate it but—"

"It's not even close to as good," Kat interrupts. "Like, I swear, you put some kind of magic in it at Sip."

"I've told you, it's not *just* chai and coffee," I remind her for the hundredth time. "But I'll make you one on Friday."

"Can you make her a gallon of it?" Daniel jokes. "So she can bring it back to school?"

I breathe a laugh through my nose, draining the rest of my drink. All this talk of liquids has given my bladder a few ideas. "Hey, I have to pee." I turn to Kat. "Do you?"

Kat shakes her head, then plucks a credit card from her tiny leather purse. "I'm gonna grab another round, though, so I'll walk with you."

We shove up from our barstools, and Kat kisses Daniel goodbye for what will surely be a devastating five minutes that they're apart. Then it's just the two of us: Kat fighting through the crowd with me just a few steps behind. For ten precious seconds, I almost forget that tonight isn't going according to plan. It's just her and me, like always, like it used to be. As I peel off toward the bathroom, Kat squeezes my arm and offers the tiniest smile. "Hey," she says, "I'm so glad we're doing this."

"Me, too," I agree, although I'm not sure exactly what we're doing or if I actually mean it.

two

✻

t's only five minutes after 9:00 p.m., but the line for the women's bathroom is already amusement park level long, stretching to the back of the bar and rounding a corner toward the emergency exit. If morale weren't already low, it'd be in the shitter by now. Or at the very least, waiting in line for the shitter.

For a full verse and chorus of a song I haven't heard since senior prom, I consider the men's bathroom, which has no line. I could be in and out and back to the table before Kat even pays for our drinks, but not without risking the possibility of seeing a former lab partner pissing at the urinal. I opt to play it safe, stepping into line behind a chatty group of girls who are trying to do the math on the number of shots they've had so far. Young women in STEM, hard at work.

I look down at my phone, trying to seem busy in case anyone mistakes me for someone they want to talk to. I've had that annoying low storage notification for a week, and now seems like as good a time as any to clear out my camera roll. Somewhere between screenshots of takeout menus and duplicate pictures of lattes for the Sip social accounts, a new text pops up from my mom: a picture of my parents smiling on the beach with the text took this one earlier! wish you were here.

My breath sticks to the inside of my lungs as I zoom in on the sunset behind them. This is the first year I've opted out of our annual Thanksgiving Florida trip, and for what? A weekend of third wheeling? I'd be better off on the beach, letting Mom use up a full real estate commission to pay for my drinks.

By the time the line shifts up enough for me to enter the bathroom, I've cleared out nearly five hundred photos, most of my email inbox, and a handful of unrecognizable contacts. Even if the rest of the night is a wash, at least I did something productive. I pocket my phone as I pass through the swinging door, trying not to stare at Imani Reynolds from freshman biology, who is doubled over the sink crying, probably over the same guy she cried over in high school. Another medium-hot girl caught up in the drama of some crusty guy she grew up with. Now that's a story I've heard a hundred times. I keep my head down until the last stall opens up, and I've hardly crouched over the toilet when a knock shakes the stall wall.

"Uh, occupied?" I say.

"No, over here." A set of blue-painted fingernails wiggles beneath the side wall. "I'm out of toilet paper. Do you have any?"

I rip off more squares than anyone could possibly need and place them in the offending hand, then carry on with what I came here to do. When I go to wash my hands, crying Imani Reynolds is long gone, replaced with a short blonde in a black halter top and a pair of red corduroys stacked over Doc

Martens. She's scrubbing between her fingers, humming "Happy Birthday" under her breath. When she reaches for the soap, our eyes lock in the mirror, a spark of recognition dancing in her pale blue eyes.

"Murphy?"

My throat closes up. Am I allergic to forgetting people's names? "I'm so sorry, you're . . . ?"

"Ellie?" There's a quiet hope in her voice. I study her smile, her pale cheeks dotted with a spray of freckles. My brain starts to whir, placing her face in memories of art and gym class. Right. Ellie. I think she was a year or two older. She was ultraquiet, usually rocking heavy eyeliner and brown hair down to her butt. Now, her white-blonde bangs barely skim her forehead, and her silver septum ring looks like it belonged there all along.

"Ellie. From art." My eyes slip down to her blue fingernails. "And from the stall over."

"Oh yeah, thanks for the toilet paper." She laughs softly, and I hang on to the hint of a dimple on her left cheek. I don't remember her having a dimple, but I guess I don't remember her much at all. She was always a friend of convenience, someone I talked to if we had a class together but never saw outside of school.

"So where'd you end up after high school?" She asks, slouching out of the way of the sink so I can step up and wash my hands.

"Uh, here. I go to community college." I aim my words toward the drain, praying they'll rinse away. "But hopefully transferring to U of I next semester."

"That's where I go! Great school for softball." She hesitates, then adds. "I mean, do you still play softball?"

"Not since I got injured junior year."

"Oh." Ellie winces. "My bad."

"You're fine," I say. "College sports are tough anyway. It's like, you dedicate your whole schedule to it and then you graduate and then what?" I look up from the sink, and Ellie blinks back at me, smiling politely, but without much recognition in her eyes. Wrong audience for this conversation, I guess. I try something else. "Do you still do art?"

"Yeah, I'll graduate with an art degree this spring. What about you? What's your major?"

"I'm just doing gen eds right now, but I do social media stuff for work, so I'm thinking maybe marketing."

"Cool," she says. "U of I is perfect for you, then."

"Anything would be an upgrade from where I'm at."

Ellie pulls a fistful of those scratchy brown paper towels from the dispenser and hands them off to me, her eyes flashing from my lips to my hips and back up again. It's over so quickly that I nearly miss it. "I don't know, community college seems to be treating you all right."

"Not as well as U of I seems to be treating you." A smile pulls at the corner of my lips, and when she meets my eyes again, she winks, sending me into a minor spiral. Is this flirting or just an overly friendly drunk bathroom moment? Either way, I don't have much interest in loitering in here any longer than I already have. It smells like someone puked and rallied a little too early.

"Well, I should get back to my friend," I say, tipping my head toward the door. "Kat Fleming? Do you know her? She was in my grade."

Ellie's laugh is louder this time, bouncier. "Yeah, we used to walk the mile together! Do you mind if I say hi?"

I shrug. "Sure. Our table is up near the front."

"Daaaamn, you got a table?" Ellie crumples her paper towel and sets it on top of the overflowing trash can. "You're lucky."

"Do you want to tell your friends where you're going?"

"Nah." Her nose scrunches as she shakes her head, whipping her bangs back and forth. "I just came here with some AP art kids, but we're not really close. Half of them never even showed up." She picks a chip of blue nail polish off her thumb and flicks it onto the black-and-white tile floor. "They won't miss me. Let's go."

With Ellie following close behind, I cut through the crowd shoulder first, avoiding a run-in with a former student teacher and my freshman year homecoming date. Memory lane is too crowded. It'd be better off as a one-way street.

Back at the table, Kat and Daniel are practically licking each other, so they don't notice my return. "Helloooooooo." My voice carries over whatever forgotten radio hit is currently shaking the walls, but it's still not enough to pry them apart, so I wave my hands like I'm trying to startle off a wild animal. "Hey! Lovebirds! We have company!"

Daniel jolts back, nearly toppling off his barstool. "H-hey, welcome back," he sputters, turning a pale shade of pink. Kat, on the other hand, looks a little proud of herself.

"Murph, I got you another . . ." She gestures toward what looks to be another vodka soda waiting at my seat, but her hand freezes in midair when she spots my new plus-one. "Wait." Kat chews her cheek. "I'm so sorry. You look familiar."

Ellie introduces herself the same way she did to me—wide-eyed and hoping to be remembered. Kat's memory jogs quicker than mine did.

"Oh my god! Ellie from GYM!" Kat leaps off her stool and straight to Ellie's side, grabbing her new-old friend's forearm in a way that has me betting she finished her second round a little fast. "I looooooove your hair! And wait, don't you go to U of I too? I just transferred there."

"Yeah, I'm in the art school. You?"

"Hospitality management, music minor," Kat rattles off. "Do you know Daniel? Honey, let Ellie have your seat."

"I'm fine to stand," Ellie insists. "You look familiar, Daniel. Are you an art major?"

He shakes his head. "Music ed. My roommate is, though. Josh Segal?"

"I love Josh!" Ellie presses her hand to her heart. "Wait. Didn't he host that Halloween party where they had to call an ambulance?"

Kat howls with laughter. "Twice! We had to call an ambulance twice!" She holds up two fingers on one hand and smacks the table with the other, dislodging my cardboard wedge again. Dammit.

"Oh my God." Ellie fans herself with her hand as she catches her breath. "That's practically U of I lore now. Josh and I had a nine a.m. together the Monday after Halloweekend, and even Professor Howell was asking for details."

"No way. You have Howell?" Kat draws a line through the air between herself and Daniel. "We met in Howell's psych lecture."

"I thought you met in Music History," I interject. My one and only contribution, but Kat barely acknowledges it.

"I mean sure," she says, "but technically we had psych together first. Hey Ellie, don't you think Howell's mole is, like, so distracting? I literally just want to. . . ." Reaching over the table, Kat mimes plucking something off Daniel's face, and the three of them launch right back into their laughing fit.

"I, uh. I'll go look for another seat," I say, but I don't think anyone hears me over the U of I pep rally. I slink away with a huff, ducking between crowded tables and half-familiar faces in search of an empty barstool. How the hell did Daniel find one so quickly earlier? The place is packed. After a thorough search, I return with fractures of gossip from former classmates and some early predictions on who's hooking up tonight, but no leads on additional seating. Which sucks for me, it turns out, because Daniel has taken my seat, Ellie has taken Daniel's seat, and none of them seem the least bit bothered with where I went.

"I-L-L!" Kat shouts.

"I-N-I!" Ellie and Daniel echo back, and I rejoin the group just in time to see Kat hand my vodka soda off to Ellie before clunking her own drink against it.

"Hey, that's mine." I'm horrified to realize that the source of that whiny, childish voice is *me*. I close my mouth, but I can't take back the words, and Kat's eyes are already drilling through me, fully mortified.

"My fault," Ellie says, holding the cup out to me with an apologetic smile. I can't make myself accept it.

"I'll just get you another one, Murph," Daniel volunteers.

He jumps to his feet, but he doesn't take so much as a step before I lose it entirely.

"Murphy," I snap. "My name is Murphy." Apparently my filter is entirely off tonight. I want to say I regret it, but I don't. He can't call me Murph. He doesn't know me like that.

Kat's shooting daggers at me. "Murph. Don't." She sounds more like she's scolding a dog than speaking to her best friend.

"And I want that one," I continue, pointing to the sweaty drink that should've been mine, the one I'm still not taking from Ellie because it's not really the point. "I want the one I was supposed to have." I aim a pointed look toward Kat. "Like we planned." I wish I'd stop talking. We could've had a seminormal night if I could've kept my dumb mouth shut. But there's only so much sitting back and listening to your friends gush about the campus you should be living on, the parties you could've gone to, the things you might've known if you were smart enough to pass accounting on the first try.

Kat forces a soft, airy laugh, her eyes darting between Ellie and Daniel. "Murph, do you wanna maybe go to the bathroom with me?"

"No, Kat. I don't." I ball my hands into fists to try to stop them from trembling. "And I really don't want to fight with you, so—"

"So maybe we should call it," she finishes, her voice a shaky sigh as she slides off her barstool. "For tonight, you think? So we have time to cool off? I don't wanna ruin things for tomorrow."

I want to tell her that she's already ruined tomorrow, and our belated twenty-first birthday celebration, and probably my chances of ever getting along with Daniel. But I know I'm to blame too. "Yeah," I choke out, "you're probably right."

As Kat shoves an arm into her puffer coat, the tiniest smirk twitches at the corner of her lips. "I'm always right," she says, tugging her zipper up to her chin. "Can't remember a time I've been wrong." While Kat makes the rest of her vodka soda disappear, Daniel and Ellie make small talk about some campus bar, and I make prolonged eye contact with the laces of my shoes. Guilt curdles with the vodka in my stomach. Even if I'm not the only one to blame for this bullshit night, I'd still rewind and try again if I could. I'd find a way to have a better attitude about all this. But it's too late now.

"You want a ride home?" Kat offers, tipping her head toward Daniel.

"Nah," I say, "I can walk."

"You sure?" She doesn't bother leaving a beat for me to answer before moving past it. "Get home safe then." Kat squeezes my forearm, then wrangles me into a hug, once again smothering me in her red puffer coat. If anything, she squeezes me a little tighter than she did when she first arrived.

"You get home safe too," I grumble into her shoulder. "Text me when you make it."

Ellie and Kat make some vague plans to reconnect on campus, and I say goodbye to Daniel with an awkward and definitely forced side hug. He gives me some last-minute niceties that I certainly don't deserve, and then, as quickly as they rolled in, they're out the door. Kat Fleming, the center of my social life and my primary reason for staying in Geneva this weekend, is gone, leaving me to brave a bar full of our classmates who wouldn't have known the difference if I never showed up tonight. Except for Ellie, of course, who is sitting across the table, fluffing her microbangs with a small, sorry smile. "You okay?" She asks.

"Yeah," I say on instinct, but we both know it's a lie. I feel rotten and rejected, like roadkill or the weird lumpy pumpkin no one brings home from the patch. "I guess I should probably head out too."

Ellie dips her chin in a quick double nod. "I get it." She bites her lip, and her gaze wanders away from mine and toward the bartender. "Or."

"Or?" I repeat.

She paints her tongue over her lower lip, bites it again, then tips her head toward the bar. "We could grab one more drink. Maybe try to save a shitty night?"

My laugh is more of a grunt. "It might be past saving."

There's a flicker in Ellie's eyes, a spark of a challenge. "Well," she says, "only one way to find out."

three

✳

swear on my life. U.S. History with Miss Carlisle."

Ellie props up her elbows on the edge of the bar, chewing tiny zigzag patterns into the end of her cocktail straw. For efficiency's sake, we traded our table to a couple of townies for a pair of seats at the bar. We've already doubled Ellie's initial offer for just one more drink since then, and she's spent the better part of an hour proving her memory of high school, specifically what classes we had together, is far superior to mine. So far, we've confirmed we had art and one semester of gym together. History, however, is currently up for debate.

"I know I had Miss Carlisle. She had the . . ." I draw invisible vertical lines on my forehead with four fingers.

"Stringy bangs," Ellie translates, tucking her own hair behind one ear. A gold turtle-shaped stud sparkles back at me.

"Right. Who else was in that class? Mostly people in your grade, right?"

Ellie uses her fingers to count out our classmates, starting with her thumb, but each name is a complete blank for me. "Zack McMillan? C'mon, you remember Zack McMillan."

I shake my head.

"Come. On. Zack McMillan, the football player? He just got married to that girl from the volleyball team." She wiggles her phone out of the back pocket of her corduroys, blue fingernails flying across the screen until we're both looking at a picture of a girl in a poofy white princess dress, standing next to a familiar-looking man who is presumably her husband. "You didn't see this?"

"Wait, that's Isha . . . something. It starts with a *B*?" I snap my fingers over and over, trying to summon the name. "Her mom is a regular at Sip. Bowman?"

"Burman," Ellie corrects me, pulling up Isha's profile and swiping to her content. "Do you not follow her? She was in your grade."

"I'm only really on social media for work," I admit.

Ellie raises her eyebrows without taking her eyes off her phone. "Seriously?"

"I run the accounts for Sip. You know, the coffee shop? When half your job is creating content and responding to comments, it kind of takes the fun out of it."

"Wow, they had a baby already!" She holds her phone out again, showing off the same vaguely familiar couple, each of them kissing the cheek of their new mini-me. "I didn't even know Isha was pregnant."

"Doesn't surprise me," I say with a shrug. "Isha's mom never shut up about wanting to be a grandma."

Ellie's nose scrunches. "I didn't realize you two were best friends."

"Did you ever go to the original Sip?" I ask. "The seating area was really small. I have zero clue why people thought it was such a good place for private conversations. I could run a tabloid with all the gossip I've heard over the years."

"Oh yeah?" Ellie ditches her phone on the bar top and leans in, intrigued. "How long have you worked there?"

"I started when I was sixteen," I say. "So, what, five years?" Hearing myself say it out loud feels like a sucker punch. Five whole years perched just above minimum wage. At least taking on marketing has been a bit of an upgrade. "The renovations are really cool. You should come to the reopening this Friday."

"Hmm, maybe." Ellie taps one chipped blue fingernail against her lower lip and stares up at the ceiling. "Depends. Is the new space bigger? Or are you going to eavesdrop on all my conversations too?"

"It's way more spaced out," I promise. "So as long as you're not publicly breaking up or making out with someone, you'll be okay."

Ellie smiles, but it's a sadder, softer smile than I've seen from her so far. "I'm fresh off a breakup, actually." She punctuates the news with a hefty gulp of her drink. "So I think we're safe on both of those fronts."

If I could swallow my tongue, I would. Way to bring the vibes down, Murph. I rack my brain for something witty or encouraging to say in response, but all that tumbles out is, "I'm sorry to hear that."

"Not as sorry as me." Ellie dodges my gaze, a soft pink shading in the skin around her freckles. "Or my family. I think they were really counting on me marrying a business major."

"Were you engaged?"

She shakes her head, gathers up all of her hair like she's going to put it in a ponytail, then drops it again. It's barely long enough to drape over her shoulders. "We weren't, but maybe someday? Probably. Not anymore, obviously."

Thus begins my campaign for Biggest Asshole of the Night. Poor Ellie tried to save my evening, and now I'm turning hers into a major downer. "Well, that's the business major's loss," I say, lifting my cup in the air. "Because you've really glowed up since high school."

Her laugh stays trapped behind closed lips, but those lips quirk back up to a smile, and I like knowing I'm responsible for it. "Is it bad if I say you look exactly the same?"

"Sort of. But I deserve it." I let the ice hit my teeth as I down the last of my drink. She's right. I dabbled in box dye a few times in middle school and cut my hair stereotypically short when I first came out, but once I grew out my side bangs and committed to an eyebrow shape, I was a fully evolved Murphy by age sixteen. I wave down the bartender, shaking my empty cup and holding two fingers in the air. He nods, and moments later, we have a fresh set of vodka sodas.

"Wait. I got it." Ellie thumps her palm on the bar, spooking the couple next to her. Not that she realizes. "On Miss Carlisle's desk. Do you remember if she usually had a Big Gulp?"

"You're still on this?"

"Just try to remember," she pleads. "Did she?"

I scrunch my eyes closed, catapulting myself back into what I thought was a dead conversation about a memory I smoked out. I try to place Ellie in that history classroom, picturing her face at one of the carefully arranged pods of desks. I remember the terrible blue carpet, permanently coated in eraser shavings. The big pull-down map. Miss Carlisle's grating nasal voice and, as mentioned, her stringy bangs. And on her desk, next to a tall stack of ungraded papers . . . yup. A Big Gulp.

"I think so," I finally say.

"If she did, you definitely had her sixth period with me," Ellie says. "She'd always go to the 7-Eleven across the street during fifth-hour lunch." She speaks so matter of factly, like she's reading from the actual U.S. History textbook.

I open one eye, suspicious. "How do you remember that?"

"How do you forget?"

Before I can reply, a triple tap on my shoulder interrupts us. When I turn around, I'm nose to nose with one of the girls from the bathroom line, offering up her phone. "Would you mind taking a picture of us real quick?" she asks, gesturing behind her to her gaggle of gal pals.

"Yeah, no problem." I take the phone, and she scampers back to the rest of her group, finding her place in a pose that looks too good not to have been rehearsed. One girl pinches her straw and sips her drink while another laughs out loud despite no one saying anything funny. I snap half a dozen pictures from slightly different angles before passing the phone back.

"Thanks so much," the group's representative says, then spots Ellie over my shoulder and wags a finger between her and me. "Do you want one of you two?"

"Sure," Ellie says, thrusting her phone forward. "Why not?"

Our photographer steps back to set up her angles while I frantically try to remember if I've ever smiled for a picture without looking like a serial killer. Taking notes from the expert modeling work I just witnessed, I fake a laugh, and Ellie rests her head on my shoulder, her blonde hair falling into my face just enough to tickle my lips.

"So cute." Our photographer returns Ellie's phone with a smile. "Let me know if you want me to take more."

"I'm sure these are perfect," Ellie insists. "Thanks so much."

As the amateur models turn their attention to another round of drinks, Ellie practically throws her phone at me. "Put your number in so I can send it to you."

I do as I'm told, but when three new photo messages appear on my phone from an unknown number, I instantly regret agreeing to a picture in the first place. All three are nearly identical, and in all of them, I look absolutely unhinged, like I'm trying to bite off a lock of Ellie's hair.

"We're so cute," she says, and suddenly I don't care that I look like a hair-eating gremlin. Ellie thinks we're cute. So cute, in fact, that she zooms in on the shot and sets it as my contact photo.

I cringe at the close-up. "Not my best look."

"I like it," Ellie says. "It's proof that we had a fun night."

"Did we?" I pause, weighing the events of the evening with my first and final attempt at a not-so-candid photo. "I guess we did."

"And it's not over," she reminds me, double-checking the

time on her phone before pocketing it. "It's not even eleven. Want to hit one more bar?"

There's a moment between us, a split second of stillness in an otherwise noisy crowd. For a sliver of a fraction of a second, all that's in this bar is the squint of her eyes and the curl of her lips, and me, drinking her in, deciphering the endless parade of signals she's been sending. All I can see are hundreds of spinning green flags.

"Sure," I say, "let's do it."

She slams her cup down on the bar top definitively. "Perfect. Just lemme grab my coat and say goodbye to the art kids."

My mental color guard momentarily trades their green flags for yellow ones, signaling for the parade to slow down. I forgot she didn't come here alone. "You sure it's okay to ditch your friends?"

"Generous of you to call them my friends," she says, snorting a laugh. "We've barely spoken since graduation. I doubt they've even noticed I've been gone."

"That can't be true," I say. Not that I have any evidence to back it up.

Ellie lets out an unimpressed puff of air. "You'd be surprised. But hey, I'll be right back."

We part ways momentarily, just long enough for her to find her coat and for me to close out our tab. She meets me back at the bar, dressed for the weather in a camel-colored knee-length coat and a gray Carhartt beanie that her bangs just barely poke out of.

"Ready?" I ask.

"Ready ready." She takes a few initial steps into the shoulder-to-shoulder crowd before reaching back to grab my hand, towing me behind her as she motors through. Her head grooves to the beat of the bass as we bump and stumble past old classmates, but I'm stuck on the warmth of her palm pressed to mine. It's easy and secure, and I almost regret how quickly we make it through the chaos. I wouldn't mind a bar twice as crowded if it meant holding her hand twice as long.

Outside, the November air has dropped a few too many degrees. Chicagoland has officially crossed over into that chaotic time of year when any kind weather would be normal, but I would've preferred snow to this bitter cold. Nothing could stop the merrymaking, though, and a line has formed on the sidewalk, stretching from the front door of the bar to well past the old courthouse down the block. "Sheesh." I crane my neck, trying to spot where the line falls off. "I'm glad I got here early."

"So am I," Ellie says with a wink. The second wink of the evening. One more and I might develop a complex. "Where to next?"

I scan my mental map of downtown Geneva. "Wanna check out the new wine bar on Third Street?"

"I didn't know there was a new wine bar on Third Street," she admits. "I'm following you."

Past the line of shivering hopefuls, we turn down a quieter side street, where a few stragglers are tripping over drain covers while they wait for their price-surged Ubers. Compared to the madness of the bar, it feels borderline silent, and to my surprise, I don't feel inclined to fill the quiet with small talk. When we turn onto Third Street, Ellie's stride breaks, the tiniest gasp fogging the air around her lips. Geneva has put on its holiday best: white Christmas lights line each storefront, and a lush green wreath and glossy crimson bow hangs like a necklace around every other light post.

"I forgot how pretty Geneva is around the holidays." Ellie tips her head back to admire the lights, which cast a twinkly glow over the apples of her cheeks. "It's like a Christmas card or a picture book."

"It's definitely our best season," I say, one of several canned responses I keep handy during holiday rushes at work.

"That's not fair," she pushes back. "What about fall, when they do the wine festival? Or summer? Geneva is so cute in the summer."

I try not to visibly wince. With summer comes the swarms of middle schoolers flooding into Sip, ordering one iced vanilla latte to share and taking up an entire table for the better part of the day. "I think I'd like downtown Geneva better if I didn't work here."

Ellie stops for a moment, nodding as she considers me with thoughtful eyes, then makes up her mind. "*That's* your problem," she says. "You haven't learned the secret to loving your hometown."

"Which is?"

"Leaving it."

I huff a laugh. "I'm working on it."

For the remainder of the walk, Ellie stays a few paces ahead of me, pointing out every tinsel wreath and light-up Santa in the store windows. Third Street really is enchanting; it's just been so long since I've had a reason to slow down enough to notice.

When we pass by Sip, Ellie smiles over her shoulder, and her eyes twinkle like Christmas lights.

"When did you say the big reopening was?"

"Friday."

"Friday," she repeats to herself, like she's trying to stamp it into her memory. "I can't wait. It's so cool that you were a part of all this."

Warmth flutters in my chest. I haven't thought of my job as cool since I first got bumped from full-time barista to part-time marketing-manager-who-picks-up-barista-shifts-as-needed. When I'm not filming videos or coordinating events, I'm mostly trying to blend in with the espresso machine and avoid conversation with the new batch of sixteen-year-old baristas. But if Ellie says it's cool, maybe it is.

"Can we look through the windows?" she asks, lacing her fingers together like she's praying for a yes. "Is it cheating to sneak a peek before the opening?"

I shove a gloved hand into my pocket, fishing out my keys and mentally discarding my employee handbook. "Y'know, I think I can do you one better."

four

❄

By the light of my phone flashlight, Ellie and I are two tipsy spies, sneaking around dumpsters and hopping over garden beds on a top-secret mission we've assigned ourselves. Is it a good idea to make a midnight visit to my place of employment? Absolutely not. But I've got a few vodka sodas worth of confidence, so we're going in. Through the back entrance though. I'm a risk-taker, not a dumbass.

"Watch your step." I waddle penguin-style over a slick patch of ice on the brick path. No sooner have I cleared it than I hear the slippery shuffle of Ellie's boots as she follows suit.

"I didn't know Sip had a back door," Ellie murmurs, snapping a twig beneath her Docs. To my anxious ears, the sound is on par with a car accident, and when I fumble with my keys, I might as well be banging cymbals. Everything seems so loud when you're trying to be quiet.

"We've gotta keep it down," I whisper. "The cops are probably crawling for DUIs tonight. Let's not give them a breaking-and-entering charge too."

"You literally have a key," Ellie says flatly. "I don't think that counts as breaking and entering."

"Okay, fine, but I still probably shouldn't be doing this, so at least try to stay quiet."

My pulse quickens a few beats as we approach the door. Could be anxiety, or maybe I'm just excited to finally show off what our team has been busting our asses over. I carefully sort through my keys, trying not to let them jingle too much as I locate the newest one, still silver and shiny as it was when I added it to my keyring in early October. I twist it into the lock, and the door swings open with a whine that, given the state of my nervous system, mimics a siren. All these renovations and we still haven't greased the hinges, huh? Go figure. I point my phone flashlight toward the glossy new hardwood floor ahead of me, motioning Ellie in.

"Can we turn a light on?" she asks, one hand hovering over a switch.

"Not that one. There's another on the far side of the bar. Just stay close to me."

"Staying close," she confirms, hooking a finger through one of my belt loops. It triggers a highway of goose bumps down my side. "Lead the way."

With roughly three feet of visibility, I feel my way past the kitchen and behind the bar, where I flip a light switch—just one. A single bulb illuminates the counter, and I recoil, blinking into the brightness. My contacts are still shifting into place when I hear Ellie gasp through her nose, launching me into a minor panic. "What? Is everything okay?"

"It's fine, it's fine," she whispers. "It's just . . . this is unbelievable."

By the time my eyes adjust, Ellie has already wandered to the other side of the bar and started nosing around the seating area. Her face blooms into a smile that gets bigger each time she spots a new detail. The old library-card-catalog-turned-coffee-table has been a Sip staple for as long as I can remember, but the paint on the enormous community mural behind it has barely dried. I rest my forearms on the bar, supervising Ellie's self-guided tour. The newness of it all hasn't entirely worn off for me, but it's gotten a little less exciting with all the long hours and manual labor. Her fresh set of eyes has me soaking in the specialness all over again.

"How much of the furniture is new?" Ellie runs her blue fingernails along the back of the green-velvet bucket chairs huddled near the fireplace. Never have I wanted to be a chair so badly.

"Almost none of it," I say. "It's all just reupholstered or repainted. Except for the bookshelves. Those are built from the old floorboards."

"I love that. Like the shop is built out of its own history."

In the dim glow, Ellie's shadow dances behind her, rounding the corner toward what used to be the screened-in porch. It's now a proper room with floor to ceiling windows, more appropriate for Illinois weather year-round. She disappears out of view, and for the first time, I'm alone in the new space. I've worked my fair share of closing shifts, but I've never seen Sip like this—late at night and with no one around. I expected it to feel spooky; instead, it's almost sacred.

"How long did all this take?" Ellie asks from the room over. Her hushed voice carries through the emptiness, echoing off the back wall.

"Which part?"

"All of it."

"Ten months-ish for the major renovations?" I count out the months on my fingers to check my math. "Construction wrapped up in September, and we've been getting it ready to reopen since then."

When she wanders back into view, Ellie's coat is unbuttoned, and her blonde hair stands up straight with static where her hat just was. "Can we hang here for a little while?" she asks.

"Of course," I say. "Make yourself at home."

If Sip had a tagline, that would be it: *Make yourself at home.* Like most shops and restaurants on the main drag of our little downtown, the building was a historic house back before any of us were born. The first floor is still laid out like a living room, and even as an employee, walking into Sip has always felt a little like visiting an old friend's house. An old friend with a big, noisy family and very expensive taste in espresso machines.

Gingerly, Ellie drapes her coat over the butter-colored couch, then plunks herself down in one of the bucket chairs. Her red corduroys against the green velvet make her look like a Christmas decoration, and under different circumstances, I'd hand her a mug and ask her to pose for some photos we could post to announce our holiday hours. I snap a mental image instead, hanging on to the way her thumb traces circles on the velvet armrest.

"I like the new logo," Ellie says, tipping her chin toward the clean, simple Sip logo painted over the bar and the matching stacks of to-go cups on the counter beneath it.

"Thanks. I designed it."

"Impressive," she says. "Did you do the interior design stuff too?"

"Nah, I had nothing to do with that." I wander her way, hugging the walls to avoid any sightlines from the front windows. "I just helped haul furniture and made the behind-the-scenes videos."

Ellie folds her arms over her chest, blocking the hint of nipple that was previously poking through her halter top. Sort of a loss for me. "I have a hard time believing that's all you did," she says.

"Does designing the website count?" I offer. "I helped with the rebranding, but that's just because I have tenure and basic Photoshop skills. And I've been coming to Sip since I was twelve and barely out of the closet, so I know this place better than . . . almost anyone." I sink into the chair next to her, and for the first time since we paid our bar tab, Ellie's eyes are level with mine. They're extra blue against the pink of her windblown cheeks, and I'd tell her that if I weren't so sure I'd trip over every word. Something has me feeling unsteady, but I'm not sure if it's the vodka sodas or the glisten in her sea glass eyes.

"This is really impressive, Murphy." Ellie tilts her head, still staring at the logo over the bar like it's an optical illusion. "I bet you could do this sort of work full time. You could work in branding or be, like, a small business marketing consultant."

Privately, I'd need to consult with Google on what either of those jobs entail, but for now, I just say, "Thanks."

"You know, I almost worked here too," she says. "My brother was a barista here and was supposed to refer me, but he quit before I was old enough to work."

"Your brother? Would I know him?"

"I don't know. Marcus?"

Marcus, Marcus, Marcus . . . I rack my brain, twisting my chair side to side. I forgot these things could spin. "I don't recognize the name," I finally say with a shrug. "Must've been before my time."

"Yeah, he's older," Ellie says. "He was a senior when we moved here."

"You moved during his last year of high school? Ouch."

"Brutal, right? And yet he still managed to land a cool job, popular friends, and graduate top of his class." Her voice has the tiniest bit of bite to it, but her face doesn't show it.

"Where is he now?"

"San Francisco," she says, her tone instantly bored. "He's an engineer, and he's engaged to a corporate litigation lawyer."

My laugh comes out louder than intended. "Oh, so they've got *money* money."

"Yeah. My parents are thrilled. And Mom definitely plays favorites. I think she's spending more on just their reception than they're contributing to my college tuition."

"Your parents are bankrolling the wedding?" Between a corporate attorney and some kind of engineer, I can't imagine this couple couldn't foot their own bill.

"Yeah, both of my grandparents on my mom's side passed away this summer," Ellie explains, "so Mom inherited quite a bit."

"Ah." I look down at my shoes, eyeing a new streak of dirt along the laces. Probably from trying to jump over those garden beds. "I'm sorry," I finally say.

"It's okay. They were in their nineties. It's a shame they couldn't make it another year to see Marcus get married, but they'd be happy knowing that's where their money was going."

I breathe a sigh of relief. Thank God I haven't ruined the evening by taking us to dead grandparent territory. I look back up from my shoes. "What about you?"

Ellie's lips part an inch. "What about me?"

"Is there enough money to help pay for your wedding too?"

She sputters a laugh. "After witnessing this planning process, I'm not sure I want a wedding. But I'm planning on getting my master's, so I'm hoping Mom and Dad will let me put the money toward that."

"That's cool, what in?"

"Art therapy."

"A way worthier cause than a party," I point out.

"Maybe if I was smart like Marcus," she says, and I can hear the bite creeping back into her tone. "But who knows. I haven't mentioned it to my parents yet."

"Why not?"

"I was planning to bring it up in a few weeks, after acceptance letters go out." Her lips fuse together, flattening into a line. "But everything sort of went on the back burner after the breakup."

And I've steered us back into yet another bummer. Maybe next we can talk about her dead pets or 9/11. I fold one leg over my knee in a figure four, careful not to let my dirty laces touch the upholstery. "The breakup with the business major," I remember aloud. As long as we're here, we might as well talk about it. "When did that happen?"

Ellie's eyes dip to the floor. "Three weeks ago."

"And how long were you together?"

"Almost a year."

"Woof," I say.

"Yeah."

"Can I ask why it ended?"

Her first response is a shaky sigh. "I might overshare, but if you really want to know . . ." She glances toward me, and I give my permission in the form of a nod. "So we were really serious really fast, right? We started dating last December, and over the summer I visited her at her internship in New York. We crafted this whole five-year plan where we'd move there right out of college, she'd take a job with that same company while I was in grad school, and then we'd settle down somewhere on the coast. Sounds great, right?"

"Great," I agree, pocketing her ex's she/her pronouns. "And stable. Sorta like Marcus and his fiancée."

"Exactly."

"So your parents must have loved her."

Ellie pauses, breathing a laugh to herself. "Actually, they were supposed to meet this weekend. But then a month ago, she got scouted by this company in Raleigh, and she came to me all excited about accepting the job. Like I was supposed to drop everything and move to North Carolina with her, no questions asked." She laughs again, but it's wobblier this time. "Like, was I really even a priority to her? What about my dreams?"

"Are there no art therapy master's programs in North Carolina?" I ask, half joking.

"Literally no," Ellie says. "And even if there were . . . we were supposed to be planning a life for *us*. Together. But she was only planning for her."

"Ouch."

"And then she had the audacity to suggest long distance, even though she knew how difficult that was for me just for that one summer she had her internship . . ." Ellie trails off, shaking her head, but she can't shake the sadness out of her eyes. "Maybe some people are cut out for that, but I'm just not. No matter how much I love a person. It's just too much."

"I get it," I say, although I don't really. My only frame of reference for long distance is my friendship with Kat, and as difficult as that has been the past three months, we're just friends—and only a three-hour drive apart. "So the breakup was mutual, then?" I ask, only slightly worried that I'm getting too nosy.

"I guess," Ellie says. "But I mostly feel like I got dumped for a state south of the Mason-Dixon."

A laugh slips out of me with panic immediately behind it. That probably wasn't meant to be funny. Before I can apologize, Ellie laughs along with me, a low, closed-lip chuckle that rumbles in her throat like an engine trying to kick over. I hope it feels as natural to her as it does to me.

"So the ex is off to Raleigh," I say. "What about you? Still New York?"

Ellie crosses her fingers on both hands, and the sadness in her eyes dissipates as she nods. "Both my dream school and backup school are in Manhattan, so the only problem will be getting the money from Mom and Dad."

"I'm sure they'll be on board," I say with more confidence than I'm entitled to.

"We'll see." Ellie blows a sigh straight up into her bangs. The short blonde hairs flutter like wheat in the wind, then resettle across her forehead. "Mom is the real problem. She doesn't exactly love that I'm an art major, and she'll probably think I'm just throwing money away on grad school to 'find myself' post-breakup." She pauses, swallows, then adds, "And maybe she'd be right."

It's quiet between us for just a little too long, and I find myself fixated on Ellie's hand draped over her right knee. It's just a few inches away from mine. I could reach over and grab it, or even just lay my hand over hers. Would that be sweet? Or weird since we were just discussing her getting dumped? Am I over-thinking this? Her fingers twitch, and I'm sure we're thinking the same thing until she smacks her thighs and launches out of her chair.

"Enough of my sob story," she announces, brushing her palms together like a carpenter clapping off sawdust. "Where do I place an order?"

I shake off my internal hand-holding debate and point to the register across from me. "For coffee? Right there. But not until Friday."

"Oh come on." Ellie whines. "We're already here."

"Yeah, which is pushing it enough. The owners will definitely notice if I test-drive the new espresso machine before Friday's grand reopening."

"Fine," she sighs, stretching one word into two exasperated syllables. *Fyy-nuh.* "But you owe me a chaicoffski."

"If you come to the reopening, it's on me."

"Deal," she says. "I wouldn't have missed it anyway." She smiles at me, and something about it feels different from any smile I've seen from her so far. It spreads up and crinkles the corners of her eyes, which twinkle in the low light, and my breath catches.

And then Ellie picks up her coat and fishes her phone out of the pocket, and the moment ends. "I guess I should probably call an Uber."

"Oh, yeah, probably." If I hadn't gone so hard on vodka sodas, I would've offered her a ride, but if I'm drunk enough to be sneaking into work after hours, I'm certainly too drunk to drive. "I hope it's not too pricey." No sooner are the words out of my mouth than Ellie's eyes stretch to the size of gumballs.

"All right." She laughs in disbelief. "Ninety-five dollars."

"Are you shitting me?"

"I wish." She blows a deflated raspberry at her phone before pocketing it and pulling on her coat. "Ricardo will be here in seven minutes."

My chest squeezes tight. Seven minutes is way too soon. Before I fully realize what I'm about to say, I speak up. "Cancel it."

Ellie's nose scrunches. "What?"

"Cancel it and stay with me." I stop, swallow, backtrack. What am I really offering? A place to crash, or something more? Either way, no part of me wants to let her leave, and I'm hollow at the thought of going back to an empty house. "I live a ten-minute walk from here," I explain, "and I was fully prepared for a sleepover with Kat. Snacks, air mattress, everything is set up. Just crash at my place."

Ellie's eyes narrow as she reaches for her phone in slow motion. "Are you sure?"

Am I sure? "You're not paying a hundred bucks to drive across town," I say.

"Ninety-five bucks," she corrects me.

"Before tip."

"Fair point."

Her blue fingernails float across her phone screen. "I guess I'll tell my mom I'm crashing with a friend."

Her word choice irons my nerves flat. Right. A friend. She's fresh off a breakup and bound for New York, and I'm just some girl from her hometown with her sights set on U of I.

Ellie hits send on the text, cancels her ride, and then, just when my nerves have fully settled, she laces her fingers into mine.

My body lights up like Third Street after dark. Crashing with a friend, my ass. Yeah, we might have entirely separate trajectories, but maybe, just for tonight, we can take things off the track.

I flip off the singular light with my one free hand and guide Ellie through the pitch black and toward the back door.

"God, when's the last time I had a sleepover?" she asks the darkness, giving my hand the gentlest squeeze.

"I was just thinking the same thing," I say. It's almost true. As we step back into the cold I wonder: when's the last time I spent this much time with someone—anyone—who wasn't Kat?

five

❋

Blacking out feels sort of like one giant, full-body blink; like somewhere between your seventh and eighth drink, God pressed the skip forward button on your life. It's sudden and surprising, a slur of a vodka-soaked memory that barely clings to the edges of your brain. One moment you're enjoying a perfectly messy evening, sneaking into your place of employment with a girl you've known for either three hours or five years, depending on who's counting. Next thing you know, you're stumbling home together, laughing and pouring shots from your parents' liquor cabinet, and then . . . well, then you're waking up on an air mattress in your living room, just like you'd originally planned, only not next to the person you expected.

I open just one eye at a time, hoping it'll make things half as bad. If the hangover wasn't punishment enough, the living room floor is a minefield of Oreo shards and half-eaten bags of pita chips, and it looks like we pulled all the cushions off Mom's white leather couch, presumably for some kind of pillow fort that didn't seem to have come together. The knocked-over bottle of Tito's scares me fully awake, but a quick survey of the area suggests it was already empty before it tipped over. Thank God. I have until Sunday to replace it and get this place back to Mom's standards.

I shift onto my right side, careful not to disrupt the blankets too much. Beside me, Ellie's body rises and falls with slow, even breaths. Just looking at her makes my chest wind tight. She's curled up remarkably small, a tiny, sleeping angel still in last night's clothes. I pull back a blanket just enough to check my own status—still fully dressed in last night's jeans and T-shirt. Given the empty bottle of vodka, that's probably for the best. The few clues I have—the bottles, the snacks, the faintest memory of a pillow fort—suggest that Ellie and I ended our night on a high note, albeit a fully clothed one.

A low vibrating noise hums from across the room, and I startle, then check to make sure it didn't wake Ellie up. It didn't, thank God. I haven't figured out what to say to her yet. I trace the humming sound to the coffee table, where my phone somehow ended its night safe and sound on a charger. After several attempts to stand up off the air mattress without disrupting Ellie's sleep, I opt to logroll off and onto the floor, then scramble to my feet, tiptoe across the room, and turn my phone over. A bright glowing image of my mom flashes on the screen, then dips to a notification for a missed call. Shit.

I yank out the charger and make it halfway up the stairs before Mom calls a second time, and although I pick up right away, I don't say a word until I'm safe in my bedroom and way out of Ellie's earshot. "Hello?"

"Morning! Did I wake you?" Mom's voice buzzes with caffeine and sunshine, two things I haven't seen yet today.

"Sure did," I manage through a yawn. I'm not as hungover as I deserve to be, but the unmistakable cement-like feeling pouring from my forehead to my sternum hardly has me in "talking to my parents" shape.

"Oh, I'm so sorry! Go back to bed, we'll call you later."

"No, it's fine," I lie, tugging open my junk drawer in search of eye drops. Blackout Murphy may have been responsible enough to charge her phone, but not quite enough to take out her contacts.

"Well happy Thanksgiving," Mom chirps, reminding me that I'm not just hungover, I'm hungover on a holiday. "We're so thankful for you, sweetie."

"And we're thankful that this place has a swim-up bar!" Dad shouts in the background. Classic.

"Are you guys at the pool already?"

"What do you mean already?" I can hear the frown in Mom's voice. "We're an hour ahead! It's nearly noon!"

I pull my phone away from my face to verify. Jesus, ten thirty already? I could've sworn it was the crack of dawn.

"Well, it sounds like you're having fun. I miss you guys."

"We miss you too, sweetie," Mom says. "How's Kat?"

I bite the inside of my cheek. How *is* Kat? I haven't heard from her since her grand exit last night. "She's good. Her boyfriend's nice." I tug the junk drawer out a bit more and get back to rummaging.

"Oh, I didn't know he was joining you!" Mom says, and her

excitement on the subject feels borderline insulting. "Is Kat still loving U of I?"

"Yup." I grit my teeth. "She's obsessed with it."

Mom is quiet for a moment, leaving me enough time to scrounge up some eye drops and pry out my crusty, dried-out contacts. "Did it get you excited about next semester?" she finally asks. I don't speak fluent Parentese, but I believe that roughly translates to "are you moving out of my house soon?"

I push a long breath out through my nose as I flick my contacts into the trash like boogers. "Still working on the transfer app, Mom. I'll be all set so long as Professor Meyers doesn't flunk me again." The only people who want to see me off to U of I as much if not more than I do are Mom and Dad.

"Well, let's not blame this on Professor Meyers when you're the one taking the tests." She's using that playful, pretending not to be bothered tone, a Susan Konowitz classic. I guess she's sick of telling the other agents at her brokerage that her daughter "isn't quite ready for U of I."

"Yeah yeah yeah, responsibility for my actions," I rattle off. "Listen, I should go . . ."

"Hang on," Mom stops me. "At least tell me about your plans for the day. When are you headed over to the Flemings?"

My stomach churns, and for a second I think I may need to hit my knees and snuggle up to my trash can. Throwing up would be a great excuse not to discuss the only subject more depressing than my accounting grade. "I don't know," I say, breathing through the nausea. "I'm not sure if I'm going."

The silence on the other end of the line feels heavy with disapproval. "What do you mean you're not going?" Mom finally asks. "Wasn't that the whole reason you didn't come to Florida?"

"I said I'm not sure," I correct her. "It's a whole thing. I'll tell you more about it when you get back, but I'm definitely not skipping Florida Thanksgiving again." I sandwich my phone between my face and my ear, grabbing a bottle of Tums from the back of my junk drawer. Expired. Damn.

"All right, well, we'll be home Sunday afternoon," Mom reminds me. "I have a few showings on Tuesday and Wednesday, but I'll send you a few nights that might work for family dinner this week." That's the Mom I know, on vacation and still coordinating both her real estate and family life.

"We'll figure it out, Mom. Just enjoy your trip."

"Right, right," Mom grumbles, sounding like she needed the reminder. "We'll let you go, but we just wanted to call and say that we love you."

"And don't drink all my beer!" Dad calls out.

My stomach goes full spin-cycle mode, and in desperation, I shake out two expired Tums into my palm. "I don't think you need to worry about me drinking anything anytime soon."

"All right, well. Love you!"

"Love you back, bye."

I end the call, pop the Tums, and give myself a moment to recalibrate before opening my texts. No word from Kat—not even a text to let me know she made it home. I flop down on the bed and start crafting a message that functions both as an apology and a reminder that she's not off the hook for being a dickhead last night.

"Admiring our pictures from the bar?"

I fumble my phone, pressing a hand to my heart to keep it from jumping out of my chest. "Jesus Christ, you scared me."

"Sorry." Ellie leans against my door frame, using her ring fingers to scrape the crust from the corners of her eyes. "Is this your room?"

My cheeks go hot as I start to stammer. "Oh, um. I, uh." I'm not usually so self-conscious about living in my childhood bedroom, but I'm also not usually giving tours to girls who make wiping away eye boogers look cute. If I weren't so hungover, I'd make up an excuse for all the teenage decor, but my head feels like it's been dragged behind a semi from here to Chicago, so all that comes out is "Yup."

Ellie nods and takes one cautious step inside, then another, then a third. It's almost like she's waiting for me to stop her; when I don't, she starts to walk the room's perimeter, and my heart rate climbs with every book or softball trophy she picks up for closer inspection. "Have you always lived in this house?" she asks.

"My whole life."

"And how long did this take you?" She gestures to the giant collage of posters, pictures, and ticket stubs on the far wall, years of memories layered so thick, you can't even tell what color the paint behind them is.

"The Wall of Fame? I think I started it sometime in elementary school."

Ellie hums in thought, studying the wall like it's a two-page spread in a Where's Waldo? book, and my chest constricts a little around my breath. I don't even remember what all's up there. Nothing I would want to hide, obviously, or I wouldn't have taped it to my wall, but the longer she stares, the more it feels like she's sorting through the intimate details of my personal history. I toss my phone on the bed and stand up to join her, trying to follow her gaze over the chaos in case there's anything incriminating that warrants an explanation.

"I was in that." Ellie points to a light-blue piece of paper: the program from our high school's production of *Grease*. "Just in the ensemble. The only show I ever did."

"Yeah? Kat played in the pit orchestra."

"What about this one?" Ellie points to a photo of Kat and me, blue lipped and baby faced in matching Cubs hats.

"Kat's first Cubs game. It was her eighth grade graduation present from my parents. We housed, like, four snow cones each."

"Huh," Ellie says with a nod, but I don't miss the tiny pinch of her eyebrows that has me concerned that I've accidentally built a wall-size shrine to my best friend. It's not my fault that most of my favorite memories include Kat, but it does mean she takes up about a third of the wall. The early stages of my panic spiral are interrupted by Ellie's snort-laugh. "Is this you?"

I follow her finger to an even older photo of me and my family on one of our first Florida trips. Mom hadn't committed to growing out her bangs yet, and Dad's wire-framed glasses are half the size of his face. Between them, I'm a third grader with one front tooth missing, grinning behind purple heart-shaped sunglasses.

"That's me. That might've been our first Thanksgiving in Florida."

"Is that where your parents are now?" she asks.

"Yup."

"And you're not there because of . . ."

That's a fill-in-the-blank question with multiple correct answers. "Kat, finals, and the Sip reopening," I list off. "In no particular order."

"Gotcha." Ellie steps away from the Wall of Fame, seemingly remembering her hangover. She scrunches her face tight, groans, then relaxes it again. "God, I feel rough."

"I can offer you Tums, but they're expired."

"That's okay," she says. "We have some at home." She pulls her phone out, checking the time. "I should probably get going anyway."

"I can drive you," I volunteer. "If I can find my keys."

"If they're the ones with the, uh . . ." she taps her thumb against the rest of her fingers as she searches for a word. "The key chain thing? The pink one?"

"Oh, the bottle opener that says 'dyke' on it?" I laugh.

The corner of Ellie's mouth hooks into a smile. "Yeah. They're on the counter downstairs."

I follow Ellie out of my bedroom, but not before catching my reflection in the mirror and immediately wishing I hadn't. Last night's minimal eye makeup has melted into two not so minimal smudges, and my hair has committed to falling in every direction at once. Not exactly the look for impressing a cute girl who just spent the night. I'd love to at least brush my teeth, but I don't want to make Ellie wait, so I grab a swig of mouthwash and call it good enough. If we're gross, at least we're gross together.

Downstairs, Ellie points out my keys on the counter before hunting down her coat, which was ditched somewhere among the living room snack pile. She's done a little cleanup since I've been down here—the couch cushions are back in their place, and the air mattress is almost fully deflated. "Do you want help cleaning the rest of this up?" Her lip twitches toward some pita chip crumbs crushed into the carpet.

"I've got it," I say. "It'll give me something to do today."

She pins her twitchy lip with her teeth. "You're not going to Kat's?"

I toss my keys from one hand to the other, then back again, letting the "dyke" key chain knock against my wrist a little harder with every throw. "Oh, uh, yeah. I've gotta figure that out."

In lieu of repeating this painful conversation for a second time this morning, I launch into some diatribe about Mom's obsession with keeping a clean house. Ellie nods along while I shove my arms into my coat, yammering without even knowing what I'm saying. My brain is too dedicated to creating a pros and cons list for going to the Flemings this afternoon. *Pro: I get to see Kat. Con: It's all about Daniel. Pro: I'm not alone on Thanksgiving. Con: I'm playing third wheel to the happy couple.*

Ellie graciously cuts me off midsentence. Only then do I realize how heated I was getting about carpet cleaner. "Ready?"

"Yup." I zip my coat to my chin. "Let's hit it."

It's a quick drive, and we're quiet for most of it, leaving me plenty of headspace to work on my pros and cons list. *Pro: Kat's Thanksgiving will have stuffing made out of challah bread. Con: Kat's Thanksgiving will have Daniel. Pro: I'd love to see Mr. and Mrs. Fleming. Con: Mr. and Mrs. Fleming are going to be way more interested in getting to know their daughter's boyfriend.*

"Right here." Ellie points toward a dusty-blue Subaru

turning down an approaching side street. "That's my parents' car. Just follow them."

As advised, I pull up behind the Subaru into the last driveway on the block. I can practically hear my mother going full realtor mode in my head. *A two-story colonial! Great curb appeal! Just steps from Colfax Elementary!* I imagine her playing up the big yard to Ellie's parents. Who knows, maybe she did. There are only so many realtors in this town. There's a nonzero chance Mom sold them the house.

"Thanks for the ride," Ellie says, pulling me out of my head yet again and back into reality, where I'm missing my chance.

"Yeah, um, hey." I labor through a dry-mouth swallow while Ellie's chipped blue fingernails linger on the door handle. Planning how to ask out the girl in my passenger seat would've been a better use of time than my stupid pros and cons list.

"What's up?"

My throat constricts. It's not like I haven't asked a girl out before, but the beads of sweat between my palms and the steering wheel are an unwelcome reminder that I'm very out of practice. "Last night was fun," I start, "and I was wondering if you're around the rest of the weekend? I'd love to, uh . . . maybe I could buy you dinner after the Sip opening? I'm sure I'm gonna clean up on tips."

Ellie's face doesn't change much, but there's something sad hovering in her eyes, and I pray to God it's not pity. "Last night was perfect." She says it like she means it. "I'm so glad we reconnected, and I wish I would've known you sooner. But—"

"Skip the but." I flick my wrist and fumble her gaze. I should've known this was too good to be true.

Ellie exhales through her nose, and her eyes close for a moment. When she opens them again, they're cloudy and sad. "With the whole moving to New York thing, and the just getting out of a relationship thing, I'm really not looking for anything serious. And I don't really do casual hookups, so . . . I'm not really looking for anything. At all."

My chest deflates in what has to be my body's attempt to make itself as small as I feel. Right. Of course. The details of last night's conversations fade back into view: the breakup and grad school and moving to New York. I'd remembered the flirting but forgotten the facts, and I think my brain might've done that on purpose. "For sure," I say. "Well. Can't say I didn't try." I can't hold her gaze, so mine bounces from her smile to the passenger side of the Subaru parked ahead of us. A short man in an enormous coat is struggling out of the car with an oversize bag of charcoal.

"I hope we can be friends, though," Ellie says, then follows my eyes to the man who must be her father. "Oh, Jesus. I forgot Dad is smoking the turkey this year. God help him."

But God doesn't help him, and neither do we. Instead, we lean our heads back on our headrests, marinating in the double discomfort of my rejection and her father's attempt to close the car door without dropping the charcoal. We're a silent, captive audience, breathing a few tandem laughs as her dad booty-bumps the car door closed. It must not close all the way, though, because he has to reopen it and try again.

"I think I'd like your dad," I say, and Ellie's laugh dissolves some of the tension.

"You probably would," she agrees. "I'm less sure about my

mom though." She smiles at me, then looks past me, tipping her chin up. "Speak of the devil, I think she wants to say hi."

There's a triple tap on my window, and I try out a laugh, too, just to see if it clears up the rest of the awkwardness. That same laugh catches in the back of my throat, though, the instant I lock eyes with Ellie's mom. Outside my car, a familiar set of horn-rimmed glasses sits above a wide, toothy smile, a better reaction than any of my accounting grades have ever earned me.

"So," Professor Meyers says. "You must be Ellie's girlfriend."

six

＊

After two semesters in her classroom, there's no shortage of titles I'd expect Professor Meyers to give me. *Most frequently tardy* would be appropriate, or maybe *least improved*. I figured she thought of me only as the slacker sidekick of her favorite student, Kathryn Fleming. But referring to me as Ellie's girlfriend—her *daughter's* girlfriend—isn't just unexpected. It's downright nonsense that I can't make heads or tails of. The longer I stare out the open car window and into the expectant eyes of my accounting professor, the more my brain spins out of orbit. *You must be Ellie's girlfriend.* I'm more capable of reversing the full two miles home than collecting the words to correct her.

"I . . . me? What? You're . . . I'm . . . It's not . . ."

Ellie cuts off my stuttering with a soft squeeze of my thigh, which simultaneously shuts me up and sends me into yet another spiral. A fresh wave of nausea hits, and I'm not sure whether the hangover or the situation is to blame. Either way, I shut my mouth and wait for Ellie to jump in with a correction that smooths over whatever weird misunderstanding we're caught in, but when she speaks up, it's only to say, "We'll meet you inside, Mom."

My jaw drops in solidarity with my plummeting stomach. Ten seconds ago this girl said we were just friends. Now she's squeezing my leg and letting her mom jump to conclusions? There's a ten-car pileup of questions just behind my forehead.

Before I can protest, Ellie's grip on my thigh tightens, and I close my mouth again as she smiles and waves her mother back into the house. Once we're alone, she lets go of my leg and lets out a long, blow-out-a-birthday-candle-type breath. Like she's the one who's going through it.

"So," I say, "wanna tell me what the fuck that was?" I fold my arms tight over my chest, waiting not so patiently for some much-needed answers from Ellie. Ellie Meyers, that is. As in Professor Meyers, the woman with my grade in her hands and a complete misconception of my relationship with her daughter. Jesus, I'm too hungover for this.

"It's an honest mistake," Ellie says. "I told you, my ex was supposed to come home with me to meet my parents this weekend." Her teeth start to chatter as she rubs her hands up and down the arms of her coat, trying to spark some warmth. "Aren't you freezing? Turn the heat up."

I ignore her and shove my hands into my coat pockets, both for warmth and to stop myself from grabbing Ellie by the shoulders and shaking answers out of her. "Why didn't you let me correct her?" I ask. "Why did you lie to your mom?"

"I didn't mean to," Ellie says, sounding flustered. "I just . . . I don't know. I panicked. And I haven't . . ." She stills for a moment, and her guilty gaze flits from the Subaru to the stereo, anywhere that isn't me. I'm confused at first, but when the explanation dawns on me, my jaw unclenches and falls open with a gasp.

"Oh my God." I breathe a laugh of sheer disbelief. "You didn't tell your parents you got dumped."

Ellie's shoulders droop, and her gaze finally settles on her own feet. "I haven't had a chance."

"Did you also not get a chance to tell them her name?" I ask. "Because whatever it is, I bet it's not Murphy."

"It's Mary," she says flatly. "And I'm not exactly close with my parents, okay? I don't think Mom and I have had a personal conversation longer than ten minutes since sophomore year when I told her about the whole bi thing."

My stomach bottoms out. "The whole bi thing?" I repeat back to her, spacing each word out to give it room to breathe. *The? Whole? Bi? Thing?* I lock eyes with the plastic red flag on their mailbox.

"You know what I mean," she says. When I turn back to face her, her features stiffen, but she still won't quite look me in the eye. "You know."

A breath leaks through my gritted teeth. I try to put myself in her shoes, to remember how things felt when I first came out. It was an endless parade of firsts—first kiss with a girl, first date with a girl, first girl I brought home to Mom and Dad—all set to the tune of constantly slipping up and falling flat on my face. It was clunky and wobbly and new, like testing out your first baby steps in a pair of stilettos. Or maybe not stilettos. Maybe Doc Martens. A new pair that still needs breaking in. But I was a kid, and everything sort of felt that way. Coming out was just another portion of puberty for me, and as hard as it was to be the only gay kid in my grade, there are perks to knowing who you are from the get-go. I've had nearly ten years of practice navigating the queer world, so my shoes are well worn, but I *do* know what she means. I've been there, too, and I remember the blisters, even if they healed long ago.

"I do know," I admit, and my jaw softens as I catch her gaze for the first time since her Mom showed up. "I get that breakups are hard. I get that telling your family about it is hard too. But you can't just lie your way through this one. You really need to go tell them I'm not Mary."

"Right," Ellie says. She swallows, then in a small voice adds, "Well . . . or . . ."

"Or?!"

"I know it's a lot to ask, but if you could just go with it for a second, it would really save me a world of hurt."

I blink back at her in disbelief. "I . . . what?"

"It doesn't have to be a huge deal," she says. "You don't know how obsessed with Mary my mom's been. She's gonna think it's my fault, that I let a good thing go, and I just . . . I can't deal with that right now. So can you just come inside for a second, say hello, maybe mention something about the New York internship? And then you can go and I'll deal with the rest. I know it's weird but . . . please? I'd owe you one."

I stare at her, dumbfounded, my mouth forming a perfect O.

I'm sure she's gone off the rails until I remember I have one major detail that she doesn't. "What does your mother do for a living?" I ask, shouting as much as a whisper allows.

She jostles her legs with impatience. "What does that have to do with anything?"

"Just answer the question."

Ellie huffs. "She's an accountant."

"And an accounting professor," I add, drawing out my words to give her time to process. "*My* accounting professor."

The slight annoyance on Ellie's face slips into a pale, ghostly expression. "Oh my God. I didn't . . ." she trails off, blinking in bewilderment into the early winter wind whipping through the window. "She only teaches one class."

"Right," I say. "My class. The one I'm failing." A deranged laugh leaks out of me and, by the way Ellie's pupils are dilating, I'd say she's feeling a little off-kilter herself. She pushes out a shallow breath that fogs the air, then takes the words right out of my mouth.

"This is unbelievable."

"Unbelievable!" I echo, then dial my voice back a few notches. "No one could make this shit up."

"And she thinks you're my girlfriend," Ellie mutters to herself. The pieces are just now falling into place, showing her the whole messy picture. She rakes her fingers through her hair, slowly shaking her head. "God, that's so awkward."

"So you get it," I say. "You need to tell her the truth."

"Right," Ellie says, but her frown doesn't budge. "Well, or . . ."

"Again with the or?!"

"Listen, I know this sounds crazy," she says, "but I think this might actually be a good thing."

"You're right," I say. "You sound crazy."

"I'm serious," she whines, and I watch her reddish-blue fingers roll into fists for warmth. That or she's about to deck me. Time will tell. "Please," Ellie begs, "just hear me out."

And I do. Because what the hell, we've made it this far.

With a twist of the key in the ignition, hot air blows full force from the vents, chapping our faces in a welcome way. I roll up the window and shift sideways in the driver's seat, propping my arm on the steering wheel and my head in my hand. "I'm listening," I say. "Shoot."

Ellie lowers her voice to a hush that can barely be heard over the full-blast heat. "As far as my parents are concerned, Mary was the best thing I had going for me," she says. "A future CEO. A Marcus type. She was the first girl I ever seriously dated, and they were all-in on the two of us. But without her, I'm just their wild card daughter who wasted their hard-earned money on an art degree."

I wait for more of an explanation, but I get none. "So?"

"So they're not going to give me more money for grad school if they think I'm just wasting it, which they will, if I don't have my totally-has-her-shit-together girlfriend on my side."

"What are you saying?"

"You've got this whole marketing thing going with Sip," Ellie says. "We could spin that as you having a job lined up, starting your own business as a marketing consultant." She drums her fingers on the center console, and I can practically hear the motor in her brain whirring and overheating. "The marketing department is part of the business school, I think, so it's not that much of a stretch to call you a business major. And I didn't—"

"Enough." I slice my hand through the air, miming my own decapitation. "I see what you're getting at, and it's not gonna happen. I'm not cosplaying as your girlfriend just so you can go to grad school."

A flicker of something wicked flashes through Ellie's eyes. "That's fair. But would you do it to pass accounting?"

I blink back at her, my mouth opening and closing like a dying fish. "Do you think . . . could that actually happen?"

She shrugs. "I already told you. Mom plays favorites."

I rake my teeth over my lower lip, remembering Kat's strategy to pull off a passing grade in this very class. She wasn't a star student, but she was charming, so Professor Meyers liked her anyway, and it paid off with a passing grade. What better way to make her like me, too, than to play the part of her daughter's stable, successful girlfriend? It's a wild idea, but what are my other options? Schmooze Professor Meyers on my own? Unlikely. Pull off an A on the final? Borderline impossible. This could be my ticket out of community college—or it would be, if I had any confidence that we could pull it off. I don't give Ellie a yes or a no, just a single fact. "You're overestimating my acting abilities."

"Am I?" Ellie lifts a brow. "Not to be rude, but is it that far of a stretch to pretend to be into me? You asked me out, like, ten minutes ago."

My cheeks go hot with a twinge of embarrassment. "Yeah," I grumble, "before I found out you were my accounting professor's daughter. Now I look at you and I see equations."

"Bullshit." Ellie huffs a laugh and folds her arms over her chest. "Look me in the eye right now and tell me all you can think about is math."

I roll my eyes before allowing myself to look into hers. Ellie is partially right—my first thought has nothing to do with accounting. Instead, I'm wondering how those sea glass eyes might look behind a set of horn-rimmed glasses. She's not a carbon copy of her mother, but that hooded stare of hers is straight from the playbook of Professor Meyers. "You look a little like her, you know."

"Then it's a good thing we're not actually dating," she reminds me. "You can look past the resemblance for a day, can't you? Not even a whole day, either. Just for Thanksgiving dinner so we can make each other look good and both get what we want."

I twist the dial and bring the heat down a notch, but it doesn't stop the sweat pooling near my lower back. "But then what?" I ask. "What about after?"

"Then I get to go to grad school and you pass accounting. You'll transfer to U of I and I'll eventually tell them we didn't work out. Easy."

"You're really putting this plan together quickly," I mutter.

"Thanks." Her lips quirk up in a proud smile. "So you'll do it?"

"No."

"Come ooooooooon." Ellie stamps her feet either out of frustration or just to circulate blood flow to her thawing toes. "Please?" she begs again. "Why not?"

"Because this isn't some Hallmark holiday movie," I say. "This stuff doesn't actually work in real life."

Ellie bites her cheek to hide an incoming smile. "Of course it's not a Hallmark movie. Have you ever seen two gay women star in one of those?"

"Exactly! Fake relationships for the holidays? This is some straight people shit, Ellie!"

"Oh come on." Her voice drops to a low grumble, and if I hadn't just turned the heat down, I might not hear what she says next. "It's not like you were planning to do anything else today."

My heart trampolines up to my throat before burying itself in a newly formed pit in my stomach. She's hitting below the belt now. I direct my words more to the steering wheel than to her. "You don't know that."

"Yes I do. You were just saying how cleaning the house would give you something to do." There's something in her voice I don't like. Some know-it-all tone, like the worst of the sixteen-year-old baristas I work with. "And you weren't really talking that quietly on the phone with your mom, either. I heard what you said about skipping Thanksgiving with Kat."

The silence is too long, both of us waiting for the other to give in. If we'd known each other even a little bit longer, she'd know better than to try to out-stubborn me. "Murphy," she finally says, her voice steadier than it's been all morning, "I know what it's like not to be the favorite."

I want to tell her she's wrong, but she's not. Marcus is the favorite child, and Kat was the favorite student. I wasn't even my own best friend's first choice of company this weekend.

"Will you at least think about it?" Ellie pleads.

My lip twitches at the compromise. "Fine," I say. "I'll think about it. But I'm thinking about it at home. I don't want your mom coming back out to ask why I'm idling in her driveway."

"Okay," Ellie says. "Just let me know." She reaches to open the passenger door, but for the second time today, her fingers pause on the handle for just a moment too long.

"Did you forget something?" I ask.

"No. I just . . ." She reaches over the console to squeeze my thigh again, and regardless of who her mother is and where she's headed next fall, my skin lights up like a sparkler at her touch. "No matter what you decide, I'm glad we met, okay?"

"Me, too," I say. I can feel my cheeks turning pink.

"Good." Ellie smiles just enough for her dimple to show. "Because I really do want to be friends."

"Right," I say. But I can't quite make myself agree.

seven

❋

She's her MOTHER?!"

Kathryn's voice is a shrill speakerphone squawk echoing throughout every inch of my car. She's lucky I'm at a stop sign when I break the news, or I'd be at risk of running straight off the road with a reaction like that. We have plenty to talk about so far as last night goes, but I couldn't bury the lede on what is undoubtedly the most uncomfortable moment of my life. Some things just take precedence, and this is undeniably one of them.

"HER MOTHER!" I screech back. "Professor fuckin' Meyers. She literally tapped on my car window. It was a goddamn jump scare."

Kat wheezes a laugh. "I'm dead," she announces. "I was dying and now I'm officially dead."

"Same," I agree. "RIP."

"So wait, back up a little bit. After we left the bar . . . Ellie spent the night at your place?"

"We kept drinking and Ubers were expensive," I explain. "It was a last-minute call." Under normal circumstances, I'd replay every joke, talking point, and low-level trespassing charge that went down after she and Daniel left, but I'll pocket all that so long as Kat and I are ignoring the drama between the two of us from last night. For now, I'm sticking to necessary details only.

"So you drove her home, and Professor 'Mommy' Meyers is there to welcome you?"

"That isn't even the worst part." I grip the steering wheel extra tight, rolling the last stop sign on my way out of the subdivision. "She thought I was Ellie's girlfriend."

Kat howls like a hyena on laughing gas. "I *knew* she was gay! Daniel, didn't I call that last night? I knew it!" Her self-righteous victory lap is hardly what I need right now.

"Can we focus, please?"

"Right, right, sorry." Kat clears her throat, resetting herself. "So wait, does she have a girlfriend?"

"*Had.* Her parents were supposed to meet her this weekend, but they broke up, like, two weeks ago. Maybe three?"

"And she didn't tell them?"

"Guess not," I say. "And then Ellie tried to sell me on playing along with it. Like if I pretended to be her girlfriend, maybe her mom would actually pass me."

This time, Kat's cackle sounds more like a dying goose. The girl has a whole zoo trapped inside her. "That's simultaneously the best and worst idea I've ever heard," she says. There's a crumpling sound, and she lets out a tiny *ope*. "Hang on. Out of Cheez-Its. Be right back."

To the beat of Kat's footsteps, I round the corner into my neighborhood at nearly twice the speed limit. The big lawns and sky-high oak trees are always a warm welcome, but in the thirtyish minutes I've been gone, a smattering of unfamiliar minivans has appeared, each one overflowing with relatives carrying tinfoil-topped casserole dishes. For half a second, I had almost forgotten it was Thanksgiving.

"I'm back," Kathryn chirps, ripping into what I assume is a new box of Cheez-Its. "You're on speaker though. Daniel's here."

"Hey, Murphy." His voice is quieter than Kat's, more distant, like he's talking to me from the bottom of a well. He'd be more welcome there than he is on this call, but I'll tamp that down for now. "How's it going?" he asks.

"It's going," I say, but even that feels generous given the events of the day so far. As I come careening back into my driveway, the bump of the curb bounces me out of my seat with a full Mississippi second of hang time. Maybe I need to slow down.

"Soooo, what happens now?" Kat asks, steering the conversation back to where we abandoned it. "Are you gonna play along?"

"Of course I'm not going to play along. I'm desperate, but I don't think I'd ever be *that* desperate." I kill the ignition and take my phone off speaker, then climb the last bit of driveway at double speed, grimacing against the cold. "We did get along, though, so maybe we'll hang out again when she's back in town." Just in case, I rap my knuckles against the garage door for good luck before punching in the code. It's as close to knocking on wood as I can get at the moment.

"Hang out? Or *hang out*?" I can practically hear Kat

punctuating the second iteration with a suggestive shoulder shimmy.

"The first one," I say decisively. "Nothing happened."

"Yet," Kat says.

"Or ever. She's fresh off a breakup."

"It won't always be fresh."

"And she's moving to New York City," I add.

"So?"

"And she literally told me flat out that she only sees us as friends."

Kat pauses, then sighs. "All right, fine," she says. "I can't really argue with that, I guess." Whatever she says next sounds like mishmash beneath the whirs and squeaks of the garage door.

"One more time?" I say.

"Oh nothing, Daniel's just being cute." Kat giggles—the kind of flirty, airheaded giggle I've only heard her do when she's talking about Harry Styles. Maybe Daniel is the real deal after all. "Anyway, I need to start getting ready, but you are telling me *everything* when you get here. What time are you coming over?"

My stomach swan dives as I struggle out of my coat with only one free hand. I'm feeling a little caught in my own trap. "I, uh. Actually." I kick off one shoe, then the other, each of them hitting the mudroom wall with a *thud*. By the time I complete my escape artist act, my mind is made up. "I think I'm gonna hang back today."

"To go to Ellie's?"

"No, I just really need to clean." I fling my coat over a kitchen chair in passing, trying to play off this whole moment as casually as possible. "My mom would kill me if she saw what the house looks like right now."

"But she's not home till Sunday," Kat reminds me, not that I've really forgotten.

"Sure, but work is going to take up most of the next two days."

I tug open the fridge and pop the top on a can of lemon La-Croix, waiting for a response that doesn't come. "Kat? You there?" I pull my phone away from my face just to verify the call hasn't dropped.

"I'm here," she says, but her voice is raw. "I just don't love the thought of you staying back from Florida just to spend Thanksgiving alone. Especially when the whole plan was to spend the day together."

My breath rattles around my lungs as I try to form a response that won't immediately start a fight. Since when does Kat care about sticking to the plan? She sure didn't care last night. Maybe if she had, and Blackout Wednesday had gone as intended, I wouldn't be so opposed to third wheeling today. I step over an open bag of Cool Ranch Doritos and collapse onto the white leather couch, which releases a little puff of air beneath me. Even the couch is sighing.

I'm still trying to figure out what to say when Kat speaks up again, this time in a soft, unsettling whisper. "Is this about last night?"

I let an exhale leak through my teeth. Kat's not dumb. Of course this is about last night. But I really don't want to have this conversation—not with Daniel listening, not while I'm still a little hungover, and really, not at all.

"Of course not," I lie. "This is a me thing. I really need to clean and probably study, too, so I should hang back. Don't worry, I'm good by myself."

Kat pauses, trying to decide whether to believe me or not. "You sure?"

"Yeah. I'm like Macaulay Culkin in *Home Alone*, only older and gayer."

I can hear her smile through the phone, the tension breaking. "I always thought there was something gay about him in those movies. I mean, he was obsessed with those two older men."

"He was ten and they were trying to rob his house," I remind her, taking my first sip of LaCroix, which I immediately regret. It tastes like carbonated lemon Pledge. "Bleurgh. Have you had lemon LaCroix?" I ask, airing out my tongue.

"No, is it good?"

"No."

Kat laughs. "Noted."

I set the can down on a pink tile coaster. Maybe it'll taste better once I've fully squashed this hangover. "I think I'm gonna take a nap before I clean."

"Sounds good. Text me later, okay?" Kat says, sounding marginally less sad. "And if you change your mind, you know you're always welcome here."

"I know, I know. Thanks." I reach for a throw blanket, trying to spread it over my lap with just one hand. "Daniel, good luck meeting the family. Watch out, they're all just as judgy as Kat." Bonding over jokes at his girlfriend's expense is the only type of bonding I know how to do.

Daniel laughs. "Thanks for the tip. I'll put on my judgiest face."

"You're the worst, you know that?" Kat whines. Whether it's directed at me, Daniel, or both, I'm not sure.

"You loooooove me," I remind her.

"Yeah, yeah. You love me too. Bye."

I end the call, dropping my phone on the coffee table and nestling deeper into the couch. Or at least I try to. Mom has gradually transitioned the whole house into this crisp, clean aesthetic over the past few years, and although it looks sharp, I miss our ugly, comfy furniture from before she went Barbie Dream House on us. I could inflate the air mattress again or, God forbid, actually go up to my room, but somehow, that feels like more work than just leaning into the discomfort. I squeeze my eyes tight, trying to imagine that the sunlight seeping through the bay window is a warm beam of Florida sunshine. Maybe my reject LaCroix flavor is just a poorly mixed beach drink. And the hum of the heat kicking in . . . crashing waves, I guess? I give the too-small throw blanket another shake, trying to cover at least my legs, but it's too itchy to be my pretend beach towel. No wonder I've never seen anyone use it.

I ditch the blanket and scrunch my knees toward my chest, trying to make myself as small and sleepy as possible, but a piercing screech in the backyard interrupts my nap before it even begins. Maybe that's . . . an injured seagull? The screeches double, then triple, followed by bubbly laughter too loud to ignore. I sit up, peering out the window at a small flock of kids, most of whom I don't recognize. They're running laps around the neighbor's yard, tiny arms flailing in their swishy little puffer jackets, leaving a trail of miniature hats and gloves strewn across the icy grass. Their moms are supervising from the safety of the patio, balancing full glasses of wine in perfectly manicured fingers and laughing over a joke I'll never hear. Just as I'm trying to decide who I'm more jealous of, one of the husbands swings open the back door, wandering out to top off their wine glasses. When he reaches the last of the three women, he weaves an arm around her waist, pressing a long kiss onto her forehead before beginning his pour.

My heart does a pirouette in my chest. *That. That* is what I'm most jealous of. Mom is with Dad, the neighbor is with her husband, Kat is with Daniel, and I am with an itchy blanket and a reject flavor of LaCroix. What I wouldn't give to be someone's first choice.

I turn away from the live action made-for-TV movie unfurling outside the window, drawing in a deep breath and holding it there. Anything to temporarily fill the hollow feeling. And then the voice in my head reminds me of the thing I'm desperate to ignore: *It doesn't have to be this way.*

I rub my lips together, weighing my options. What's worse: acting out a lie that makes you happy, or sitting lonely in the truth? Before I can decide, my phone buzzes on the coffee table, and I lunge for it. One new text from Ellie with a link to a *Tribune* article about Sip's reopening. Cool. It's sweet of her, but it doesn't affect me half as much as the trio of pictures from last night perched above it in the thread. Tipsy Ellie smiles at me from the screen in all three. She's barely propped up by Tipsy Murphy, who is faking the world's least convincing laugh.

Neither of these poor, inebriated idiots knew what we know now, but if they did, would they have done anything different? I'll take the awkward morning after if it means I get to keep last night. I hold my thumb against the pictures, saving all three, and warmth flickers in my chest as the blackout curtains on my memory part just an inch, just enough to access a hint of a moment from last night. It plays like a fuzzy vintage film in my head: me and Ellie, laughing as we battle the air mattress pump and test the firmness of our bed for the night. I can still hear her laugh, like jingle bells caught in a spin cycle, as she fell onto her back, deflating the mattress. I can still see a shadow of something warm and curious in her eyes as she caught her breath. The memory fades, and I know that whatever last night was, it was never supposed to last, but I can have it again—and hell, maybe save my grade and Ellie's grad school dreams too. My fingers fly across my phone and hit send on a text before I have the better sense to stop them.

is the thanksgiving offer still on the table?

eight

❋

n hindsight, braving the grocery store on Thanksgiving Day was a rookie mistake. Doing it hungover? Now that's just plain stupid. But here I am, slogging back into the house sweaty, demoralized, and forty dollars poorer.

I drop my armful of grocery bags onto the counter with a *thunk*, peeling off my coat to admire the red indents the bags left in my forearms. When I asked Ellie to swing by to pick me up in an hour, I pictured myself dressed and ready to go with a pre-made pumpkin pie in hand, but according to the clock above the stove, that was fifty-five minutes ago, and I'm still in last night's clothes with nothing but ingredients to my name. You don't con your way into a passing grade by showing up to your fake girlfriend's family Thanksgiving empty-handed.

I tug my laces loose and kick my no-longer-even-close-to-white Converse into the corner before I can track any more of November's worst into the house. On top of all the remaining sleepover damage, I guess I'll be cleaning the floors before my parents get home. Before I can organize my mental to-do list, the doorbell rings.

"Be there in a sec!" I shout, although I'm not sure why. No way Ellie can hear me over the long, melodic doorbell song my parents have programmed. Assuming it's Ellie at the door, of course. I guess it could be a neighbor's cousin who mixed up the address, or maybe a mailman who doesn't observe federal holidays. I'd welcome anyone who would buy me just a few more minutes, but one peek through the window and the flash of Ellie's white-blonde hair confirms that there'll be no such luck. Damn. I knew I should've built in buffer time.

I shuffle toward the door, checking my reflection in a foyer window on my way. Last night's clothes look about as good as you'd imagine after wearing them for eighteen hours or so, and the half-assed pile of hair on my head is less of a messy bun and more of a disheveled knot. The whole look is only made worse when I tug open the front door. Unlike me, Ellie has showered off any and all evidence of her hangover.

"Hey again," she says with a playful smirk. "I parked behind you. Hope that's okay."

The home security system beeps twice, and I punch in the code to turn it off, thankful that my parents haven't made good on buying that doorbell with a camera yet.

"Come on." I wave her inside. "You're helping me bake."

"You didn't say anything about baking," Ellie says, shedding her coat to reveal a worn black band T-shirt tucked into an emerald silk skirt. And, of course, her Doc Martens. "I thought I was just picking you up."

"I thought that too before the grocery store was out of pies."

The look she gives me would be better suited for someone toying with the idea of scaling Everest. "You tried to buy a pie *today?*"

"It's my first Thanksgiving not poolside," I remind her. "I'm doing my best."

Having caught on to the very obvious "no shoes" vibe the house gives off, Ellie pairs her Docs neatly by the door, then trails behind me into the kitchen.

"Sorry it's still a mess." I wave a hand toward the deflated air mattress that's still sitting in the center of a fairy ring of crumbs.

"Don't apologize," she says. "I helped make the mess, remember? Let me help clean it up."

"You don't have to do that."

"And you don't have to bring anything to Thanksgiving," she says with a knowing look. Touché.

"Aren't we supposed to be buttering up your mom?" I remind her. "I can't do that if I look like a freeloader, showing up without any contribution."

"Fine, fine," Ellie concedes, "so long as you promise never to use the phrase 'buttering up' in regard to my mother ever again."

I snort. "Scout's honor." Digging into the grocery bags, I pull out two slightly dented boxes of Rice Chex, two jars of peanut butter, and way too many bags of chocolate chips. "This shouldn't take long."

Ellie squints at my grocery haul. "Muddy buddies?"

"In this house, it's puppy chow." I wedge my thumb beneath the tab of one of the cereal boxes, pry it open, then reach for my phone. The recipe is still pulled up in my browser, and I scroll past the pages of pointless storytelling every food blogger feels inclined to write before landing on the actual instructions.

Step one: In the same bowl, combine one jar of peanut butter and two bags of chocolate chips. Melt until smooth.

I twist the top off a peanut butter jar, peeling back the paper while Ellie collects an armful of last night's snacks from the living room floor. We work silently for a few minutes—her, cleaning up our mess; me, making a brand new one. Once she has the air mattress crammed back into its storage bag, she wanders back to the kitchen, munching on some leftover pita chips. "These are still good," she says, holding the bag out. I politely decline.

"Can you make sure there's nothing in this your family is allergic to?" I ask, fully aware that I should've asked an hour ago. I slide my phone across the counter, and Ellie taps the screen, taking her turn with the recipe.

"Only allergy I know of is Aunt Carol, who can't have shellfish." She looks up, a no-nonsense look in her eyes. "How much shrimp were you planning to put in these?"

"Three, maybe five bags," I joke, ducking down into the cabinets and sizing up a gradient of pink mixing bowls. "Should we make a single or a double batch?"

"Depends," Ellie says, "Are we using three bags of shrimp or five?"

A laugh explodes out of me, bouncing off the vaulted ceilings. "Double batch it is." I grab two bowls on the bigger and pinker end of the spectrum, then unleash a chocolate hailstorm into one of them as I rip open four bags of chocolate chips with my teeth. "Grab that rubber spatula, wouldja? We need to scrape both jars of peanut butter into here."

Ellie pauses, eyeing the mixing bowls. "Are those micro-wave safe?"

"Probably. Let's find out."

While I dump the first box of Rice Chex into the empty bowl, Ellie meticulously scoops every last smear of peanut butter onto the pile of chocolate chips. She's an artist at work, scraping every inch of the jar with laser focus. The pink tip of her tongue peeks out between her lips in pure concentration, and I'd tease her about it if it weren't so cute. I can't imagine being so diligent about a recipe that boils down to *dump a bunch of good stuff in a bowl and stir.*

"Can I help you with something?" Ellie asks, glancing up just long enough to catch me staring.

"It's okay if you don't get all of it. You know that, right?"

She juts her chin toward my phone. "The recipe says two jars of peanut butter."

"Yeah, but it doesn't have to be perfect to be good."

Her attention doesn't budge from the jar. "But if we can make it perfect, why wouldn't we?"

"I think you'd have a lot in common with my mom," I mutter.

Ellie breathes a laugh. "Just what every girl wants to hear." She drags the edge of the rubber spatula along the lip of the mixing bowl, adding a fraction of a gram of peanut butter. "Are the two of you close? You and your mom?"

"Closer than it sounds like you and *your* mom are," I say, al-though based on previous conversations, that's not saying much. "I think we'll get along better once I move out though. Like, even now, I'd love to be in Florida with them, but the time apart is sort of refreshing." I look up from the second box of cereal

I've been struggling to open, locking with Ellie's narrow gaze. "All relationships need a little space, right?"

"Makes sense," she says, then mushes her lips together in thought. "Do you think that's true for you and Kat too?"

"I . . . I don't know. This semester is the first time we've been apart."

"In how long?"

"Since we met," I say. "Since we were six."

"Wow." Ellie's hand stays suspended in midair, wielding the rubber spatula like a magic wand. "I wish I had a friend like that. The longest friendship I have is from"—she squints out the window as her lower lip stiffens—"second semester freshman year, I think."

"Of high school?"

She shakes her head. "College. We moved around a lot when I was a kid, and I just never really clicked with anyone once we got to Geneva. Even with the art kids, I always felt like a weird extra because everyone else had been friends for so long." Deeming the first jar of peanut butter officially empty, Ellie picks up the second one and resumes her work. Meanwhile, I'm fighting off the pity creeping into my chest. Everyone deserves a friend like Kat, the kind of long-term friend you can show all your cards to without questioning the consequences. The kind of person you can answer a FaceTime call from while you're on the toilet, who, even the morning after a fight, will pick up your call on the first ring. Some of that is just the side effects of a fifteen-year friendship, but I imagine there are other ways people end up that close.

"I don't think it's always about how long you've known a

person," I say. "If it were, we'd all be best friends with our moms."

"Fair," Ellie agrees. A golden thread of hope outlines her voice. "So you have newer friends that you're close with?"

My argument collapses. "Well, no," I admit.

"Oh."

"But I've also barely left Geneva," I remind her. "I'm not really meeting people out here. Before remeeting *you* last night, it's been years since I've made a friend." My own word choice doesn't sit well with me, and my stomach churns in protest. Are Ellie and I friends? That's what she wants, right? Maybe we're just partners on the world's most deranged group project. In a different world, we might've been something more, but given the circumstances, I'd be stupid to waste my time on what-ifs.

Before either of us is brave enough to break the silence, the microwave does it for us with three loud beeps. I pull the bowl out, confirming that the peanut butter and chocolate are sufficiently nuked. "Wanna stay on scraping duty?"

Ellie bows a little. "It would be my honor."

The churning in my stomach subsides with her smile, and I hand the bowl off to her and watch as she scrapes it onto the cereal with expert precision, leaving only a few skinny streaks of glossy chocolate and peanut butter behind. When I rinse the bowl, the water runs just about clear.

"Are you this much of a perfectionist about everything?" I ask.

"I prefer detail oriented," Ellie corrects me. "It's what makes me a good painter."

"So painting is your main . . . thing? Art form?" This seems like the sort of thing a convincing girlfriend should know.

"Medium," Ellies corrects me. "It's my primary medium. You can get a generalized art degree, or you can get a concentration in your medium, so I'm an art major with a concentration in painting. And I picked up a psychology minor to help with grad school apps."

"You didn't mention the psych minor last night," I point out.

She smiles, a tiny, tight-lipped smile that holds back a laugh. "And you didn't mention that you were failing accounting with Professor Meyers," she says. "So I guess we both left things out."

I flip the faucet off and dry my hands on my jeans. There's no arguing against that.

"That's a good thing to know going into today though," Ellie goes on. "That I have a painting concentration. Mary would've known that, obviously."

"Right. And what are we telling your parents about the fact that my name isn't Mary?"

"That they're getting old and they must've misheard me when I said Murphy," Ellie says.

"Okay, so gaslight your parents," I say. "Got it."

Ellie goes on without acknowledging my joke. "And like I said earlier, I think we should stick with the story that you're opening a small business consulting firm after you graduate." My hand instinctively hovers over my phone, ready to google the details of what that entails, but Ellie does the work for me. "Essentially, you would be doing all the stuff you do for Sip now, but for lots of businesses instead of just one."

"Got it." I stamp the air with my chin with one firm nod.

"Out of curiosity, though, what do you actually want to do after you graduate?"

"U of I, remember?"

Ellie rolls her eyes. "After *that*."

I plant my forearms on the counter, leaning my weight against the quartz. "Move to Chicago. Same as everyone around here."

"Not everyone," Ellie says. She wiggles her fingers in a wave. Right. I'm in the presence of the great midwestern exception.

"What exactly is it about New York that makes you want to move?" I ask. "It just seems like a bigger, more overwhelming Chicago."

"It's less about the city and more about the schools," she explains. "I'd move to the middle of nowhere if that's where the best master's programs were. I'm glad I don't have to, though. Especially after four years at U of I, which is essentially in the middle of a cornfield."

I snort a laugh. "One girl's cornfield is another girl's dream school, but I guess anything beats staying here."

Ellie pinches a stray piece of cereal off the counter and adds it to the bowl. "I promise you'll think Geneva is cute once you leave it."

"Yeah," I agree. "Like I said. All relationships need a little space."

Ellie and I take turns mixing, switching off whenever our wrists get tired and only crushing some of the Chex along the way. When the cereal is sufficiently coated, she watches me rearrange the freezer drawer like a bad game of Tetris, maneuvering ice packs and bags of frozen vegetables to create enough space for the mixing bowl. It won't quite fit, so in true midwestern form, we set the bowl out on the back patio, letting Mother Nature's freezer do the job. Once the rest of the dishes are stacked in the sink, I grab Ellie a LaCroix (avoiding the lemon for her sake), then glance at the time. Three o'clock. Could be better, could be worse.

"What time are we eating?" I ask.

"Around five thirty or six."

"Perfect." I tip my head toward the staircase. "Cool if I go get ready real quick?"

Ellie frowns. "You're not ready?"

I snort a laugh, but when Ellie doesn't join me, I make a face that can only be described as "frog that's been run over by a truck." "You know these are the clothes I wore last night, right?"

She lifts a shoulder, looking a little too pleased with herself. "And they look good on you."

"Almost as good as they smell." I pinch the collar of my Cubs shirt, pretending to take a whiff. Only when you've been wearing the same clothes for two days, there's really no pretending. I smell rank. "Be down in twenty, 'kay?"

I take the stairs two at a time and slink into the bathroom, locking the door behind me and stripping down before turning the shower handle all the way to the right. It feels like there's half an inch of bar grime that needs to be singed off my skin, but speed is the top priority today. The water hasn't even heated up to the temperature I like by the time I step out and towel off.

I catch my reflection in the mirror, wishing I had showered

long enough for it to fog. The bags under my eyes are beyond what concealer can save, even if I had the time, and my eyebrows haven't been tweezed since senior prom. I'm not sure I'd be particularly proud to bring me home to my parents, but I guess it's nothing that Professor Meyers hasn't seen before.

Once I'm dry enough not to leave footprint puddles behind me, I sprint across the hall in my towel to dig through my closet, then opt for the first decent, clean outfit I can find: a loose-fitting tan sweater and black jeans. Better than I've ever dressed for class but not as nice as I would for our family's semiannual pilgrimage to Catholic Mass. If only I had a pair of Docs like Ellie's to give the look the edge it desperately needs.

After two pumps of moisturizer and an ungodly amount of dry shampoo, I deem myself *good enough* and head back downstairs, where Ellie is posted up at the counter, her back facing me. It's strange to see her in my parents' kitchen, almost like we're in high school again and I volunteered my house for a study session. It's closer to the truth than I want it to be. After all, she and I are working for a grade. My grade.

"Ready," I announce, and Ellie jolts a full inch off her stool, a puff of powdered sugar erupting around her as she whips her head over her shoulder. The Tupperware I left out is sealed and waiting at the end of the counter, presumably full of puppy chow, and as I get closer, I see she's been drawing in the thin layer of powdered sugar on the countertop. There's half a dozen loops, a handful of hearts, and her own name scrawled in the light dusting of white. Part of me wishes she would've cleaned up instead of finger painting, but another part, an increasingly expanding part, would watch her create anything, even a mess.

"The puppy chow seemed pretty cooled off," she explains. "So I went ahead and finished up. Hope that's okay."

"More than okay. Thanks." I nod toward her powdered sugar art. "Impressive work," I say, and her smile comes on all at once.

"Speak for yourself." Ellie dusts the powdered sugar off her fingertips, her eyes drawing a straight line from my thin gold necklace to my worn wool socks. A buzzy warmth traces the same route along my nerve endings.

"The sweater seemed family friendly," I say, holding my arms out like a paper doll. "Bland. Nonthreatening. Does it work?"

"It works," she says, chewing her lower lip. I pause in the silence—a warmer, more inviting silence than any we've suffered through today.

"There's, um." Her eyes flutter over the crown of my head. "You've got some dry shampoo marks." She gestures toward her own roots, and I rub the heel of my hand against my scalp, trying to remove any proof that this hair hasn't been properly washed in four days.

"Worst-case scenario, we say it's powdered sugar," I joke, then crouch down, leveling the top of my head with her line of vision. "Is it better?"

"Mmm . . . Just let me."

Ellie waves me a little closer, then pushes her fingers into my hair and starts fluffing. Her tongue inches past her lips, focused again. So am I, on the crinkle of her brow, the twitch of her bright blue eyes as she tousles the white residue away. Her fingers linger a little longer than they need to, but not nearly as long as I'd like. "There. All better." She leans back to admire her work. "You look . . ."

I blink back at her, waiting for her to finish the thought. I look what? Tired? Unshowered? Like a convincing fake girlfriend?

"You look like exactly my type."

My chest locks tight, and I've never been so aware of the volume of my heartbeat or the flutter of my breathy laugh. How am I supposed to respond to that? Breeze past it? Thank her? Go back in time and ask her to homecoming? Before I can iron out the details of time travel, Ellie's hand floats back up to my scalp, giving my hair another gentle tousle before trailing her fingers down the frame of my face, landing on the stretch of skin just below my earlobe. She's tender and deliberate, the pads of her fingers resting on a part of me people don't usually notice or consider or ever, ever touch. But here she is, tracing the shadow of my ears, her fingers searching for the parts of me worth forgetting. My lips part on a breath, the beginning of a question, but Ellie steps back before I can ask.

"Perfect," she says, admiring her job well done. "If I didn't know better, I'd think you washed your hair today." With a small smile, she adds, "My mom won't question a thing."

Every bubbling feeling in me goes flat.

"Right," I choke out, forcing a smile of my own. "One totally-has-her-shit-together girlfriend, reporting for duty."

The twinkle of a ringtone interrupts this sinking ship of a moment.

"Shit." Ellie jumps down from her stool, and the fingers that rested so gently on my skin moments ago are prying her phone out of her back pocket and holding it up to her cheek. "Hey Mom, yup, almost ready, be over soon."

If there's more to the conversation, I don't hear it over the sound of my own heartbeat pounding in my ears. Her mom. Of course. We have a dinner to attend and a show to put on. When Ellie hangs up, she smiles sheepishly, just enough to show her top teeth. "We should go."

"Sounds good," I say, but my nervous laugh gives me away. "Let's get this show on the road."

I fumble with my sneakers and slip back into my jacket, and at the front door, I watch as Ellie pinches a stray blonde hair off her camel-colored coat, letting it float to the ground next to her. I can't quite explain why it makes my toes curl. Maybe just knowing there will be evidence that she was here. God, I need to get it together. "Ready?" I ask.

"Yup." She hands the puppy chow container off to me, but before I can reach for the door, her eyes narrow into that signature Meyers stare. "Real quick, though. I wanted to ask: what made you change your mind?"

I flinch. "About what?"

"About coming today," Ellie says. "And, well, playing pretend."

I roll my lips over my teeth and fidget with the zipper on my coat as I weigh out a portion of the truth. "Well, it's like you said. I want to pass accounting, you want your mom to pay for grad school."

Ellie nods, and I pause to watch as she lifts a thumb to her lips, wets it with the tip of her tongue, and rubs a blotch of powdered sugar out of her T-shirt, all while seemingly oblivious to the way it has me hypnotized.

What I don't say is the acting isn't going to be nearly as hard as I thought.

nine

*

t's an eight-minute drive from my house to Ellie's—at least that's about how long it took this morning. It's all residential roads, too, so we don't hit any holiday traffic. We're running behind schedule, so this should be good news, and under normal circumstances, it would be. Too bad today is anything but normal. I would need about eight hours to gather the amount of information on Ellie that would make me a convincing girlfriend, but we can only work with what we have, and what we have is eight minutes. Maybe ten at the snail's pace Ellie is driving to buy us a little more time.

"Okay, your favorite color is navy, your favorite movie is *Back to the Future*, and you don't have a favorite book because you don't really read." Ellie recites my own information back to me with the flat apathy of a doctor's office confirming your appointment details. Hand over hand, she turns the wheel in slow motion, pulling into her neighborhood at a crawl.

"Perfect. And for you, favorite color red, favorite movie *27 Dresses*, and favorite book is some poetry collection."

"Which poetry collection?"

I bite my cheek and hazard a guess. "Something by . . . Mary Anderson?"

"Mary Oliver," she corrects me. "But not bad."

"One more question." I just barely raise a hand, feeling like I'm back in Professor Meyers's class. "Are we going to Thanksgiving or a taping of *The Newlywed Game*?"

Ellie glosses over my joke, which was honestly too dated for either of us. Clearly my audience has been my parents for too long. "I'm just trying to be safe. Mary and I were together for almost a year, remember? You never know what will come up."

I picture Ellie and me seated at a kitchen counter with a panel of her entire family on the other side, grilling us on the sort of questions we put on our elementary school "About Me" posters to determine whether our relationship passes the reality check. "I feel like there are more reasonable things I would know about you after a year of dating. Like . . ." I pause to think, unsure if the car is even moving at this point. "Like what's your roommate's name?"

"Rachel," Ellie says. "What's yours?"

"Um." I pick at a loose hangnail. "Mom and Dad?"

"Oh right." She rolls her lips over her teeth. "Sorry."

We spend the last few seconds of the car ride wading out of an awkward silence, and by the time we're turning onto her street, I have three fun facts and a roommate's name. With that amount of basic info, I wouldn't even believe I was this girl's dental hygienist, but here we go anyway. As her house comes into view, so does the dusty-blue Subaru. It's been joined in the driveway by an olive-green Jeep, bringing another obvious question to mind. "Who all am I meeting?"

"Just my dad and my mom's sister, Carol," Ellie says.

"Right, because Marcus is with his fiancée's family." I wait for my verbal gold star for remembering, but instead all I get is:

"Right."

The car jostles beneath us, trading asphalt for concrete as we pull into the driveway. A closer view of Carol's Jeep gives me a half dozen more questions I don't have time to ask. While the geometric mountain design plastered on the back wheel cover is an odd choice for the famously flat Chicago suburbs, the bright pink NASTY WOMAN sticker on the bumper is a nice touch. I'm still trying to count exactly how many crystals are lined up on the back windshield when Ellie kills the ignition and hops out of the car, jogging over to the passenger side to get my door.

"Quite the gentleman," I murmur, handing off the puppy chow while I unbuckle. "You think your mom's watching from the window or something?"

She lifts a shoulder, drumming her fingers on the Tupperware lid. "Could be. Mostly I just don't want you spilling the muddy buddies."

"Puppy chow," I correct her, motioning for her to hand the Tupperware back. "We're gonna need to be a united front on that."

We trudge up the limestone pavers to the front porch, where the flower pots bookending the door have been given a festive makeover with craft maple leaves and tiny plastic pumpkins.

Ellie pauses, her fingers hovering just over the doorknob. "You ready?"

My stomach tucks into itself. There's no such thing as ready. Even if the drive over had been ten times longer, if we had known each other twice as many days—even if Ellie was actually my girlfriend, there's still no version of me that's prepared to spend Thanksgiving angling for a passing grade via my professor's daughter. "Ready as I'll ever be," I admit. One final bit of honesty before the performance starts.

"All right." Ellie pushes a sigh through the tight circle of her lips. "Let's do this." She cranks the doorknob to the right, releasing the thick, buttery smell of midstage dinner preparations as we step inside and into character.

"We're back," Ellie shouts to no one in particular, then kicks off her Docs and ditches her coat over the banister. I try to follow suit, but I'm still battling a stuck zipper when a scraggly looking dog with an impressive underbite trots toward me. With wispy white whiskers and crusted-over eye boogers lining his big black eyes, he's adorable in a nasty way. He yaps twice, then jumps up on my leg, his little paws barely reaching the tops of my shins.

"I think you forgot to mention someone I'd be meeting," I tease, pinching one tiny paw between my thumb and forefinger in something close to a handshake. "Nice to meet you, sir or madam."

"This is Bo." Ellie crouches to scratch behind his ears. "Carol's dog." Bo sniffs at the Tupperware of puppy chow tucked under Ellie's arm, taking the dessert's name a little too literally. "Nooo," Ellie warns, "this isn't for puppies."

"Don't let him pee on you!" A shrill voice echoes from somewhere deeper in the house, and Bo scampers off toward it. We follow shortly behind, stepping into a kitchen that feels like a suburban Mom's Pinterest board brought to life. Every stretch of the canary yellow walls offers a different word of inspiration to remind me how lucky I am to be here. Above the table, GATHER. By the fridge, THANKFUL. And over the big copper farmhouse sink, the word BLESSED is printed in big white letters on a plank of repurposed wood. If an AI were to develop a dream kitchen for the average white, midwestern mom, this would be it.

"Welcome back, girls." Professor Meyers leans against the cream granite countertop, muscling open jar after jar of pre-made cranberry sauce. Her stained apron and worn-in house shoes humanize her, but I'd recognize that stern, disappointed look in her eyes anywhere. She glances from her daughter to the clock on the stove: 3:55. "What took so long?"

"We were baking," Ellie says. "Well, sort of. Combining ingredients, at least." She turns to the other side of the counter, where a thin woman with silver tent-shaped hair and a mess of colorful necklaces is raking a vegetable peeler over a potato, sending the skins flying off in sheets. "Hi, Aunt Carol. Good to see you."

Aunt Carol looks down at Bo, who is vibrating at her feet, then toward Ellie. "Did he pee?"

"I don't think so." Ellie scans my jeans for any non-preexisting stains. "We may have gotten lucky."

"Thank God." Carol blows out an exaggerated breath of relief, the kind you might expect from someone who narrowly dodged a car crash. "He hates the doggy diapers, Kara," she goes on, returning her attention to the potato she's peeling. "Chews 'em right off."

"Um, Carol? Were you planning on saying hello to Murphy?" Kara shakes a colander of freshly boiled potatoes over the copper kitchen sink, offering me a small smile through the steam.

Whatever hypnosis the potatoes have Aunt Carol under shatters at the sound of my name. "Murphy! Ellie's girlfriend!" Her big dark eyes stretch with excitement, and I can't help but notice she more closely resembles her dog than her sister. Both the potato and peeler drop from her bejeweled fingers and onto the counter. The clatter sends Bo into a barking fit, but Carol just raises her voice over the noise. "Kara told me everything about you!"

My heart rate doubles. *Everything*? What constitutes *everything*? Was she pulling from two semesters' worth of tardies and half-assed assignments or the sparse catalogue of information Ellie's shared about her ex? I'm desperate to know, but there's no way for me to ask. It's probably better that I don't know anyway. I accept Aunt Carol's awkwardly limp hug, trying not to get tangled up in her necklaces and praying she can't feel my heart race through her oversize knit sweater. When we pull away, Carol grabs my forearms, holding me in front of her for further examination. Her eyes crinkle as she studies me, tilting her head back and forth. Bo looks up at me from her feet, his head following a similar tilting pattern. When she finally speaks, it's to Ellie, not me. "She's beautiful, El."

"Thank you," Ellie and I say in perfect unison.

"I mean it," Carol insists, speaking to me this time. "I'm telling ya, Ellie brought home some real jerks in high school, some real clunkers. I always knew she'd eventually find a sweet guy or—" She cuts herself off with a cackle, leaning into her grip on my arms. I try to laugh along with her, only because it seems like she wants me to.

"Geez, Car, let the poor girl out of your death grip," Kara scolds, waving the potato masher at her sister.

"Oh hush, Kar, I was just looking at her, is that such a crime?"

I bite my cheek, trapping the threat of nervous laughter. I'm not sure if I hate or love the parents who gave their daughters two nearly identical names, but if we run into one another in the afterlife, I want to shake their hands. You have to respect that level of commitment to chaos.

Carol loosens her grip on my arms a little, just enough for me to feel the blood flowing to my fingertips again. Her eyes, however, don't budge from my face. She pushes her lips out, scooping her chin toward the cowl of her burgundy sweater in slow, deliberate nods. "I feel like I know you already," she says.

"Can we not do the hippie-dippie stuff today?" Kara pleads, sounding her usual level of annoyed.

"No, not that, I mean I think I've seen her in the shop before." Carol tucks her silver hair behind her ears, showing off a pair of dangly gold earrings in the shape of peacock feathers that glisten under the fluorescent kitchen lights. "I've got this little jewelry and accessory store in downtown Geneva called—"

"Monarch," we both say, our voices overlapping.

Carol's eyes flicker. "Did Ellie tell you?"

"No, but I've been in the store a few times." I sneak a second look at her mess of necklaces, wondering how many are from her own inventory. Monarch has sourced my mother's Christmas presents for more years than I can count.

Carol flashes her sister a *told-you-so* look, then swivels back to me. The flicker in her eyes has grown to a full-on gleam. "I knew it," Carol says. "I knew I'd seen you around. Do you work downtown?"

"Yeah, I've worked at Sip since high school."

Kara perks up. I've used one of her trigger words. "Marcus was a barista at Sip in high school too."

"Murphy's not just a barista though," Ellie says. She balances the Tupperware on her hip and loops her free hand around my waist, pulling me so tight against her that her hip bone digs into the side of my thigh. It's bony and persistent, but I don't particularly mind, except that it's revealing some major holes in our plan. I know her roommate's name and her favorite movie, but I don't know our boundaries so far as physically playing the part of her girlfriend. Do I hold Ellie's hand at the table? Do I snuggle up to her at every chance?

"Murphy does all of Sip's marketing and social media too," Ellie goes on, blissfully unaware of the panic kicking me in the gut. "Like I told you, Mom. She's really good at business stuff."

Kara smiles just enough to prove that she heard her daughter, but not enough to convince anyone she's impressed, then pulls out her phone without saying a word. Luckily, Carol has enough words for all of us, launching into a lengthy spiel about how Sip has changed the fabric of downtown Geneva. By the way that Professor Meyers looks up from her phone every few sentences, I get the feeling she thinks her sister is spewing nonsense, but I'm eating up every word. It's a nice distraction from the list of worries compiling in my head vis-à-vis: how I should and shouldn't touch my fake girlfriend. I'm sure Carol and I could babble on for hours about Sip's impact on the downtown demographic, the need for fewer high-end stores and more shops that fit a Sip customer's needs and budgets. I could weigh in, but my attention is tied up in Ellie's hipbone, the way my skin warms around her hand on my side. I could babble on about that too.

"Here it is," Kara interrupts. She flips her phone around to show off a low-resolution photo of a teenage boy wearing an apron with the original Sip logo. He looks a little like Ellie did in high school—dark hair, blue eyes, a little on the short side—but his smile is wide and bright like something out of a Crest Whitestrip ad.

"Aww, Little Marcus." Carol lays a hand over her heart, her stack of silver bracelets clattering and clinking together. "You've gotta put that one in the slideshow for the rehearsal dinner."

"I'm sending it to him now." Kara flips her phone back around and thumbs out a message. "When we talked this morning, he said his fiancée's family Thanksgiving is going to be twenty people. Can you believe that? Twenty! No wonder the guest list for the wedding is so long." She pauses, then looks up at me to add, "Ellie's brother is spending Thanksgiving with his fiancée and her family in Sacramento."

"She knows, Mom," Ellie says. "She knows all about Marcus."

After a few scattered pieces of conversation about plus-ones and whether or not there should be a bride's and groom's side during the ceremony, the kitchen returns to the task at hand: Thanksgiving dinner. While Kara opens the last of the cranberry sauce, Carol resumes her post at the counter, putting her full weight into slicing a quarter-size eye off a potato. Ellie joins her, shaving potatoes at twice Carol's rate. She's gotten two done in the time it takes her aunt to whittle off that eye, which flies across the room and onto the floor, becoming Bo's afternoon snack. Playing the role of vacuum cleaner, the dog is officially more helpful than me. As I look around for something to do to give the illusion of helpfulness, I spot the Tupperware among the potato scraps. "I uh, brought dessert. Where should I put it?"

Kara lifts a brow. "What is it?"

"Puppy chow," I say, ready with an apology. "I know it's not really a Thanksgiving food, but . . ."

"But it's perfect," Ellie says, then lifts her cheek in what I think is a wink, but it's over so quickly, I'm not totally sure.

"You can put it with the pie on the credenza," Kara says, and although I don't know what a credenza is, I do know what a pie is. I scan the room, locate the foil-topped pie tin, and set my bowl down next to it. Out of curiosity, I peel the foil back half an inch. Pumpkin. Good thing the store was out.

"Is there anything else I can help with?" I ask, praying for a *yes*. I'm not sure how much longer I can stand around feeling completely useless.

Kara pauses to think. "Want to check on Otto? He's been fussing with that smoker all day. I'm starting to wonder if we'll even have turkey this year."

"Backyard, right?" Ellie hops down from her stool, rolling a half-peeled potato toward the middle of the counter. "C'mon, I'll introduce you."

"Uhp-uhp-uhp!" Kara protests in the sort of stuttering, finger-wagging way moms are experts in. "You're not going anywhere if we want all these potatoes to be done in time." She gives me a knowing look over her horn-rimmed glasses before adding, "She was supposed to have them done before she picked you up."

A twinge of guilt pinches my stomach. So far, my campaign for the title of teacher's pet is looking grim.

"I'll meet you out there," Ellie assures me, returning to her post at the counter. "Promise." And as much as I don't want to go out there alone, I want to stand around and feel useless even less.

I grab my shoes and coat from up front and verify one last time that there's *really* nothing I can do to help in the kitchen— *You're sure there are no more vegetable peelers? And only one potato masher, really?*—before I slip out the back door, following the low grumbles of frustration to the far end of the brick patio. The backyard is quintessentially suburban, white picket fence and all. Unlike my neighborhood, the few trees they have are newly planted and only a bit taller than I am, allowing plenty of sunlight to warm up the air. Behind a smattering of wrought-iron patio furniture, Otto is crouched over a small black pod with stainless steel legs, the bright red pom of his Cubs stocking cap bobbing as he futzes with something. When I step on an especially crunchy leaf, he looks up, startled out of his close watch on the smoker.

"Who are you?" His voice is gruff, if not a little accusatory.

"I'm Murphy. Ellie's girlfriend." I stop a few feet away from him, leaving a patio chair between us. I'd shake his hand if his gloves weren't covered in charcoal.

"Girlfriend?" Otto's face twists up. The word must sound as weird to him as it does to me. His eyes roll skyward, scanning his memory. "Yeah, I think El Bell mentioned ya. Hey, ya ever used a smoker before?"

"Can't say I have."

"Me neither," Otto says. He shoves a gloved hand into his pocket, digging out a crumpled instruction manual and holding it at a distance. "Guess I should've read this thing first. No clue if I'm doing this right."

"I'm sure it's fine," I say with more conviction than I have any right to. "How long have you been out here?"

He checks his watch. "Six hours, give or take? Although if you subtract however long the neighbor kept an eye on it while I ran out for more charcoal . . ." His laugh is more of a grunt as he stuffs the manual back into his pocket. "I don't know. Kara's the one who's good with numbers, not me."

"I'm no mathematician either," I admit, nudging a few loose wood chips into a pile with the sole of my shoe.

"Yeah?" He lifts one thick, furry brow at me. "Whatcha do for work?"

Shit. I guess I set myself up for that.

"I'm a student. And . . . a turkey smoking consultant," I joke, and his laugh turns my nerves down a notch.

"Any insights on how I'm doing, then?"

I suck my teeth, shaking my head as I study the little black jetpack of a smoker between us. "Yeah. I'd say this turkey had a serious nicotine problem. No surprise he died so young."

This time, his laugh is a full-body guffaw that shakes his shoulders. "Atta girl," he says. "You can stay."

Before we can fully settle into the comfortable lull in conversation, Otto pulls his phone from his pocket, swiping unsuccessfully at the screen with gloves on three or four times. He finally peels one off and pockets it, punching his pointer finger against the screen and thumbing up the volume until we're listening to the brassy voice of a sports broadcaster shouting about the third down. "You like football?" he asks.

I pinch the air, holding my thumb and forefinger just far enough apart to show that my football knowledge isn't zero. "More of a baseball girl."

"Cubs or Sox?"

"Cubs."

He smiles, pulling his glove back on before tugging his hat over the red shells of his ears. "Right answer. Hand me some more of those wood chips."

We work in silence for a while, feeding wood chips into the smoker and taking turns being the one to stoke the embers and the one to hold their hands up near the flame, although I'm not sure if it's to block the wind or just to keep our hands warm. We communicate in head tilts, grunts, and nods. Otherwise, the only sound between us is the carnival barker–level football commentary blaring from his phone speaker. When the Cowboys score, Otto shuts it off with a huff.

"Gonna be another Bears loss, I bet," he says in a voice more deflated than Tom Brady's football. "Stick to being a baseball fan. At least the Cubs manage a win from time to time."

"Enough to keep us hopeful every once in a hundred years," I say.

"Yeah, 2016 was a good year." He tilts his head back, checking the sky for a memory of the last Cubs World Series win. "I think I might fly out to Arizona this year for spring training since I won't make it to Wrigley much with the wedding this summer." He pauses, then looks down from the sky and back at me. "Are you coming to the wedding?"

I speed through my answer. "We haven't discussed it."

Luckily, Otto seems more interested in talking baseball anyway. "What about spring training? You ever been? It's a fuckin' party."

One f-bomb from him and any remaining tension in my body dissolves. "I've never been," I admit.

"You've been to Wrigley though, right?" His tone has shifted to concerned father mode.

"Dozens of times," I reassure him. "Don't worry. My dad raised me right, pulling me from school at least once a year for Cubs games."

"That's a good dad."

"Yeah, he's the best," I say. "He came to all my softball games growing up too."

"And what is your Cubs fan Dad up to today?"

"He's in Florida." The wind whips through the yard, an unwelcome reminder of the weather I'm missing out on. "We always go to Florida for Thanksgiving."

Otto nods, but his frown doesn't budge. "Why aren't ya there, then?"

I rub the zipper of my coat between my thumb and forefinger. Why *aren't* I there? If only he knew how many times I've asked myself the same question over the last twenty-four hours. "I hung back to . . ." I pause, revising my story in real time. "To see Ellie," I finish. "And to meet you guys, of course."

"So you're not down in Champaign?"

"Not yet. I'm trying to transfer next semester. Just gotta pass accounting first."

Otto nods and grunts. "You should ask Kara to help you," he says, oblivious. "She's an accountant. Even teaches a class at the community college."

I could correct him. I probably should. But instead, I just smile and say, "Great idea."

"How's it looking?" A familiar voice interrupts with stellar timing. I turn toward the house, where Ellie has slid the kitchen window open just enough to yell through the screen.

"Like a turkey!" Otto shouts back.

"Murphy, did you talk him into reading the instruction manual?" Ellie asks, holding up crossed fingers.

Before either of us can form a snappy reply, Kara's distant voice clucks in the background about letting the cold in, and Ellie slides the window closed again, only to reappear moments later outside the back door. In her long tan coat and a giant pair of white New Balances, she shuffles across the patio, trying not to trip on her oversize shoes.

"What, didja leave all of your shoes back in Champaign?" Otto teases. "Have to steal mine now?"

"I didn't feel like lacing up my Docs," Ellie says, shaking one giant white sneaker toward her dad. "These are cool. You know Dad shoes are back in style again?"

"Oh good," Otto snorts. "You know how I always have to be in style." He drags the side of his glove beneath his nose, wiping snot away. "Colder than a witch's tit out here."

Ellie cringes at the expression, but it gets an honest laugh out of me. It's the kind of thing my dad would say, the sort of nonsensical phrase he probably got from his own father. It makes me miss him.

"What's your level of familiarity with witch tits, Dad?" Ellie asks, tilting her head to the side to feign innocent curiosity. I have to dig my fingernails into my palms to keep from making an obvious joke at Professor Meyers's expense.

"Is that what you came out into the cold to ask us?" Otto asks gruffly.

"No, I came out here to check on Murphy." Ellie steps behind me, rubbing her hands up and down my arms for warmth. "And the turkey. We're getting close to being ready inside."

"Murphy's doin' great," Otto says, and I don't even mind him speaking on my behalf. "Hey, why didn't ya tell me you were dating a Cubs fan? We coulda gone to a game together this fall, maybe grabbed a few beers at Murphy's Bleachers." I hear the sharp inhale as he realizes what he's said, and he turns toward me with an open-mouthed smile. "Hey! *Murphy's* Bleachers!"

My smile matches his. "I was named after that place. I introduce myself that way sometimes. Murphy, like the bleachers."

"Only works if you're in this part of the world though, huh?"

I replay my clumsy exchange with Daniel from last night. "Even then, not everyone gets it."

"Well I guess they can't all be Cubs fans," Otto says wistfully. "Somebody has to cheer for the losing team."

"Dad!" Ellie interrupts. "Focus! The turkey? How long until it's done?"

"Right, right." Otto shifts the cover off the top of the smoker just long enough to get a read on the meat thermometer. "Thirty, forty-five minutes? No later than five thirty."

"Gotcha," Ellie says. "I'll tell Mom. Cool if I steal Murphy to help me set the table?"

With the thumbs-up from Otto, Ellie weaves her fingers into mine, pulling me toward the house and out of earshot. "How'd it go?"

I ignore the tingle that runs across the hand she's holding. "Good, I think."

She frowns. "Just good?"

"Excellent? I like your dad."

She pinches my thigh and loops a thumb into one of my belt loops, giving it a gentle tug. "I figured you might. It seems like he likes you. And Carol won't stop talking about how you're some kind of sign from the universe."

My nose scrunches. "A sign of what?"

"I'm not really sure, but it seems to be a good thing. The point is, she likes you too."

"Yeah, well." I suck in a deep breath and let it out on a sigh. "Two down, one that actually matters to go."

"Give Mom some time. She'll warm up in time for dinner, and then we'll bring up grades and grad school." Ellie tugs on my belt loop again, pulling me toward the side of the house. "C'mon, I gotta show you the garage."

I arch a skeptical brow. "We're setting the table in the garage?"

"Noooooo," she says, dragging out the *o*'s as she shuffles her giant shoes against the brick. "Trust me. There's something I need to show you first."

ten

✳

There's less than a foot of driveway between the garage door and the rusted front grille of Carol's Jeep. It'd be plenty of room for all five foot nothing of Ellie were she wearing normal shoes, but she's still sporting her father's size 14 New Balances, so watching her try to squeeze through to the garage door opener is like watching an old slapstick comedy. Lucky for all of us, she narrowly avoids a fall onto the hood of Carol's car, but when she mashes her pointer finger against the light-up numbers of the garage door opener, the buttons flash back in warning. Three wrong codes in a row.

"Do you need me to go in and ask someone?" I suggest, but Ellie either doesn't hear me or doesn't care to respond.

"What year did the Cubs win the big baseball thing again?" she asks.

"The World Series? 2016."

This she hears loud and clear, and when she punches in

2-0-1-6, the garage door grinds to life. "You're gonna love this," Ellie says with a brilliant smile.

The garage door creeps up inch by inch, hinting at flashes of bold reds and royal blues behind it. It's not until the door is completely lifted, hanging parallel to the Astroturf below, that I fully process what I'm looking at: a miniature, 18 x 20-foot Wrigley Field.

"No way," I whisper. "No fucking way."

Just the wooden recreation of the Wrigley Field sign would have been reason enough to drag me to the garage. Or the pitch-back, stationed in the center of the fake grass outfield. But the back wall, covered in floor-to-ceiling craft ivy; the forest-green stadium seats, which are either perfect replicas or stolen straight from the third-base line; and the sizable collection of Cubs player portraits, framed and autographed . . . I think I just stepped into a miracle.

"This is Dad's retirement project," Ellie explains, flipping on a space heater in the corner. "I figured you would appreci-ate it."

Appreciate it is an understatement. I want to *move into* this garage. I follow a few paces behind Ellie, each step weighted with the cautious excitement of a little kid entering a museum. "This is wild," I say, not really to anyone but myself, but Ellie breathes a laugh anyway.

"The original plan was to build it in my room when I left for school," Ellie explains, "but I like this better than sleeping in the garage when I'm home. Although Mom hates that she has to leave the Subaru in the driveway."

I trail my fingers along the taped-off square in the center of the pitchback. It's a little worn, but not enough to suggest any real use. "Does your dad play?"

"No, that's leftover from Dad's *last* project. Turning me into a softball star." Ellie's smile is small and apologetic. "He gave up on that one somewhere between sixth and seventh grade."

"So you played?"

She sputters in dissent. "What part of me walking the mile would make you think that?"

I'm tempted to mention that not all softball players are runners, but it hardly feels like a relevant argument. "I guess the crossover between AP Art and extracurricular sports is . . ."

"Zero."

"I believe it." Beside the pitchback, a white paint bucket filled with baseballs catches my eye. The mitt balanced on top doesn't have an autograph or any kind of sticker labeling it a collector's item, so I slip my hand inside. It fits like, well, a glove.

"Remind me exactly when you quit playing again?" Ellie asks.

"Midseason junior year, when I tore my rotator cuff. Just in time for the recruiters to show up to watch me ruin my career in real time." I select a baseball from the top of the bucket. Again, no autographs, no stickers, no nothing, so I throw it into the mitt, adjusting to the size and weight of it. Softballs are heavier, but the brace of my wrist and the clap of a ball against leather is the same. A prickle of familiarity inches up my forearms and toward my chest, and I fight the urge to imagine a life where I never had to take the mitt off. If everything had gone according to plan, I'd be gearing up for a third season pitching for a DI team—ideally U of I, but I would've gone anywhere with a persuasive recruiter who could guarantee I'd be pitching all four years. It's all fantasy now, but unlike most days, my reality isn't so bad. It's a decked-out garage, a mitt that fits, and a girl who's waiting to see what I've got.

After a centering breath, I adjust my stance, wind up, and throw a knuckleball dead center into the pitchback. The net recoils, launching the ball right back into my mitt. *Thunk*. God, I missed that sound.

"Oh wow," Ellie whispers. "You're like *good* good."

"Not like I used to be, but I still remember a little." I wind up again. Curveball this time, right into the sweet spot. The pitchback does what it's meant to do. *Thunk*, right back into the mitt.

"Seems like you still remember a lot."

I turn the ball over in my hand, inspecting it for scuffs. "It's like riding a bike. Once it's in your body, it stays there."

"Deep," Ellie teases.

"Shut up." I throw a third pitch, hitting the corner of the tape this time. Not my best. "See?" I point at the pitchback as evidence. "They're not all perfect pitches."

A flicker of something wicked and wild dances through her eyes. "It doesn't have to be perfect to be good," Ellie says, and the breathy rhythm of her voice tests my balance more than I'd ever admit.

"Using my own words against me, huh?"

"You know it."

For the next few pitches, she watches me closely, her eyes hot on my skin with every throw. Eventually, she stops following the ball, examining only me. "How'd you hurt yourself?"

she finally asks. The inevitable question anytime my softball career gets brought up.

I tap the mitt against my right shoulder. "Overuse. I kept pitching even when my shoulder started to bug me, and then during a tournament it just . . ." I shudder the memory away, unwilling to relive the details. "Long story short, bad form did me dirty."

"Really?" Ellie arches a brow. "You look good to me."

My stomach twists. She steps up behind me, and on my next pitch, I can feel her mirroring my movements at half effort, like a dancer marking her choreography. When my weight shifts, her weight half shifts. When I follow through, she half follows through. When I turn around, she blushes, caught in the act.

"You need a mitt if you're gonna catch it," I point out.

"Or you could just catch it for me." Ellie rests a hand on my shoulder, watching her own thumb as it strokes tiny circles against the knit of my sweater. There's no one here to witness her tenderness—not Kara or Otto or even Bo—but no part of me wants to remind her of that. "How's your arm now?" she asks.

"Better. I can throw a little." I tip my head toward the pitchback as if it'll agree. "If I took it easy, I might be able to play in a community league or something." Just the possibility sparks a little hope in my belly.

"You should," she says. "It's cool to see you do your thing."

I slip off the mitt, and Ellie takes her hand off my shoulder. I shouldn't have moved. "What about you?" I ask, wiggling the tension and the fluttery feeling out of my fingers. "What's your thing? Apart from painting."

She tilts her head, searching the ceiling for a response. "I dunno."

"What do you mean you dunno?"

"I mean, there's painting for pleasure, and there's painting for school." She holds out her hands with her palms facing up, weighing pleasure and school against one another. "It feels like two separate things, ya know?"

I nod, but I don't know, really. Work feels like work. School feels like school. Getting high and watching *RuPaul's Drag Race* feels like getting high and watching *RuPaul's Drag Race*. I've never known a world with overlaps, one where I'm so passionate about one thing that I do it for more than one reason. "So what's the difference?"

"For school it's like . . . timed drawing and painting exercises and practicing different styles, right?" Ellie snatches the baseball from my mitt, holding it to the overhead garage light. It casts long, oval shadows, the perfect scene for a still life. "And I don't get to just *paint* either. There's so much art history and figure drawing and classes like Current Issues in Art. But when I'm just painting, then it's just for me. No deadline or distractions. I can just make something because I want to."

"But then what?" I press. "What if painting becomes your job? Say you're the next Monet . . ."

She cuts me off. "I won't be the next Monet. After grad school, I'll be a health-care worker with a paintbrush."

"And you're cool with that?"

"Cool with it? I love it." She tosses the ball underhand to me, but I have to lunge to catch it. "No one's getting rich as an art therapist, which is why grad school debt is such a no go, but it'd be nice to actually help people. Then I can paint just to paint. On my own terms, you know?"

I study the crinkle of a smile reaching the corners of her eyes, feeling every bit the asshole for what I'm about to ask next. "And what if your mom won't pay for grad school? Then what?"

As suspected, her smile falls. "Then I've honed a skill that I'll use for a lifetime of homemade presents for my parents. So that's something, I guess."

I snort a laugh. "I bet your dad would love that though." I tilt my head toward the curated collection of autographed player pictures. Even from across the garage, I recognize Fergie Jenkins' mustache and a young Sammy Sosa, pre-corked bat incident. "You could paint his favorite player, or like, Wrigley Field."

"Or Yankee Stadium," Ellie suggests, and a tiny bit of disappointment curdles in my stomach. Right. Even standing right in front of me, her heart is in New York.

I toss the ball back to her as gently as I can. Without a mitt, she fumbles for it, then chases it across the Astroturf. "Are you gonna show me how to throw this or what?" Ellie finally asks, cradling the ball in both hands like a baby bird. I've never seen someone so unnatural with a baseball.

"I can try." My gaze dips down to her feet. "But I'd ditch the clown shoes first."

Once Ellie's down to her socks, I find her a mitt and position myself behind her, fighting every instinct to close the we're-definitely-just-friends amount of distance between us. I move her arm into pitching position, but the moment I let go, her arm drops a half inch, so I guide her elbow back into place with a gentle nudge of my fingertips. I like having a reason to touch her, even if it's just like this. "So the secret is to keep your feet and shoulders squared off toward your target." I plant my feet one at a time to demonstrate, drawing invisible lines between my shoulders and my toes. "See?"

Ellie nods and mimics me, peeking back over her shoulder to be sure she's the perfect reflection of every shift of my weight and bend of my elbow. Set, aim, follow through. I mime throwing an invisible ball right alongside her.

"Like you're throwing a dart," I say, squaring her shoulders for her. She pulls back and proceeds to throw the ball straight past the pitchback, nearly knocking a framed Ron Santo picture off the wall.

"Should I take up softball?" she asks, full sarcasm.

"You're not as bad as you think," I say with a shrug. "You could probably join a community league."

She squints at me. "You're lying."

"Of course I am."

With a full-throated laugh that goes straight to my ego, Ellie chases down the ball again and gets back in position, wiggling her butt a little for effect. This time, the ball hits the netting, but when the pitchback does its signature and only move, she shrieks and ducks out of the way. I reach out my mitt to catch it. *Thunk*.

Ellie's eyes stretch with horror. "You sure you weren't a catcher?"

"What can I say? I'm a woman of many skills."

After two more throws, Ellie starts holding up her own mitt. Five more and she catches it for the first time, startling herself a little when she does. Ten or so down the line, she throws one within the tape, and it shoots back right into the pocket of her glove.

"There you go!" I shout, sounding just like my old warm-up coach, but feeling twice as proud. "You did it!"

Ellie stares at me, slack-jawed and blinking in disbelief. "That was good, right?" she asks, barely holding back excitement.

"Yes," I assure her. "That was really good."

"That was really good!" She throws her arms into the air and the ball goes flying as she runs a miniature victory lap around herself. "New York Yankees, here I come!" As she stretches out her celebration, pride swells like a rising tide in my chest. At least I think it's pride. Whatever it is, it's warm and full and alive, and I hope it never goes away.

"You can pitch!"

"I can pitch!" she echoes, my very own verbal pitchback. She rounds out her victory lap, positioning me as her finish line, and she skids to a stop just in front of me, bright eyed and grinning from ear to ear. "Thanks for the help, coach," she murmurs, then plants her mitt on my bad shoulder and, before I even realize what's happening, presses her lips against mine.

When it comes to first kisses, Ellie Meyers is not a long, fireworks-and-butterflies type; she's soft and simple, and it's over before I can get a hold on what's real. The head rush is instant, though, as is the certainty that if that's acting, I need an encore. My hands find the curve of her waist through the emerald silk, drawing her back up onto her tiptoes and guiding her mouth to mine again. With a brush of my tongue, her lips part like two tiny ballet slippers, opening in a way that's gentle, giddy, and so perfectly Ellie. A fluttery feeling bridges the arches of my feet, and with each sweep of my tongue against hers, I wade deeper into something I'm supposed to only pretend to have. Friends don't do this. Group project partners definitely don't do this. But here she is, and here I am, and nothing about it feels pretend. She tastes like coffee, and I'd drink her all afternoon if she would let me. Cancel Thanksgiving. Cancel Christmas too. Give me weeks and months to learn the plush of her lower lip, the way it rebounds when I release it from my gentle bite. Her kiss feels like hope, like coming home, and I never want to go anywhere else.

"El Bell! Can you come here for a sec?"

We startle apart, and I could choke on my frustration if my heart weren't already lodged in my throat. Ladies and theydies, it's the queer cock block and royal pain in my ass, Kara Meyers. She's really outdone herself: not only has she cut short my make-out session with her daughter; she's left us no time to discuss what it means. We stare at each other for a long moment and if my face looks anything like Ellie's, I'm the color of a near-ripe raspberry. We're frozen in the silence until she clears her throat.

"That's, uh. That . . . that's my cue," she stutters. She slides the mitt off and passes it to me with trembling hands, and I watch as her cheeks turn a pale shade of pink. So we're both shaken up. That's sort of reassuring.

I open my mouth to ask a question, but I can't seem to land on which one to ask. "Did you . . . what did . . . maybe we should?" My head feels like an overflowing aquarium, and each flopping fish of a thought dies before I can form a complete sentence.

"El Bell!" Kara yells again. "Did you hear me?"

"Y-yes Mom, coming!" Ellie shouts back, then lowers her voice to the volume of a sigh. "I guess we should get back inside."

"You go ahead," I say with a wave toward the door. "I'll, uh, be there in a sec. I . . . I'm gonna check in with my parents." I ditch both mitts and retrieve my phone from my back pocket, ready to invent some sort of important business that needs my attention just to buy myself some recoup time. Conveniently, I have three texts from Kat, so I won't have to improvise after all. I'm about to open the notification when I feel Ellie's warm gaze over my shoulder.

"Who the hell is Big Booty?"

My chest flattens against my lungs, completely bulldozed by embarrassment. "Oh, uh. That's Kat." I hit the side button, and the screen dips to black. "It's just a joke."

Ellie's brows pinch together for a moment, but it's so quick that I'm sure I imagined it. "Um, okay. See you inside." Just like that, she's gone.

When the door to the house clicks behind her, my sweaty palms and shaky fingers fumble to swipe open Kat's messages. I could use a distraction from . . . all of that. It was what I wanted, right? For Ellie to kiss me? And it was better than I ever could've hoped. But was it a fluke? Did she change her mind about us just being friends? Or maybe she's doubling back on her "no casual hookups" rule? I'm surprised to feel my heart squeeze, to learn that's definitely not all I want from Ellie Meyers. Maybe she just got . . . carried away, and so did I when I pulled her back in for more. It's more than I can make sense of, so I focus on my phone instead. Kat's provided plenty in the way of distractions. She's sent over two pictures in the last hour—one of their family dog, George, with his paws on the table and his giant basset ears dipping into the gravy bowl, and one of a Scrabble tile rack with the letters arranged to form the word QUEEF. Beneath the pictures, a quick text:

> accurate portrait of how thanksgiving is going so
> far. how's cleaning going???

I breathe a near-silent laugh at the pictures, but there's a kick of guilt behind my rib cage at the cleaning comment. If I'd been honest with her about today's change of plans, we'd be overanalyzing the hell out of that kiss right now. I'd walk her through every fact and question and messy feeling, and she'd hang on to every word, the way we both always do. Kat would probably crack a joke about my fake girlfriend being more complicated than her real relationship, and she'd have just the right pep talk to get me back in that house to do what I set out to do: schmooze. But I can't tell her any of it, and without my usual sounding board, the unknowns feel too scary to face alone.

I don't have a choice though. At least not for the moment. Eventually, I'll have to admit that I chose Thanksgiving with Ellie over more time with Kat, and she'll inevitably get every detail out of me. But not right now. Not when we're both juggling chaos, and certainly not when we're facing true tragedy, like a missed opportunity to play QUEEF in Scrabble with your Bubby. I keep the conversation focused on Kat instead.

scale of one to ten, how bad is it?

A full three minutes pass without a response, validating my choice to keep quiet on the drama of my day. Kat's busy. Of course she's busy. She's introducing her boyfriend to her parents and grandparents and all bazillion of her cousins. She doesn't have time to text me, and she wouldn't have had time for me if I were there today. The uneasy feeling in my stomach levels out a smidge. Ellie is confusing, sure, but at least I don't have to vie for her attention.

I pocket my phone and, before heading inside, slide the mitt back on for one last pitch: a fastball. No spin, no curve, just a steady, reliable pitch. *Thunk*. Straight into the center of the pitchback, then right into the center of my glove. I wish everything could be that straightforward.

eleven

❄

Do you have enough room, Murphy?"

I sidestep into my designated place at the kitchen table, a folding chair wedged in with the four-piece oak dining set. None of us has any personal space, but crammed in with my back against the bay window, I've certainly got it the worst.

"Of course," I lie, then fold my arms mummy style so I don't bump Ellie or Carol on either side as I settle into my seat. Any backward movement and I'll bang my head on the window; forward, I'll dunk an elbow in the cranberry sauce. As long as I don't move, Thanksgiving should be a breeze.

"How'd we ever fit at this table with Mom, Dad, and Marcus?" Carol asks as she scooches her chair another half inch away from mine. It's a nice gesture, but it doesn't do much good.

"I'm fine," I insist. "Promise." I'd hold a hand up in oath if there were enough room to do so. I'm not fine, really, but that has very little to do with my lack of space. It's entirely the fault of the extremely cute and brutally confusing girl seated beside me, the one whose thigh is pressed against mine just enough to make my head spin. In the wake of our little off-script moment in the garage, every little touch feels magnified, more electric, and in turn, more confusing. I've lost the line between real and pretend, but for better or worse, that doesn't impact our plan. We've got two critical topics to bring up, and neither of them are our feelings.

"All righty, where do you want me to put this?" A booming voice interrupts. Otto, the only one not seated, saunters in with a giant bowl of mashed potatoes balanced between his belly and his forearm. By the eye daggers he's getting from Kara, you'd think he'd walked in with his own head on a pike.

"There's no room," Kara growls, sweeping a hand through the air across the width of the table. "This is why I told you to use the green bowl."

Otto lifts a shoulder. "But there were a lot of potatoes."

The two of them tumble into an argument, and I'm glad to have the attention off me for a second. No wonder people complain about the holidays. There are so many moving parts and people and traditions. And this is only five people. Marcus's Thanksgiving has twenty. My parents knew exactly what they were doing starting the Florida Thanksgiving tradition before I was old enough to know any other version of this holiday.

The bickering dies down, ending in a compromise: the potatoes will remain in the big ornate bowl for the sake of not dirtying another dish, but they'll stay on the counter, and anyone who wants them will simply need to go get them. A perfectly reasonable solution, although you wouldn't think it by the tick of Kara's jaw.

"The turkey smells awesome, Otto," Carol says. "And Kara, the rest looks absolutely delicious."

"Well, the stuffing is a little burnt," Kara grumbles, "but thank you."

I can hear Ellie's voice in my head from earlier this afternoon. *If we can make it perfect, why wouldn't we?*

"Come on," Kara says, "let's say grace."

Everyone extends a hand to either side, and it takes me a moment to get the hint. I wasn't raised in a praying family, and I've never even eaten dinner with a hand-holding family, but when in Rome. Carol takes my right hand, and I place my left in Ellie's, simultaneously calmed and confused by the stroke of her thumb against the soft space between my thumb and forefinger. They all recite something close to a nursery rhyme, and I remember to chime in at the "Amen."

No sooner have we dropped hands than the plates start passing, a revolving door of dishes moving from one person to the next. It's methodical and silent, apart from the clanging of serving spoons against dishware and the quiet murmurs of compliments on the juiciness of the turkey or the snap of the green beans. When the carousel of casseroles has completed one full rotation, everything returns to its place, each dish settling back in to the only configuration that will allow it all to fit.

"So Murphy," Kara starts, lifting her first bite of stuffing to her lips. "Ellie mentioned you have a job lined up after you graduate?"

It feels like my brain is cracking its knuckles. I guess Ellie wasn't kidding about her mom's priorities; I guess we're getting right to it.

"Right, uh, sorta," I say. A weak start. "I'm already running the marketing for Sip, but once I graduate, I'm planning to start my own marketing consulting business." I turn to Ellie for reassurance that I said the right thing, and she squeezes my thigh under the table to confirm that, yes, I got my line right.

Kara, however, is slightly less encouraging. "You're *planning* to?" She peers at me over her glasses. "It's just an idea, then?"

"No, I'm *going* to," I correct myself quickly. "It's, uh, already in the works. You wouldn't believe the number of small businesses in Geneva who are trying to work with me." That's not entirely a lie. She really wouldn't believe the number: zero.

"Add Monarch to that list," Carol chimes in, bumping that number up to one. "We could use the help."

"I'll put you on the wait list," I say to Carol with more confidence than I'm entitled to. Look at me go, marketing my nonexistent company.

"So you're planning to stay in the area, then?" Kara asks. It's directed more toward her daughter than me.

"We're figuring it out," Ellie says. "Murphy still has at least a year of school left after I graduate. We have time."

Kara nods toward her daughter, then turns her attention back to me. "I can't imagine the suburbs can compare to your summer in New York." If she sees me flinch, she doesn't acknowledge it. The easy part of the lie is over; we're on hard mode now.

"Oh! Yeah. My internship." I pick up my fork and skewer a few green beans. "New York was cool."

The silence that follows feels light-years long, and Kara looks at me, stone-faced, through all of it. I don't even taste the green beans as I chew them; all I can focus on is my own heart beating in my ears. When Ellie nudges me with her thigh, I swallow hard and try again. "I mean, I could even see myself living there. In New York, I mean. I could see . . . us . . . living there." I turn toward Ellie, whose limp smile reads as less of a good job and more of an eh, you could've done worse. It's enough of a smile to show her dimple, though, which feels like a win to me.

Carol waves a spoonful of cranberry sauce as if to command our attention. "Lemme get this right. You'd live in New York and work with shops in Geneva? How would that even work?"

"Um, yeah." Panic creeps up my throat like a stubborn pill. I gulp it down with my green beans and try again. "Yeah, I would. There's so much you can do remotely these days, and . . ."

"And we're figuring it out," Ellie says for a second time in as many minutes. "What's important is that things are looking great for Murphy's business already."

Kara lifts a brow. "Oh?"

"Yup," Ellie continues, and I unclench my glutes while she takes the lead. "We'll have no trouble affording a nice apartment, and I'll be able to pursue my next steps wherever we are. Los Angeles, New York . . ."

"Hey," Otto interrupts, wiping turkey grease from his lips, "what about Chicago? Ever thought about livin' in Wrigleyville?"

I work up a smile before letting him down gently. "I'm not sure I'd want to live in Wrigleyville," I say. It sounds nicer than the truth: that Wrigleyville is a petri dish of overgrown frat boys and, therefore, a complete no go for anything but a night on the town.

"Wrigleyville is right by Boystown," Carol points out. She looks quite proud of herself for knowing that.

"That's true. I could definitely see myself living there," I say.

"Except we don't really see ourselves in Chicago." Ellie spits her consonants a little extra, nudging my thigh with hers again.

"Oh. Right," I agree, but the disappointment on Otto's face has me padding the landing. "I'll probably be in the suburbs this summer though. Maybe Ellie and I can catch a home game at Wrigley if we're up there for Pride in June." The words come easier to me than I can rationalize. I didn't expect making fake plans with my fake girlfriend to feel this natural.

Kara frowns at her daughter. "June? The wedding is in June."

"We don't have to block off the whole month, Mom," Ellie reminds her, then turns back to me. "I've never been to Pride. That'd be fun, if I'm in town."

I bite my cheek, curbing my excitement at the thought of bringing Ellie to Hydrate or Roscoe's or any of the other legendary gay bars that have thrown me and my fake ID out onto Halsted Street. I haven't been back since turning twenty-one in September, mostly because I've had no one to go with. Kat is so far from Chicago, and even if she was more local, taking my straight best friend to a gay bar feels sort of like riding a corporate float in the Pride parade. Fun enough, but a little forced. Ellie, on the other hand? I can easily picture us cheering and posing for pictures in front of rainbow balloon arches. In my mind's eye, we're kissing in those pictures . . . but that's not allowed, is it?

"We should all go to Pride!" Aunt Carol pipes up, interrupting my gay daydream. "I've always wanted to see the parade."

Kara clears her throat in her sister's direction. "Pride isn't for you, Carol."

"Pride is for everyone," I assure her. "I mean, as long as you're not homophobic or anything. I know plenty of people who bring their family."

"See?" Carol waves her fork at her sister. "It's called being an *ally* to your bisexual daughter."

"Is that how you . . . what is it, *identify*, as well?" Kara lifts a brow at me. "Bisexual? I try to keep up with all these terms, but it seems like they're always inventing a new one."

Ellie tenses up next to me. I can feel it. Maybe because she's only about an eighth of an inch away. "We're not inventing anything," she says, overarticulating each syllable. "We're—"

"Gay," I interrupt. "I'm actually just gay. Plain old gay. Pretty easy to understand." I hope that will be the end of the conversation, but when Kara clears her throat again, it feels like we're teetering on the edge of something worse.

"When did you and your last girlfriend break up?" she asks.

I tilt my head, trying to scare up the name of the girl I briefly dated two summers ago. If you can even call it dating. She might've just been using me for my Sip discount. "Who?"

"The dark-haired one." Kara twirls her fork around her head, suggesting curls. "You two were attached at the hip. She was such a pleasure to have in class."

My whole body goes numb apart from the slow burn of heat creeping over my cheeks and down my chest. There's only one verified pleasure to have in class that I know, and we've certainly never dated. I swallow hard, forcing a too-big bite of stuffing down my throat. It goes down with a fight. "That's Kathryn,"

I choke out. "She's not my girlfriend. I mean, she was never my girlfriend. She's straight. We're just friends."

"Kathryn, yes, that's it." Kara straightens in her seat, unfolding and refolding her cloth napkin before dropping it into her lap. "You two just seemed really close is all."

"We are close," I say. "Close friends."

Kara looks skeptical, but she doesn't push the point. "Well, regardless. I really liked Kathryn."

I force a smile that I hope reads as polite. *I know. That's why you passed her.*

Otto looks up from his plate for the first time since the conversation strayed from Wrigleyville. "Wait. Kara's your teacher?" His bushy brows smush together, and when no one says anything, his big belly laugh rumbles the silverware on the table. "Wow, that's a hoot." He wags a finger between me and Ellie. "Is that how you two met?"

If I thought my cheeks were hot before, they're surely on fire now. "Uh, no . . ." I turn toward Ellie, panic bouncing from my eyes to hers. "I mean . . ."

"We met in high school and reconnected last year," Ellie says, as breezy and calm as I am tense. "Murphy insisted that she didn't want any special treatment in class just because she's dating me, so we opted not to tell you, Mom."

I almost choke on my turkey. I can't believe how opposite that is from the truth.

"That's quite mature of you, Murphy," Professor Meyers says, the threat of a smile twitching at her thin lips. "I'm impressed."

The table is quiet apart from Carol's open-mouthed chewing, until Otto gets our attention with a phlegmy cough. "Anyway. *Murphy*." He says my name like it's the perfect joke. "Ms. *Bleachers*. We're glad ya came."

"Hell yeah, we are," Carol echoes.

"We're thankful to have you here," Kara says, her lips finally giving way to a toothy grin.

"Is that an official thankful submission?" Carol leans in to ask, the wispy ends of her hair dipping into the gravy.

"Not yet!" Ellie's eyebrows leap up her forehead in warning. "Not till dessert!"

I frown at Ellie. "We can't be thankful till dessert?"

"Did El Bell not tell you?" Carol asks. "During dessert, we all say what we're thankful for. It's tradition."

I turn toward Ellie. Did she tell me? I don't remember, but admittedly, we were speed running through each other's personal lives. I'm liable to have missed a detail or two.

The squeak of Kara's chair rivals sneakers on a high school gym floor. She gets up, and for a moment I'm sure she's walking out. Instead, she heads for what I now know is the credenza. "Did she tell you we keep a journal?"

"I don't think I brought it up," Ellie says.

Her mother tugs open a drawer and starts riffling through a stockpile of takeout napkins. "Here it is." She returns to her seat, shifting her plate to make room for a small notebook with gold spiral binding and a pale-blue cover featuring a watercolor-style hummingbird. "We've been doing this since the kids were little." She turns back the cover, running her finger along the smudged pencil script. "Here it is. 2004, Marcus is thankful for Mom and Dad. So sweet. Ellie is thankful for grape juice."

"Still true," Ellie murmurs into her wine glass.

"Otto was thankful for no snow, Bruce Springsteen, and that he has tomorrow off work. Grandma was thankful for Grandpa and vice versa, I was thankful for my new teaching job, and Carol was thankful for"—she squints and frowns at the page—"her divorce lawyer."

"Also still true," Carol says. "I might say that again this year."

"No repeats," Ellie says. "That's another rule. Except for Grandma and Grandpa. They got to be thankful for each other every year."

"It's a bullshit rule," Otto grumbles. "If I'd known *that*, I wouldn't have listed multiple things those first few years."

"Try having a crappier life," Carol says. "Then you'd have less to be thankful for."

"Or more," Kara says. "We were extra thankful during the recession." She flips a few pages, presumably landing on 2008. "Marcus is thankful for his Xbox, Ellie is thankful for her slippers, Grandma and Grandpa are thankful for each other again, Otto is thankful for . . ." She draws in a deep breath, then rattles off about fifteen household items from the toaster to the towels.

"I did towels already?" Otto groans. "We have different towels now, does that count as a repeat?"

"Still counts," Ellie says, a tiny satisfied smile pulled across her lips. Why do I get the feeling she's the one who made up this rule?

"I think it's great that you can't do repeats," I say, angling for the title of most supportive fake girlfriend. "It's a great tradition. My family never really put much emphasis on the thankful portion of Thanksgiving."

Ellie pivots toward me, her smile relaxing into something more genuine. "You're lucky. First year, fresh start. You can be thankful for anything."

I run my tongue along the front of my teeth, sucking out any turkey that might be wedged in the gaps. My instinct is to opt for something goofy: I'm thankful that my hangover didn't last. For the dry shampoo that's hiding my hair washing crimes. For the happy accident of bringing puppy chow instead of a store-bought pumpkin pie that wouldn't hold a candle to Aunt Carol's, I'm sure. It's all true, and it's all to avoid the sappy, entirely unhilarious reality: I'm thankful to be here on a day I otherwise might've spent playing second fiddle or entirely alone. Instead, I have the undivided attention of a girl who gives me butterflies—no, not just butterflies. Hummingbirds, flapping their watercolor wings at an impossible speed just behind my chest.

Ellie presses her thigh against mine again, and I turn toward her, worried that I've said or done the wrong thing. Instead, I'm met with a sheepish smile as her gaze hovers over my lips. Maybe I'm not the only one losing track of what's pretend and what's very, very real.

twelve

❉

Once the plates are cleared and the excessive compliments on the food have run out, we all retire to the family room for what seems to be a weird intermission separating dinner from dessert. I guess we all need a little time to kick back and digest—all of us, that is, except for Kara, who keeps her post in the kitchen, busily scrubbing dishes and boxing up the mashed potatoes we all forgot to eat. I must've offered a half dozen times for Ellie and me to take over as cleanup crew, which had really been more of an attempt to secure a little private time to talk to Ellie. Unfortunately for me, Kara was having none of it, and I've been booted to the living room with the other noncontributors.

Everyone else seems to have accepted their place on the sidelines: Otto is slumped into his leather recliner, snoring softly; Aunt Carol is working her way through a small mountain of Black Friday newspaper ads on the floor; and Ellie is cozied on the far end of the leather couch, half watching the football game on TV. Following their cues, I join Ellie on the couch. I loop an arm around her to guide her closer, and Ellie takes the invitation, snuggling in. With her back flush to my chest, she fits against me perfectly, like a mug in its corresponding saucer. I rest my chin on the top of her head, breathing in her grapefruit shampoo. We're barely situated when she starts to fidget.

"Hey," Ellie whispers, just loud enough for me to hear, but quiet enough to be drowned out by the football announcer and the rustle of Aunt Carol flipping through ads. "Can we talk?"

Finally, the discussion we must've both been waiting for. I was hoping she'd be the one to bring up the kiss, but this wasn't the venue I was expecting. I look from Otto to Aunt Carol, who both seem oblivious to our whispers. "Here? Are you sure?"

"Yeah, just real quick."

It's not exactly private, but it's better than going another minute without discussing what happened in the garage. I count five seconds of an inhale before agreeing with a nod. "Okay," I say. "What's up?" As if I don't already know.

"Would you mind taking it a little easier on the Chicago talk?"

I don't just flinch; my full body spasms. "What?"

"The Wrigleyville and Boystown stuff," Ellie specifies. "Can we steer things back toward New York to set up the grad school conversation during dessert?" In the silence of me trying to form a response, she scoots out of my arms and turns so we're face-to-face. "Does that make sense?"

"Yeah . . . yeah, that makes sense." I force down what feels like a fist-size lump in my throat. "I just . . . is that . . . all? Or is there anything else you want to talk about?"

She gives my hand a little squeeze. It sends a tight, tingly feeling down every nerve. "Nope," she says, "that's it."

That's it? Is that a joke? My mouth dries up, and my heart feels like it's skidding down a Slip 'n Slide hours after someone shut off the hose. If she won't bring up the kiss, I have to, but it takes a bit to generate enough spit to speak up. "Okay, but can we talk about the—"

"Get a load of this!" Aunt Carol's squawk startles us both with a jolt. Jesus Christ. The interrupting genes are strong in this family.

"What is it?" Ellie asks. "Did you find a good deal?" I guess our private conversation has gone public again.

Carol holds up a flimsy Kohl's ad that folds in on itself before we can read it. "Up to eighty percent off the whole store! How do they keep their doors open doing this sort of shit?"

"Up to eighty percent probably means only some clearance is eighty percent off," I explain. "The rest will be, like, thirty percent. But it gets you to show up." I hope that will be the end of it and Ellie and I can resume our discussion, but no such luck.

Carol straightens, craning her neck over her shoulder to get a better look at me. "El Bell is right. You are a marketing genius."

I stop myself on the verge of a venti-size eye roll. It doesn't take a genius to understand basic advertising tactics, but before I can argue the point, Ellie takes my hand and squeezes tight again.

"She's so smart," Ellie swoons. "And she hasn't even taken any marketing classes yet. Just gen eds. Can you believe that?"

"You better hurry up and graduate so I can hire you to fix

139

Monarch's marketing," Carol says. "What do you think we need? An Instagram? A Google account?"

I bury my teeth into my lip. Any chance of that private conversation is officially gone, so I guess I might as well weigh in. "I think a website is probably a good place to start," I suggest. "Have you thought about an eCommerce shop? Selling some of your stuff online?"

Carol's frown pulls the droop of her cheeks down even farther. "Sounds complicated."

"It doesn't have to be. I can show you."

"Jesus," Carol huffs. "I feel like I should be paying you already!"

"See?" Ellie says. "I told you. You'll be drowning in business as a marketing consultant the second you graduate."

Carol's nod is so aggressive, she's at risk of a neck injury. "I feel like all these new shops have something Monarch doesn't," she says. "Like Sip or that new bookstore with the dog on the sign. They're doing nutso levels of business. It's like they know something I don't. What am I missing, Murph!?" Every sentence out of Carol's mouth is a decibel louder than the last, the verbal equivalent of being shaken by the shoulders. What's worse is the way she stares at me, eyes wide and expectant, like I'm supposed to reveal the secret formula to her right here, right now.

"I think it's about making the store less of a store," I start, hoping Carol's lack of marketing knowledge will mask the fact that I'm talking out of my ass here. "Running a shop is one thing, but making it into a destination creates community, you know? Coffee shops have it easier. They're meant to be the kind of place where you sit and stay for a while, read a book, talk to a friend. And the bookstore, that's the same way. They created this setting where you could just come and . . . be."

"I don't want people to just *be*," Carol says flatly. "I want them to spend money." It's not very Zen hippie aunt of her, but I get it, and although I'm not entirely sure what I'm going to say, I keep talking anyway.

"I think Monarch is somewhere you go for a purpose, just to do something and get it done. You buy a necklace or a candle and then you leave. Whereas a place like Sip feels more like a community center. There are events and concerts and people you want to see. If you can turn Monarch into more of a destination, a community that people want to belong to, they're more likely to come by more often and spend more money." My eyes flit to Ellie, who nods, either impressed or faking it well. When I turn back to Carol, she blinks at me, slack-jawed. I guess I actually landed on something pretty good there.

"Damn, Murph. You're one smart cookie," Carol says.

Ellie's laugh shakes her shoulders without making a sound, and her blue eyes sparkle with amusement. "Told you she's a genius at this stuff."

"Not a genius," I correct her. "I just have a decent sense of how people think."

"Oh sure." She nudges me playfully. "Like a genius."

Carol laughs and slowly shakes her head as she studies us. "Geez, you two bicker like an old married couple. It's crazy to me you've only been dating a year."

"Is it?" Ellie nuzzles her head into the crook of my shoulder, close enough for me to breathe in grapefruit again. "What's so crazy about it?"

"You're just so comfortable with one another. Maybe it's 'cause you've known each other since high school." Carol steeples her fingers and presses them to her lips. "You know what it is? I think you built your relationship on a really solid friendship."

"That's true." Ellie responds a little slower than feels natural. "We started off as just friends."

It's not lost on me that we're still starting off right now.

"That really shows," Carol says. "Never lose that friendship."

"We won't," Ellie says. "Right, Murph?"

Carol launches into some parable of her ex-husband, but it's background noise to me. I'm too caught up in parsing fact from fiction, weighing the kiss against Ellie insisting there's nothing to discuss but the plan. And that friendship comment? Was she trying to say something? Or am I digging for a deeper meaning that's not there?

"Is that okay with you, Murph?"

I tune back in at the sound of my name. "Sorry, what was that?"

"Aunt Carol wants to come with me to the Sip reopening tomorrow," Ellie says. "Is that okay?"

A pinch of hope lifts the layer of fog off my brain. Ellie's still planning to come. That makes me happier than it probably should. "Oh! Of course it's okay. Everyone's welcome. But yeah, it'd be great if you both could make it."

"It's your big day!" Ellie says. "We wouldn't miss it. Plus you owe me a chaicoffski, remember?"

How could I forget? "Maybe I can give you a tour too."

I can hardly believe myself, agreeing to more plans with this family beyond the limits of Thanksgiving. I guess that means

Ellie and I will have to keep up the act tomorrow . . . right? Or are we supposed to turn back into just friends at the stroke of midnight?

"How's around three o'clock?" Carol suggests. "That's usually when I break for lunch."

"Perfect. Things should be slowing down around then."

"Totally cool." She beams at Ellie and gives her two big thumbs-up. "Can you believe it, El Bell? We're gonna get the VIP treatment." Carol claps in excitement, and the noise combined with the jangle of her bracelets startles Bo into a barking fit, which, in turn, startles Otto awake.

"What?" Otto asks, frantic eyes ping-ponging across the room. "What happened? Is it time for dessert?"

Carol, Ellie, and I look at one another, then erupt into a rich, warm laughter. A family laugh. It's enough to get Kara's attention from the kitchen. "What's so funny?" she shouts from the room over.

"Dad," Ellie calls back.

Otto grunts. "What?"

"No, I mean Dad is what's funny," Ellie says with a giggle. "He fell asleep."

"I wasn't asleep," Otto insists, but he yawns as he speaks, launching us right back into our laughing fit.

Kara ambles over from the kitchen with pursed lips and a damp dish towel slung over her shoulder. "Now that you're awake, can you put something else on the TV? I'm sick of listening to football."

"It's Thanksgiving!" Otto says. "You watch football on Thanksgiving!"

143

"Maybe *you* watch football on Thanksgiving." Carol jabs an accusatory finger through the air. "Personally, I watch the parade."

"But ya missed the parade," he sasses, "because that was in the morning."

"I recorded it." Kara gestures toward the pile of remotes on the coffee table. "It's on the DVR."

"I'm putting it on," Ellie says, and Otto grumbles something to himself but doesn't put up a fight. I watch in amusement as Ellie picks up one remote and then another, testing each one to see if it controls the DVR. Our parents may be different, but it's comforting to know that the unlabeled remote pile is universal.

"What's everyone's favorite part of the parade?" Carol polls the group. "Mine is watching the lip-synchers screw up."

Ellie moves on to a third, then a fourth remote. "I like when they show the crowd. I try to pick out any locals among the tourists."

Kara insists that the Rockettes are the highlight, and Otto puts in a vote for the giant Snoopy balloon. When all eyes fall on me, I'm only slightly embarrassed to have nothing to contribute.

"I've never watched it," I admit.

"Because you're usually at the beach for Thanksgiving!" Otto chimes in with the enthusiasm of someone who just answered a tough *Jeopardy* question. He looks toward me with a smile as wide as his face. "Right, Murph?"

I hold in a laugh. Every member of this family—well, everyone but Kara—has settled into using my nickname extraordinarily quickly, and I'm surprised that I don't mind. "Yup, my parents are in Florida as we speak," I say.

"A destination Thanksgiving." Kara gazes off into space, her face twisting as she tries to picture it. "I just can't imagine."

"Maybe we should try it sometime, Mom," Ellie says.

Kara frowns. "I don't know about all that."

"Why not? It's not like we have big family Thanksgivings now that Grandma and Grandpa are gone. You always have the week off from teaching, and Aunt Carol . . ." Ellie nods toward her aunt. "I mean, you could always have a manager watch the store for Black Friday and Small Business Saturday, right?"

"I just don't know," Kara repeats. "Maybe if you're lucky, Murphy's family will invite you next year."

There it is again, that uneasy high-tide feeling in my stomach. Excitement churning with disappointment as I'm presented with a beautiful idea set in a fictional world. I want to believe there's a version of this where it all turns out. If our plan works, I'll be transferring to U of I next semester, and Ellie and I could discuss actually dating, assuming she even wants that. Which she specifically said she didn't. Of course, that was before she kissed me. Even then, she graduates this spring, and then she's off to New York. What then? She won't do long distance, so I guess we'd have to call it quits after just a few months. Is that really the best-case scenario? A few months of dating, knowing the whole time it won't last? Worst-case scenario being she doesn't think of me that way at all? I sink a little deeper into the couch. Crushing on Ellie Meyers is more complicated than an unlabeled stack of remotes.

"Got it!" Ellie says, pumping one hand in victory while the

other navigates through the DVR, hitting play on this morning's parade.

Right away, a peppy musical theater melody trumpets from the TV, and Otto sits up a little straighter in his recliner as one of the Broadway performances starts. "Man, don't you think they're freezing their asses off in those tiny fucking costumes?" he says.

"Otto!" Kara snaps. "Language!"

"Sorry. Don't you think they're freezing their butts off in those tiny fucking costumes."

Ellie and I bubble over in laughter, a heap of giggles and grins on the couch. For a moment, I let myself forget our complicated reality for the sake of the simple stuff: how her dimple winks at me when she smiles and her laugh sounds like the swell of a cymbal against my low, bass-drum chuckle. It's good like this, just me and her, until Kara claps her hands, startling us to attention. "All right," she says, "I think we can watch while we eat dessert."

"Let's do dessert!" Otto slaps his palms against the worn leather arms of his recliner, like he's announcing a brand new idea, entirely his own.

Carol puts both hands on her belly and jiggles it twice. "I think I have room for pie."

"And puppy chow," Ellie adds.

"Yes," Carol says, "and puppy chow."

Ellie pauses the parade midperformance, and we filter into the kitchen, where all signs of our Thanksgiving dinner have been completely boxed up and washed away. The pumpkin pie has been moved from the credenza to a spot of honor in the middle of the counter, and the puppy chow has been rehomed from the pink Tupperware to an ornate cranberry-colored glass bowl with a big silver serving spoon, far fancier than it deserves.

"I hope that's all right," Kara says, nodding toward the bowl. "I just thought I'd dress it up a bit."

"It's perfect," I say. "Thank you."

Carol glides the silver serving knife along the spongy center of the pumpkin pie, laying tiny, precursory grooves where she plans to cut it. "Do those sizes look right? You can always have two."

We pass around a stack of miniature dessert plates, each one lined with tiny cornucopias. "These are cute," I say, tracing the porcelain details with my pinkie. I'll be damned, they have a full separate set of dessert plates just for Thanksgiving.

"They belonged to Ellie's grandma," Kara says when she sees me admiring them, and I grip my plate a little tighter.

"All right," Carol says. "Who wants pie?"

"Muddy buddies for Thanksgiving," Otto murmurs, scooping more than a spoonful of powdered sugar globs onto his plate. I can't quite tell if it's disapproval or just genuine surprise in his voice.

"It was just a last-minute thing," I say.

"I like it." Otto arches a bushy brow toward his wife. "Whaddya think, Kara? New tradition?"

My belly button draws back into my spine. "I didn't mean to mess with your existing traditions, I just wanted to—"

"New tradition," Kara says, not cutting me off so much as gently easing me out of my anxiety spiral. "I think it's the perfect addition to Carol's pumpkin pie."

"My only contribution," Carol announces proudly as she

slides the largest slice off the server and onto my plate. "That and peeling potatoes."

With full plates, we opt to hold off on the parade and return to our same spots at the kitchen table. The tiny corner I'm wedged into feels a little tighter one full Thanksgiving dinner later, but the lack of space is balanced by the much emptier spread on the table. I can prop my elbows up instead of gluing my arms to my sides just to fit.

"Thank you again, Murphy and Carol, for the desserts." Kara gives each of us a polite smile before pinching a clump of puppy chow off her plate and popping it between her lips.

"How is it?" Ellie asks, and I can hear the undercurrent of nerves in her voice. She's probably expecting a *needs more peanut butter* to validate her ridiculously precise behavior. I'm a tiny bit nervous myself. It was a rush job, and I didn't even sample the final product, but how bad can it be with only good stuff in it?

"It's delicious," Kara says. She grabs another piece, a single square, and places it on her tongue, letting the powdered sugar dissolve. "I haven't had muddy buddies in years."

I bounce my knees beneath the table. "My family calls it puppy chow."

Kara holds up one finger, chews, swallows, then finally says, "Call it what you want, so long as you bring it again for Christmas." She dabs the powdered sugar from her lips with a napkin, leaving behind a small, warm smile. A genuine smile. I have to make the conscious decision not to let my eyes bulge out of my head. Is this ridiculous plan actually working? Does

Professor Meyers actually like me? Is she inviting me back next month?

"Why don't we ever make this anymore, Kar Bear?" Otto asks through a mouthful of half-chewed chow. The faintest cloud of powdered sugar puffs off his lips with every plosive.

"I don't know. I guess I just forgot about it." Kara smiles at me again and adds, "Thanks for reminding us."

"Has anyone tried the pie yet?" Carol pipes up, surveying the plates. She's clearly not used to sharing dessert-related compliments.

"It's perfect, Aunt Carol," Ellie assures her. "It's perfect every year."

"Have I done a year where I'm thankful for dessert yet?" Otto scans the room in search of the notebook, but quickly gives up and gets back to his plate. "Someone check."

"I'm sure Marcus has," Kara says. "You can't repeat your own, but what's the rule on repeating someone else's?"

Ellie mulls it over, then shakes her head. "I don't think that's fair. I think it has to be original."

"I think you need to write down the bylaws," I mumble, not entirely sure if I'm kidding or not. It gets a laugh from everyone except Ellie, who just rolls her eyes.

"I'm just saying, if no one has repeated someone else's yet, I don't think we should start," Ellie says.

"But I do think we should start the whole rigamarole," says Otto. "It's about that time, right?"

The general consensus is yes, it's about that time, and Kara retrieves a pen and the notebook from where she put it—back in its rightful place in the top drawer of the credenza. When she takes her seat again, it's as though she's transformed into an old-timey scribe, ready for her official duties.

"I love that notebook, by the way," I say, greedy for extra brownie points so long as I'm on a roll.

"Thanks." Kara smiles at Ellie. "My daughter made it."

Suddenly, I'm no longer just sucking up. "No way." I turn toward Ellie, whose cheeks are turning the color of my mom's Tupperware. "Can I see that?"

Kara hands it off to me, an only slightly nervous look in her eyes. "Careful."

"Of course."

Upon further inspection, the notebook doesn't have a hummingbird cover like I originally thought—it has a black cover with a small hummingbird painting pasted over it. The edges are folded in and taped to the inside cover, next to an inscription: Ellie's name and the year. This year. "You painted this?"

Ellie just barely nods. "For Mom. For her birthday."

"It was last week," Kara says. "She didn't intend it for the cover of the notebook, but I just thought it fit."

"Mom loves hummingbirds. She has a feeder in the back."

"In the summer," Kara clarifies. "This isn't their season."

I trace the delicate edge of the hummingbird's wing with slow, careful fingers. "This is gorgeous, Ellie." I look up, meeting her soft blue eyes with a smile. "You're so talented."

Kara makes a sound that's somewhere between a laugh and a high note, all behind closed lips. "She better be for what we're paying for that art degree."

My chest tightens. This is it. The perfect setup for the grad school conversation. Or it will be, if we can shift back to that positive tone we had moments ago. I clear my throat, nudging a piece of puppy chow across my plate with the side of my fork. "It's really paying off, actually. Or, uh, from what I've seen. Ellie's learning a lot of . . . practical uses for her degree. Did you tell them about the conversation you had with your advisor, Ellie?"

Ellie's throat bobs with a swallow. "Right. I've been wanting to talk to you guys about that."

"About how you're planning to use your degree? Or about how you're planning to pay off those *private loans*?" The way Kara leans the full weight of her voice into those words—private loans—reminds me of why Kat and I made this whole "community college then state school" plan in the first place. Big Ten schools come with Big Ten price tags.

"Both, actually," Ellie starts, but her mom doesn't let her finish.

"You know, Murphy, you're smart for choosing community college," Kara says, talking out of the corner of her mouth. "That's what Marcus did. Two years at Weymouth before transferring to finish his engineering degree at Cal Poly. Ellie could have done the same and saved a lot of money."

"A good education is an investment, Mom." Ellie drops her fork on her plate with a clatter, shooting me a sidelong *save me* look as she folds her arms over her chest. What am I supposed to do? I agree with Professor Meyers. And if I'm honest, I'm stuck on the sound of her calling me smart. Is this how it feels to be the favorite?

Ellie's mother holds her hands up in defense, her mouth pinching into a perfect O shape. "I was just pointing out that your girlfriend made a very economical move."

"But money isn't the only factor when it comes to an education, right?" I chime in, and Ellie places a hand on my thigh in a silent thank-you.

"Of course," Kara agrees, but when her eyes lock with mine, they narrow with skepticism. "Did it factor into your education, though? Or was there another reason you chose community college?"

I squirm a little in my seat. There were two deciding factors that made me pick Weymouth: money and Kat. But considering Kara's earlier assumption that my best friend was my girlfriend, I can't admit that Kat was half of my major life decision. It would just raise suspicions again—and spin this conversation off in an entirely different direction. "Money was a huge factor," I finally say, only because it seems better than saying nothing at all.

"But it's not like she's doing her entire degree at Weymouth," Ellie continues. "Because her future is the main priority, and U of I is a way better school for her career goals. Right, Murph?"

I squirm again. Truthfully, I don't really know what my career goals are right now, and my main reason for choosing U of I is that it's where Kat wanted to go. But I can't say that either, and with all the back-and-forth, I feel a little like I'm being asked to pick a side on the subject of my own life.

"Some schools just have better programs than others," I say. Another nonanswer.

"Exactly," Ellie says with a decisive nod. "And U of I is . . .

well, it's U of I! No wonder Murphy's transferring next semester."

I focus my attention on the divots in the pie crust, waiting for my brain to tell my mouth what to say in order to get the attention off my life and back on Ellie's. *You're smart, Murphy. Professor Meyers just said it herself. Say something. Say the right thing.*

"Next semester?" Kara places her fork on the table with a tinny *clink*, then redirects her narrow gaze toward me. "Have you already heard back about your transfer application?"

"Heard back? No, I uh." I clear my throat into my napkin, trying to rattle the truth free. "I still need my accounting grade to submit my transfer requirements." When I look back up at the table, Kara's face droops.

"Murphy," she says, her voice airy with regret. "Honey, I write a lot of letters of recommendation for transfer students. The U of I transfer applications were due in October."

The table falls quiet, sinking into a long, horrible silence. Kara's words don't quite make it to my brain; instead, they knock against my eardrums, an unwelcome and unexpected visitor. That can't be true. There's no way that's true. I try to reference my mental calendar, checking the timeline of when Kat submitted her application last summer. It couldn't have been that far in advance . . . could it?

"October," I finally say. One word, not even a complete thought. October. Last month. That was right after the construction wrapped up on Sip, right when we started laying the groundwork for the reopening. October is when I started making overtime. My mouth opens and closes, but nothing comes out.

"Oh Murphy, it's okay," Ellie says, but this time, when she squeezes my hand, I don't even feel it. "Maybe we can call the registrar next week and see if they'll let you file for an extension. You can't be the only midyear transfer in this situation."

"October," I repeat again, blinking up at Professor Meyers with disbelief. "But I don't have my grade for your class yet. I don't know if I have the accounting credit. And I need the accounting credit to transfer into the business school. How could I apply without knowing I had the transfer credits to . . ."

"The deadline passed, Murphy," Kara whispers. "And I'm not even sure the business school allows for midyear transfers. I'm so sorry."

"Murph?" Ellie asks. "You okay?"

My internal panic must not be so internal. It feels like there's a to-do list stuck in the base of my throat rapidly unrolling down to my stomach. Is there an administrator I can email? A handbook I forgot to reference? It feels like every missed deadline is behind me and every one of my classmates is five years ahead.

"I'm fine," I choke out. "Just overthinking." Or I've been underthinking for the past two and a half years.

The rest of the table conversation sounds like it's happening underwater. Otto makes a joke. Aunt Carol squawks a laugh. Ellie says something in a voice that sounds serious, but the words themselves are smudged. When she digs her fingernails into my thigh, I have no context for what's been said or what she needs, but I know I need some air. Bad.

"So, like Murphy mentioned, I spoke with my advisor, and

she thinks I'm a great candidate for the art therapy master's program at NYU." Ellie's claws haven't risen from the shallow graves they've dug in my leg. Shit, okay, we're still doing this. I sit up a little straighter in my chair.

"You want to go into even more debt for another art degree?" Kara's voice is slow and each word is spread out a half second from the last. A scoff gets stuck in her throat, and when I look her way, she's looking back at me like I'm supposed to speak up. Like I'm supposed to take her side. I open my mouth, but all I can choke out is an airy "eh," the sort of defeated noise you might expect if I was lifting something heavy or breathing through a cramp.

Kara makes a smug little sound behind closed lips. "If that's Murphy's official stance on the subject, I'm not so sure she's on board."

"No no no," I insist, each "no" a pitch lower than the last. "It's just . . ." I have the full table's attention now, but I can't make use of it. I'm too drenched in panic, too buried beneath the rubble of my own crumbling future to say anything helpful—or really, anything at all.

"Well," Ellie says, picking up where I'm so brutally letting her down, "*I* think it's a good career path for me, and I was thinking it'd be a good use of the money from Grandma and Grandpa. Funding my education."

"So our contributions to your four years of art education aren't enough?" Kara sounds sterner than I've ever heard, and that's saying a lot. "And why New York? It's so expensive and far—don't you want to be close to Murphy?" She turns to me and adds, "Assuming you'd try to transfer to U of I next fall. Is that still what you'd want?"

"I . . . uh . . ." I push my tongue against my teeth and stare down at my plate. It's like we're back in the classroom, and just like always, Professor Meyers is asking a question I don't know the answer to. What do I want? I want to disappear from this table. I want to squeeze my eyes shut and magically reopen them somewhere else, somewhere private where I can cry. I lock my jaw to bite back the tears. "I don't know." It's my first bit of honesty since the moment I arrived, so why does it feel worse than a lie?

When I look up from my plate, Kara is still looking at me, only now, there's something sad clouding her eyes. I know that look. It's the same look Ellie gave me this morning when she turned me down. It's pity, and I can't stand it. My heart slouches into my stomach. Like mother, like goddamn daughter.

"I, uh. I have to run to the bathroom." I push back from the table, and my chair stutters against the hardwood, then my head bangs against the bay window behind me, but I don't even react. I try to maneuver past Ellie, but it's worse than trying to get to an airplane bathroom from the window seat. She stands up to clear a path, which means Otto has to get up so Ellie can move her chair. It's a circus of moving parts, and soon we're all on our feet—except for Kara, who taps her pen against the open notebook.

"We should get back to what we're thankful for," she says. "Do you want us to wait for you?"

"No, no, I'll be fast."

Ellie is watching me, her lips parted on the verge of saying something, but it's too late now. I'm already halfway down the hall before the buzzing in my pocket drags me out of my head and into an unsteady reality. Apparently, I've missed two calls and a text from Kat.

SOS. emergency. PLEASE call back.

I fixate on the first half of the message. *SOS. emergency.* I could say the same for myself. How very like us to both be in crisis mode right now. Before I can still my shaky hands enough to respond, my phone rumbles alive with a third call from Kat, and I hurry into the little yellow bathroom and turn the lock just in time to catch the final ring.

thirteen

❋

An unmitigated disaster."

That's Kathryn's official review of Thanksgiving with Daniel and her grandparents. From the moment I pick up the phone, she's a faucet of news ranging from bad (the pumpkin pie set off the smoke alarm) to worse (Daniel asked why the stuffing, made with challah bread, "tasted off"). I pace the few steps of off-white tile while she recounts every detail of a conversation between Daniel and her grandmother. "Bubby straight up cornered Daniel and asked what his *intentions* were with me."

"And?" I bite down on a hangnail. "What did he say?"

"That he and I were having *fun*." Her voice cracks more and more with every word. "Having fun. Can you believe that?"

"And that's . . . not true?"

"Of course it's true!" she shrieks. "But we're not *just* having fun! And it's not what you say to my grandma!"

Personally, I don't think any of it holds a candle to listening to your accounting professor and your fake girlfriend argue the merits of your life choices, but we don't have time for the context that conversation would need. I test the structure of the bathroom vanity with one butt cheek. When it doesn't budge, I give it my full weight, keeping my back to the mirror so I'm not tempted to squeeze the pores in my nose. "What should he have said? That he wants to marry you? You've been dating for like twelve seconds."

"He should've said that he's, like, serious about me or something." The raw edge of her voice snags on her throat. "And it's been two months, Murph. Not twelve seconds."

"Same thing."

Kat's voice shrinks. "Okay, I called for help and you're actually being pretty unhelpful right now."

My tongue presses to the roof of my mouth, barricading back everything I would say if I had been honest with her earlier. I need to ask her about the transfer app and if there's any grace on that deadline. I need to tell her about Ellie and the kiss and the work in progress that is my reputation with Kara Meyers. Mostly, I need to pull myself together, get off the phone, and get back to the table to finish what I started. But as far as Kat is concerned, I'm still on my parents' couch. I should've been honest from the jump.

"I'm sorry," I sigh. "I'm a little distracted. But you're right. Daniel shouldn't have said that. Fuck Daniel."

"Not fuck Daniel! That's not the point!"

"I'm sorry, I'm sorry!" My voice echoes off the top of the shower, and I pray they can't hear me down the hall. Just in case, I dial it back to murmur. "What do you want me to say?"

"Tell me that my family isn't going to think my boyfriend is a scumbag. That I can fix this."

"Your family isn't going to think your boyfriend is a scumbag," I repeat back to her. "But you don't have to fix anything. Your Bubby is probably glad her granddaughter is enjoying herself with a boy."

"It's Bubby," Kat says flatly. "She doesn't think anyone should be enjoying themselves until marriage."

"I'm sure she didn't take it that way. And Daniel definitely didn't mean it that way, right?"

"I don't care how he meannnnnt it," Kat whines, drawing her words out with all the drama I should expect. "I care what she hearrrrrd. She's been looking at me different ever since."

"Different how? Like bad different?"

"Way bad different. Like I'm the family slut."

I choke on my laugh. If Bubby knew what I know—that Kat had only allowed Daniel to touch her boobs as of two weeks ago—she wouldn't be concerned. "Just focus on all Daniel's Bubby-friendly qualities then. Talk about how smart he is. Talk about his scholarship."

"He doesn't have a scholarship," Kat says. Her voice teeters on the verge of tears.

"But Bubby doesn't know that," I remind her. "Or you can always talk about me. Remind her that I fuck girls. That helped the year she found out you were on birth control."

Kat makes a defeated little whiny sound. "I can't keep throwing you in front of the slut bus."

"Hell, tell her I *drive* the slut bus," I say. "Beep beep." It's a dumb joke, but it dials Kat's panic down from a ten to a seven, which is roughly on an even keel with mine.

"You don't drive the slut bus," she says between sniffles. "Unless you want to drive the slut bus."

I shrug, then remember she can't see me. "How does it pay?"

"Minimum wage."

I suck in air through my teeth. "Rough break. Any benefits?"

"Bragging rights."

"Fine, I'm putting in my notice at Sip as we speak."

Kat giggles, officially putting us beneath a five on the panic scale. Success. "God, I wish you were here. My family *loves* you."

"Because they *know* me," I remind her. "They've had plenty of time to love me. They just met Daniel. If they were just meeting me, it would probably be a disaster too." I trap a breath in the base of my throat, wondering if I'm speaking more to her or myself.

"You're right." She pauses, then adds. "I mean, no you're not. They would love you no matter what. You're the best."

I swing my feet through the air, trying to touch the hem of the hand towels with the toe of my socks. I don't really feel like "the best" right now. All I've done today is lie, lie, lie. And I'll have to keep lying the second I step out of this bathroom, but for now, maybe I can be honest. I don't have to keep up this ruse with Kat. "Hey, sorry to change the subject, but can I tell you something super quick?"

"Of course," Kat says. "What's up?"

I focus my gaze on a swirl in the towel pattern. "Ellie Meyers is up."

"What do you mean?"

"I went to her house for Thanksgiving." The words tumble out at top speed, like I'm getting them all over with at once. Kat doesn't respond, so I keep talking. "I'm sorry I didn't tell you. I didn't decide until after we talked on the phone earlier. I really was planning to stay home and clean, but then Ellie texted me and I just . . ." I run out of excuses before I figure out what to say next, but with the truth out in the open, a tiny bit of the pressure on my chest releases. "I'm sorry," I sigh, "I should've told you."

"Hang on, slow down." Kat's voice slows to a cool, measured pace. "You went to Ellie's . . . are you there now?"

"Yes."

"Where?"

"Hiding in the bathroom."

She sputters a laugh. "Does that mean it's not going well?"

"No, that's not it." I hop down from the vanity and start to pace, but something about the four and a half steps in each direction leaves me feeling too caged in. I plop down on the floor instead, running my hand back and forth on the faux suede bath mat to change the color from yellow to dark yellow and back again. "She, uh. Ellie kissed me, actually."

"What?!" The pitch of Kat's squeal seems better intended for dogs than human ears. "Oh my GOD, Murph! So it's going SUPER well, then."

"No, no. I mean kind of." The tiniest smile creeps over my lips, and I chip at a dry cuticle with the edge of my fingernail. "It's been kind of a whirlwind."

"Then why are you hiding in the bathroom? Shouldn't you be making out with Ellie or something?"

"You said it was an emergency!"

"Yeah, but that's because I thought you were vacuuming or whatever! I wanted you to feel included." Kat pauses, then in a softer voice, adds, "And I needed your advice, but it wasn't that urgent. I'm sorry."

With the tip of my pinkie nail, I draw a frowny face in the fabric of the bathmat, then wipe it away with the side of my hand. "You didn't know. I should've told you sooner."

"Well, we're all making mistakes this weekend, right?"

I flatten the tip of my tongue against the back of my front teeth. Was that . . . an apology? About the Daniel stuff? I don't have time to dig deeper on that. "Listen," I start, "I need to go. I'm missing some important family tradition right now."

"Of course. I want to hear more about that later though, okay?"

"Deal." I give a thumbs-up, then say, "I'm giving a thumbs-up right now, for the record."

"Got it," Kat says. "Thumbs-up received and reciprocated."

Our laughs blend together. "You sure you're okay?" I ask.

"Yeah, I think so," she says, then thinks again. "Wait, real quick. What kind of scholarship should I say Daniel has?"

"Did your Bubby go to college?"

She pauses. "I think no?"

"Then just make something up."

"Perfect," she says. "Thank you. I love you."

"Love you more." My thumb hovers over the end call button as I add, "Tell Daniel I say hi."

"I won't tell him you said fuck Daniel," she promises. "And tell Ellie I say hi too."

"On it. Love you."

"Love you, bye."

I pull my phone back from my face to hang up, shocked to see almost fifteen minutes have passed since I answered. I end the call, shoving up to my feet in a hurry. After practicing a smile that says *sorry I took so long*, I flush the toilet and run the sink, just in case anyone can hear the plumbing. I'm a lot less nauseated than I was twenty minutes ago, but it still feels like rush hour on every one of my neural highways. Ellie, Kat, college, transfers, accounting, putting on a convincing girlfriend act. I need to sit the hell down and eat some pie.

I tiptoe down the hall, past the family room, where Otto has resumed his position in the recliner, either sleeping or trying to. In the kitchen, Ellie is still at the table, but Kara is back at the sink, and Carol kneels over a bowl of kibble, trying to get her dog to eat. In the silence, the dishes clatter a little louder, the persistent hiss of the faucet feeling more aggressive somehow. It's like we're all in a play, waiting on one of us to remember our line. But no one does.

"Did I miss the thankful thing?" I ask.

"Yeah," Ellie says, her voice short. "It's done."

"Sorry about that." I head for the table, trying to make myself useful before someone tells me not to be. Apart from the slice of pie Ellie is still working on, only the place mats and napkins need to be bused. I scrunch each one, careful to keep the crumbs off the floor. "How'd it go?"

Ellie's eyes stay down, focused on her plate. "Fine. We missed you."

"I really am sorry. It was kind of an emergency."

"I'll bet." It's not her tone that bothers me, but the lack thereof. She's flat and cold, and a chill branches from my spine to my fingertips.

"Are you feeling all right, Murphy?" Kara asks. Maybe she felt the chill too. She turns over her shoulder and catches me with an armful of napkins. "Oh, you don't have to clean up. Just sit down and have another slice of pie, if you like." Per Kara's request, I drop the napkins in a small heap on the table, but my stomach is in no state for pie. Not so long as Ellie's being all quiet and avoidant. I settle back into my seat, hoping that, if I stare down the crown of Ellie's head, she'll eventually look up at me. "Ellie?" I try quietly, and then again a little louder. "Ellie, c'mon." I can't get her attention, but Bo does, with a bark that sounds like a squeaky toy caught in a lawn mower.

"C'mon, Bobo," Carol begs, waving her cupped hand of kibble beneath her dog's snout. "Bobocito. Boba Fett. Eat your dinner, honey." Instead of complying, Bo snarls, then barks again, and, ultimately, pees a little.

"Goddamn it, not again." Carol doesn't wince, just sighs and hops to her feet, maneuvering around her sister to retrieve paper towels and a red spray bottle from beneath the sink. "El Bell, can you let Bo out? He pissed on the floor."

Ellie nods, wiping her mouth with the side of her hand. "Where's his leash?"

"By the front door."

"I'll grab it," I offer, pushing my chair back from the table, but Ellie sticks out an arm, holding me in place.

"I've got it." She heads down the hall, and Bo follows. So do I, and we all catch up by the door, where Ellie already has her coat on and is choking the leash in her fist.

"Mind if I come with you?"

"I've got it," Ellie snaps.

"I didn't say you didn't." I try to make my voice soft and non-confrontational. "I said I wanted to come with you."

"Mm-hmm." She crouches down and latches Bo's leash on to his collar, and I grab my coat and move between her and the door, trying to stand my ground despite the spin cycle starting in my stomach. Is she really this mad that I missed the thankful thing?

"Hey. Ellie. Seriously. Are you okay?"

"Yup," she says, her voice pitched up in a way that feels untrustworthy, like she's not even pretending to pretend she's fine. It's only when she realizes she can't get out the door that she finally looks me in the eye. "Can you move? Please?"

I bite my cheek. "Only if you let me come with you."

She stares at me defiantly, but I'm not backing down. "Fine," she huffs. "That's fine."

fourteen

❋

Less than twenty-four hours into a fake relationship seems a little early to be falling into a routine, and yet Ellie and I have found ourselves out in the cold in front of her house again. Unlike this morning, we have neither sun or a car to keep us warm. We both wince against the wind, bargaining frostbite for privacy as I tug the door closed behind me.

"What do you want?" Ellie snaps. She's already shivering a little.

"You're pissed," I say, "and we should talk about why you're pissed."

"I'm not pissed." Her eyes roll a lap toward the sky, and I can barely hold in my laugh. We've both told a lot of lies today, but this has to be the least convincing among them. Not even Bo, who can't seem to sniff out the right place to pee, would fall for that. The wind picks up, whipping Ellie's blonde hair in front of her face and pasting a few strands onto her lips. She turns a cheek against it, then stares down at Bo, who is sniffing a trail along the bushes. "C'mon." She jostles his leash. "Go potty."

"Listen," I start, staring at Bo despite talking to Ellie, "I'm sorry I had to leave during the thankful thing, but I was so freaked out—"

"Can we drop it? Please?"

I roll my lips over my teeth, burying my hands in my coat pockets. "I was just trying to apologize."

"I just think it's funny how you were so invested in our agreement when it was about you and your accounting grade," Ellie says, decidedly not dropping it. "But the second I need you to support me on the grad school thing, you've got more important things to do."

"I'm really sorry," I say, putting my whole chest into each word. "If you hadn't noticed, I was sort of going through a major transfer crisis."

A tiny, unimpressed huff buzzes past her lips, but she won't even look at me. Her eyes stay fixed on Bo. "So *your* problems pull rank and you don't have to hold up your end of the bargain. Got it."

"I was trying," I say, then dial my voice back a few decibels. If her parents overhear this, it'll be over for both of us. "I set up that whole grad school conversation, didn't I?"

Ellie's laugh is more of an indignant puff. "Yeah, and that's about all you did. You just *had* to side with Mom on the whole cost of college thing, and then you completely jumped ship. I needed you."

"I didn't side with your mom. And I didn't *jump ship* either. I stepped away to take a breather."

"You stepped away to call Kat," she corrects me. "I heard you."

"No, Kat called *me* because she needed help with her own emergency."

"And?" At long last, Ellie's head snaps toward me, and I watch her jaw stiffen while her glossy blue eyes narrow an inch. "What was the emergency?"

"Family drama," I grumble. Now that I have her direct eye contact, I no longer want it, so I slip into a staring contest with a stain on the hem of my coat. Coffee, probably. "She needed me."

"So did I," Ellie says. "Listen. I get that missing the transfer deadline is a huge blow. And I get that Kat is important, but you made a promise. We were supposed to help each other."

"There's nothing to help me with anymore," I remind her. "I can't transfer. My grade doesn't matter."

"It still matters, Murphy. You heard my mom. You can still transfer next fall."

"Just in time for you to have already graduated and for Kat to have only a year left."

Ellie resets with a deep inhale that rolls into a slow, measured sigh. "This isn't about Kat. This is about me and you. *Our* lives, Murph. Right?"

"I guess."

"And if you have to think about it from Kat's point of view, I'm sure she wants to see you pass accounting, right? She knew how important it was for us to pull this off."

I swallow hard, fighting back the truth. It's gristly and thick, lodged in the back of my throat. "She, uh." I swallow again. "She actually didn't know I was here."

When I finally drag my eyes off the ground, I'm greeted with a wide-eyed stare and a small exhale clouding the air around Ellie's parted lips. "What?"

"I didn't tell her I was coming here for Thanksgiving," I say.

169

"I mean, I told her just now on the phone, but before that, I just let her think I was staying home."

"Why?"

"I didn't want her thinking I was choosing you over her."

Ellie scoffs through her nose. "You weren't choosing me," she says. "You were choosing you. Your grade and your future. Kat clearly has other priorities besides you, Murphy. Aren't you allowed to have other priorities too?"

"It's not like that," I snap. "She's my best friend. You wouldn't get it."

"Oh, because I'm a friendless moron, right?" The crack in Ellie's voice is borderline pubescent. "I have friends, Murphy. Normal friends who don't base all their decisions on one another."

"Oh yeah, your *normal* friends," I say. Bitterness inches into my tone with each passing word. "Are you referring to the friends who didn't even show up to the bar last night? Or the friends who did, but didn't remember your name or even notice when you were gone?"

"At least I have more than one," she spits. "And don't act like Kat is perfect either. We both know just how pissed you were that she screwed up your night by dragging Daniel along without telling you."

"So she made one mistake," I admit. "She was probably just nervous because—"

"Because she was choosing her boyfriend over you?" Ellie says. "And she knew it'd break your heart because you don't get to be her favorite anymore? She's clearly moving on from this freaky codependent thing you two have going, but you just won't let it go."

"We're not codependent," I correct her, "We're close."

"You skipped your family vacation for *Kathryn*. You want to go to U of I to be with *Kathryn*. When I need you to go to bat for me, you're stepping out to take a phone call because you're so in love with *Kathryn*."

"Oh come on." I fold my arms over my chest and wait for her to take it back. But she doesn't. She doesn't even blink, and I want no part of her staring contest. "Don't act like you believe that shit just because your mom thought Kat and I were a thing."

"I don't know anymore!" Ellie throws up her hands, and Bo jolts at the tug of his leash, then follows at Ellie's heels as she starts to pace. "Maybe Mom has a point. You'd do anything for Kat. And today, you had this miraculous, Hail Mary chance to save your grade by—God forbid—spending a single day with a girl you're clearly into." She halts, and I watch her shoulders pin up against her ears before releasing all at once. "You couldn't even commit to a single day without putting Kat first. Which sucks, because I'm into you too."

"You're what?" My heart drops like an anchor, holding me in place against the wind while my neurons fire a singular message throughout my body: *shut it down*. My hands ball into fists, and my jaw winds tight, trying to lock up the pins and needles behind my nose before they can surface as a full-blown cry. "Make up your mind, Ellie. You spend all of last night flirting with me, then you want to be friends, then you call me your *girlfriend* to your *mother*, but you make sure I know it's fake, then you kiss me, but refuse to talk about it . . ."

"Because I was confused!"

"Then imagine how I feel!" It's my turn to pace. "You give

me this whole speech about how you're not looking for anything, how we can only be friends, and then what? Eight hours later, you're into me? What am I supposed to think?"

"That I just got out of a relationship and I'm scared?" Ellie says, her voice growing scratchier and more raw with every word. "I like you, Murphy. I like us together."

"You don't know that," I snap. "You've known me for, like, a day."

"Whatever happened to 'it doesn't matter how long you know a person?'" She hurls my own words back at me in a sickly sweet tone. "But you're right. I don't know you that well, which is why it's not fair for me to make assumptions about you. Just because something didn't work with Mary doesn't mean it won't work for you and me."

I stop pacing and try to process. "What are you saying?"

Ellie takes a cautious step forward, and when she speaks, her voice is gentle and breathy. "I'm saying . . . why shouldn't we try this?" She softens as she takes another step, then another until she's close enough to hook one finger through my belt loop. My body responds, even if I'm not sure I want it to. "I know we're still feeling things out, but while you're in Geneva, Champaign isn't that far from here. If we date through the spring and everything goes well, we can try long distance if I move to New York or . . . wherever I end up. And when you're done with school, you could join me, you know. You said yourself you can do your business stuff remote."

"I'm not actually *doing* that business stuff, you know that, right? That was part of your lie."

"Our lie," she corrects me, and it's all I can do not to laugh.

"You don't even realize what you're doing, do you?"

Ellie blinks against the wind. "What do you mean?"

"Making yet another grand plan for you and me without even asking what I want." Her face falls, but I keep going. "Did you ask me if I would want to do long distance? Or if I have any interest in living in New York? You don't even know if I want to try a real date with you after this ridiculous day."

The color slips from Ellie's cheeks. "Do . . . do you not?"

"That's not the point. Don't you know what this is?" I don't leave her room to answer. "You're planning for you, not for us."

Ellie flinches, then her lower lip stiffens. Her eyes look like she's seen a ghost. "Don't say that."

"But it's true. What you're doing to me is exactly what Mary did to you."

"Murphy." Ellie says my name like it's a full sentence, an entire thesis, the whole point and the proof in and of itself. She says it like she knows I want to hear her say it again and again, and I wish I could pretend it could be that simple. We could forget this whole fight and tumble into an enchanting spring and summer of Cubs games and Pride parades, just like we've talked about all afternoon. I could tell her what she wants to hear. It would be easier, but it wouldn't be honest. What comes out instead is:

"I think I should go home." I turn back toward the house. Through one sidelite, the blue light of the living room TV flashes onto Otto's silhouette. Through the other, the warm glow in the kitchen backlights Kara and Carol, standing hip to hip over a sink full of dishes. At Ellie's feet, Bo lets out a soft, pitiful whine.

"Murphy," Ellie pleads. "Stay."

"No," I decide. "I gotta go."

"What about my family? Are you at least gonna say good-bye?"

I shake my head. "Tell them I have a stomachache. Too much pie or something."

"Don't be like that."

"Like what? I'm tired, El. I just want to go home."

"I'm sorry, just . . . please." She takes a step toward me, just barely placing her fingers on the tiny bit of exposed skin between my sleeve and the cuff of my glove. I steady my gaze on the front-door wreath, working overtime to keep my breath even. When I say nothing, Ellie gives in. "Fine," she says. "But it's cold. Let me drive you. Not as my girlfriend. Just as a friend."

The earth tilts and spins around me, my throat feeling tighter and tighter by the second. I swallow, and everything balances a little, enough for me to shake my head and say, "I'm not sure that I'm either."

The wind howls through the trees, and I wish it would take me with it so I didn't have to see Ellie like this, with her eyes wide and sorry and her blue-tinged lips parted just an inch, just enough to be ready should she think of something to say that would change my mind. I tug the zipper of my coat up to my chin to block out the cold, but it's too late. It's inside now, freezing me in place for just a moment longer than I'd care to stay. "See you later, Ellie" is all I manage to say as I step into the cloudy, navy night. No moon, no stars poking through. Just me and the streetlights, which are slow to kick in. I switch on my phone flashlight to light the sidewalk in front of me and start the long trek home, wondering if the houses in this neighborhood have always been kind of small or if I'm just growing up.

fifteen

❋

Everything at home is just how Ellie and I left it; not in a comforting, there's-no-place-like-home type of way, but in an eerie way, like flipping back through the pages of a scrapbook and only remembering things when a picture prompts you to. Between the dishes soaking in the sink and the air mattress I still need to haul back to storage, everything we left behind feels not quite finished—everything, that is, except Ellie's name, still drawn in powdered sugar, blending in with the quartz countertops. I wipe away her work with the side of my hand, collecting the sticky white dust in my palm and brushing it into the trash. The bag of pita chips goes back in the pantry, and her half-drunk can of LaCroix barely hisses when I empty it onto the dishes in the sink. Only then do I realize I'm one dish short; I left the Tupperware at Ellie's. Whatever. If Mom asks about it, I'll make up some excuse. I've gotten pretty good at lying today.

I drag my palms across my thighs, leaving streaks of residual powdered sugar on my black jeans, and decide the dishes can wait until tomorrow. I'm too tired for chores. Living out an entire relationship in one afternoon, it turns out, can really take it out of you. I'm better off saving up all the cleaning until right before Mom and Dad get home.

Speaking of Mom and Dad, whatever lobe of my brain makes me a decent daughter lights up. I should call them. We haven't spoken since my hangover passed, and I'm sure they'd appreciate hearing from me more than once on our first holiday apart. I fish my phone out of my back pocket, mentally adding an hour to the time before I hit dial. It's not quite 9:00 p.m. on Sanibel Island, and if this year's Thanksgiving is anything like previous years, they're drunk, sunburnt, and back in their room by now. I take the stairs two at a time as the phone rings, and Mom picks up just as I belly flop into the center of my bed.

"Hiya, Murph! I was wondering if we'd hear from you again today." She slurs every other word, confirming that, apart from my absence, this Thanksgiving is just like the rest.

"Hi Mom, how's it going?"

"Hold on one second." Several decibel-pushing scratching sounds later, she's back on the line. "There. You're on speaker. I've got your father here too."

"Who is it? Oh, Murph! How are ya?" Dad shouts, the way all dads inexplicably do on phone calls, like he needs to yell all the way into my time zone.

"Shhhhhh," Mom hisses. "People could be sleeping."

"Oh, Murph! How are ya?" Dad repeats in a more hushed tone, and Mom laughs at the bad joke, a guaranteed sign that her tequila sunrise has risen a few too many times.

"I'm okay. Just wanted to say good night, maybe hear about your Thanksgiving. I miss you guys."

"We miss you too, Murph," Mom says, her voice suddenly steady and genuine. "We wish you were here."

I lock eyes with our family photo on the Wall of Fame, the one Ellie pointed out earlier. I wish I was there too. Not just in Florida, but back in my giant heart-shaped sunglasses, wedged between my parents, without a problem in the world. What I would give to be eight again.

"What'd you get up to today?" I ask.

"Oh, it was fabulous," Mom says. "Your father got a new polo shirt at the gift shop!"

She stumbles through a story about Dad being too tall for the dressing rooms, and I throw my phone on speaker, freeing up my hands so I can change. I grab sleep shorts and shimmy out of my jeans, adding them to the "not quite clean, not quite dirty" pile draped over the back of my desk chair. My bra gets thrown on the same pile, but I opt not to take off the sweater. It's cozy and, if I'm being completely honest with myself, still smells a little like Ellie's grapefruit shampoo. Maybe that's pathetic, but it makes me feel marginally less alone. I'm back on the bed before Mom gets to the part about Dad getting a discount . . . or is he planning to go back and ask for a discount tomorrow? It's a little unclear, so I opt for the only foolproof reply: "That's crazy."

"Crazy is an understatement!" Dad is back to shouting, and Mom shushes him again, resetting his inside voice. "What's really crazy is how *crazy* good I look in this shirt!"

Mom laughs, then hiccups, then laughs again. "He really does look crazy good!" Her giggles get louder, and I can picture

Dad puffing up his chest and hitting that finger-gun pose he always does when he tries on the clothes Mom gets him for Christmas. Just the mental image has me laughing along with Mom until her giggles subside into a quiet exhaustion. "Boy, I'm telling you, I think we gotta get to bed here, Murph."

I try to curb my disappointment. "Sure, sure. I won't keep you up then."

"We love you!" Mom says.

"And we miss you!" Dad shouts over her.

"I love and miss you too," I say, but the line goes dead before I can finish the thought. I'm alone again, just me and my eight-year-old self grinning back at me from behind her heart-shaped sunnies. I wonder how she'd feel if she knew this was her future, that over a dozen years later, she'd be stuck in the same bedroom, still dealing with all the same types of drama: school, parents, crushes, and Kat. She'd probably think I was all grown up, and I wouldn't have the guts to correct her. I wouldn't want to break her little heart.

sixteen

❄

The view from behind the espresso bar is as chaotic as it is glorious. After ten months of renovations and two months of setup, Sip's doors reopened this morning to a news van, a camera crew, and a line of customers snaking two blocks down Third Street. We were expecting a solid turnout; what we got was half the county.

Over half a shift later, the line has reportedly not gotten much shorter, which checks out based on the constant crowd packed inside. The Black Friday shoppers stumble in and out between doorbusters, but everyone else sticks around to defrost and check out the details of Sip 2.0. The place is packed with familiar faces and out-of-towners alike, and in the thick of the chaos, my camera and I are capturing it all. Plenty of people mention the write-up in the *Tribune*, but just as many say they've been waiting for this all year, and I take shot after Christmas card–worthy shot of anyone willing to smile for the camera. As I set up my angle for a time-lapse video of the crowd, I try to document the moment in my memory too. The past year—the last two months, especially—have been grueling work, but it was all moving toward this. The Dream House is built, and the Barbie dolls have moved in. The PTO moms, the artsy couples, the theater cliques moving in packs—I'm so happy they're back, even if it means I barely have time to swap my SD card or catch a breath.

"Murphy, we need backup!" My manager's voice carries from behind the bar and over the customer chatter. I was supposed to focus only on capturing content today, but since a few of our fastest baristas are out of town, I've been ducking behind the bar as needed to lend an extra set of hands. For the first half of my shift, pulling triple duty as the photographer, videographer, and backup barista wasn't so bad, but around one o'clock, I got hit with the side effects of running solely on adrenaline and four hours of sleep. That part is no one's fault but mine. I shouldn't have stayed up till two in the morning scouring the U of I website for proof that Professor Meyers was wrong and I could still transfer next semester. I found nothing except proof of the exact opposite, and now I'm paying for my choices in exhaustion and eye strain.

"Murphy!" my manager calls a second time.

"Coming!" I weave between tables and back toward the bar, but I can't resist stopping to snap a few shots of a mother-daughter duo, each of them dipping their noses in whipped cream as they sip their hot chocolates. I capture them midlaugh. Perfectly candid. It should probably make me miss my own mom, but instead, my mind wanders back to playing photographer at the bar Wednesday night and my own flop attempt at a candid photo. My chest tightens a little. I like those stupid pictures of me and Ellie more than I care to admit.

I haven't spoken to Ellie since I left her house last night—not that I've had the time. Between transfer research, sleep, and work, I haven't had the headspace to even begin processing yesterday's mess. I'll need a lot more sleep before I'm really up for the challenge, but before I even started this shift, I promised myself I'd keep up the girlfriend act when Ellie and Carol swing by. If Ellie and Carol swing by. I'm not sure where our argument leaves today's plans, but I'm still sort of hoping she shows.

"MURPHY!" A third time. My manager is going to kill me.

"Yup, I'm coming!" This time, I actually mean it. It takes another minute to shoulder through the crowd and back up to the bar. The air is thick with *Scuse me* and *Can I squeeze past you* and *How long are you planning to be at this table?* Even with the new addition, the building is packed to the gills. Coffee shop customers are a liquid; they will fill whatever space they're given. By the time I'm back in my apron, I've fallen down a memory of an emptier Sip, when it was just me and Ellie, soaking in the details of the shop and each other. There's a tingle arching up my feet, but I ignore it for the moment. Right now, I've got espresso shots to pull.

"Do we have any more of this?" Brooklyn, our new holiday hire, wraps her neon nails around a half gallon of oat milk and shakes what sounds like a backwash amount left inside.

"There should be more in the basement fridge," I direct her. "Downstairs, on the right."

She nods, her braids swaying around her face. Apart from that, no signs of movement.

"Can you, uh . . . grab it?"

"Oh, right," she says. "Got it."

I watch the Gemini sign stick-and-poke tattoo on her shoulder disappear down the stairs much slower than it should. A little hustle would be appreciated, but she's probably overwhelmed; I would be, too, if this was my first real shift. While Brooklyn is gone, I pick up where she left off, working my way through the growing stack of to-go cups with orders scrawled in Sharpie on the side.

"Still waiting on those cold brews with oat milk!" the manager on register shouts over the clang of the cash drawer slamming shut.

"We're getting more oat from backstock."

She gives me a thumbs-up over her shoulder and gets back to the line of customers, leaving me to pull espresso shots in peace. Or something close to peace. The best that today can afford. Each time I snap a lid into place and slide an order onto the bar, I check the green velvet bucket chair where Ellie sat just a day and a half ago, as if she'll reappear there somehow. So much of Wednesday night feels smudgy, like a dream or a hallucination, but the memory of Ellie in that chair is hauntingly clear.

Brooklyn thuds back up the stairs with oat milk in hand, and I lock the portafilter into place, keeping the espresso assembly line going. I watch as Brooklyn sets the carton down on the counter before carefully lifting each half-filled cold brew cup, verifying the order scrawled on the side before topping them off. Detail oriented. She's a good hire, if only for the month. She pops the lids on and sets the drinks on the bar, then starts in on the next order in the queue.

"Peppermint oat milk latte with no espresso," she reads off the side of the cup. "Isn't that . . ."

"Hot peppermint milk," I say. "Probably for a middle schooler."

She breathes a scoff through her lips. "Middle school? Come on. I was drinking my coffee black by seventh grade."

"Yeah?" I arch a skeptical brow. "What required that much caffeine at age twelve?"

"Uh, have you ever been twelve? That was the hardest shit of my life."

Our laughs are a little too loud, but it's just what I need to power me through the rest of these orders. I hope we keep Brooklyn on staff after the holidays.

As I dig out the vegan hot cocoa mix from the back cabinets, my manager's gravelly voice scatters over the crowd of uncaffeinated hopefuls. "I've got two large cold brews with oat milk for Kara!"

If a name could cause an allergic reaction, I'd be reaching for my EpiPen. This morning's quad shot of espresso gurgles in my stomach as I supervise the two sweaty cups of cold brew, waiting for them to be claimed—which they are, by a thirty-something woman in a pea coat struggling through the crowd with a stroller. A hiss of air leaks through my teeth, lost beneath the whir of the coffee grinder and some indie version of a Christmas song playing over the newly upgraded sound system. It's not her. Of course it's not her. There are only four people I specifically invited today: Kat, Daniel, Ellie, and—

"Hiya, Murph!"

Carol's familiar, bouncy voice ricochets off the espresso

machine and lands between my ears. Speak of the hippie and she shall appear. At the register, her bracelets jingle like sleigh bells with every exaggerated wave. She's not wearing a coat, just a black turtleneck beneath a teal sparkly poncho, her silver hair braided down her back. "Found ya! That line was somethin' else, but the place looks unbe-freaking-lievable."

"Thanks!" When I smile at her, I look past her, searching the line for a familiar flash of white-blonde hair. There isn't one, and my stomach plunges toward my knees. Do I have any right to feel disappointed?

Carol takes a little too long squinting at the menu before I step in and order for her—one 16-ounce chaicoffski and a plain cake doughnut, made in house. I make her drink, then grab my camera and duck out past the bar under the guise of taking more pictures. It seems rude not to at least say hi, even if she's short one highly anticipated plus-one.

"Special delivery." I hand the cup off to my happiest customer, who is already covered in cake doughnut crumbs.

"Thid id unbuhleevabuh," she manages through an oversize bite before wiping her mouth with her poncho. "And what a turnout. I'd freakin' kill to have a tenth of these people in my shop in a week."

My brain instinctually switches into marketing mode, dreaming up wine nights at Monarch or jewelry making classes hosted at Sip. "I think you could pull it off."

"Maybe with a little help." Carol crumples the parchment paper from her doughnut and tosses it toward the trash can, missing by a pretty wide margin. I guess poor pitching form is genetic in the Meyers family.

I open my mouth to ask Carol if she knows anything about when Ellie might come by, but I'm instantly interrupted by a screeching toddler and the wet clatter of a mug breaking across our brand new floors. Who the hell gave someone ceramic? Today, of all days?

"I bet they're gonna need my help with that," I say with an apologetic wince.

Carol nods. "I gotta get back to the shop anyway. Spent my whole lunch break in line."

"Maybe I can give you a full tour some other day?"

"Sure, sure. And hey." Carol hands her cup back to me, freeing up both of her hands to dig through her quilted crossbody bag. She emerges with a slightly bent business card with her name and info printed in Curlz MT. "Take this. Drop me a line with your rates."

I hand over her drink in exchange for the card. "My rates?"

"For marketing stuff. For any of this." Carol twirls an index finger toward the ceiling in a *whoop-de-doo*. "Whatever you did for Sip, I gotta hire you to do the same for Monarch."

My eyes dart between Carol and my manager, who is just a few steps away at the register. There's too much noise in here for her to overhear us. "I, uh. You were serious about that?"

"Dead serious. You said there was a big ol' list of Geneva businesses who wanted your help with marketing, right?" She stretches her arms wide, seemingly indicating the length of this very imaginary list. The demonstration nearly costs her one entire 16-ounce chaicoffski. We narrowly avoid a spill, and before I can invent a lie or come clean on my nonexistent marketing business, someone shoves a dustpan and broom into my hands. The only reasonable punishment for slacking off: cleanup crew.

"I'll add you to the list," I promise her, and she grins like the Cheshire Cat.

"Thanks, Murph. You're the best."

I follow Carol toward the door, which coincidentally is also toward the crash site, and she doesn't leave without giving me an extra tight hug. "Congratulations, sweetie," she murmurs into my shoulder, then holds me at an arm's length, taking me in with a wobbly smile. "You have so much to be proud of."

As she disappears out the door and down the bricks, passing by a line that stretches halfway to her store, I let myself actually believe her.

The rest of my shift blurs toward its end, and as the line of caffeine seekers gets shorter, I start to recognize more of the customers standing in it. My tenth-grade biology teacher orders a decaf latte. One of our usuals grabs his standard drip coffee and tips a ten. Isha Burman's mom makes an appearance, showing off baby photos to the rest of the line. I point out our regulars to Brooklyn, who quickly assigns each one a code name. *Dr. Science. Drip and Tip. Proud Grandma.* As I count familiar faces, something warm and certain blooms in my chest. There's character in this building's bones that reflects on the community we've built. Even with a fancy new espresso machine and a 20 percent higher maximum occupancy, we're still the same old Sip. Same menu, new floorboards. Same staff plus new hires. Things only change as much as they're meant to.

"Hey, Murph! Over here!"

For the second time today, a familiar voice plucks me out of my head. On the other side of the pastry case, Daniel and Kat are waving and grinning like lottery winners. Kat holds up her phone to snap a few photos of me on the job, then hands photographer duty off to Daniel so she can be in a few. I guess boyfriends aren't just good Uber drivers; they make good tripods too.

"Um, hi, we have a zillion things to talk about," Kat says with wide-eyed wonder, then steps up to the counter and orders three chaicoffskis in the largest size we have—one for her, one for Daniel, and one for later, I assume. I have my manager comp their drinks, and with the amount of money we've brought in today, she doesn't give me any of her usual grief. As I scuttle around the back of the bar, Kat shamelessly talks at full volume to be sure I can hear her over the espresso machine. "How did things go at Ellie's last night?"

"Um, kind of bad, actually." I catch my manager's gaze over my shoulder. "But now's not really the time to talk about it."

"Got it." Kat mushes her lips. "Maybe we can discuss over dinner? We want to take you out to celebrate your big day."

"When?"

"How's now?"

I glance at the clock. "Um, lemme think." Technically, my shift ended ten minutes ago, but I've been holding out hope that Ellie will dash through the door at the last minute, ready to exchange an apology for a free chaicoffski. I could sell myself some excuse about her planning to come by later or how I somehow missed her in the crowd, but I know the truth. She didn't show, and even if I'm hurt, I don't exactly blame her. I probably owe her an apology too.

"Don't tell me you have plans," Kat whines, "unless it's . . . you know." She shrugs her eyebrows at me. "A date."

"No date," I say. "But maybe some damage control." I set three perfectly poured chaicoffskis onto the bar, and Kat nudges two of them toward Daniel while taking an ambitious swig of the other. Her eyes flutter closed as she smacks her lips.

"Oh my God, how is that better than I remember?" She asks from somewhere deep in a chai-induced trance. After a few more sips taken in rapid succession, she turns toward Daniel. "Have you tried yours? Hang on, I want to film it." When she's ready with her phone, he takes his first sip, clearly playing up his reaction for his girlfriend's benefit. A deep sense of knowing settles behind my chest. I guess that's what you do. If you care about someone, you go a little over the top sometimes, just to remind them you will.

"Anyway. Dinner!" Kat pockets her phone and licks cinnamon foam off her upper lip. "What's the verdict? Are you free?"

I roll my lips over my teeth, creating a vacuum seal. Five minutes ago, I would've said yes, but even with all the success of the reopening, I still have some unfinished business. My lips open with a pop. "I don't think I am," I say. "I think I need to go see Ellie."

Kat's face breaks into a proud smile. "Yeah? Keep me posted, okay?"

"Thanks," I say. "I will." I untie my apron and am headed for the office when a question I've been meaning to ask my manager turns me around. "Hey, real quick. Seven or eight years ago, did you ever work with a guy named Marcus?"

My manager turns her back on the line and fakes a gagging sound. Or at least I think she's faking. "Yes, unfortunately. That guy was such a know-it-all. We fired him after only a few months when we caught him stealing from the tip jar. Why do you ask?"

"Huh." I run my tongue along my teeth. "Interesting. No reason. See you later." I wave goodbye to her, then to Kat and Daniel one more time.

"Good luck, Murph!" Kat yells.

I'll probably need it, but if you care about someone, you do what you have to do.

seventeen

✳

There's a long list of better places I could be right now. I could be sprawled across a beach towel, soaking in the Florida sun, or cozied up in the back corner of a dimly lit restaurant, toasting to what might be my most impressive milestone to date. I could be at home, in bed, sleeping off the ten-hour shift I just finished. Instead, I'm freezing my ass off on the Meyerses' front porch. Again. How much of my life have I spent on the steps of something, waiting to be let in?

I stamp my thumb against the doorbell, squinting through the sidelites for any signs of Ellie as the two-toned chime sounds. It's a bold move to show up at a girl's house unannounced, but there's too much to discuss properly via text. Talking it out in person felt like the most practical move, or at least it did a few minutes ago when I peeled out of the Sip parking lot with a large chaicoffski sloshing in my cupholder and a half-baked apology in my head. I'm praying I'm not the only one ready to say I'm sorry.

Through the window, I lock eyes with a slightly disheveled Kara, who looks as shocked as I am about my unplanned visit. She tugs the door open just enough for a conversation to leak through without carrying the cold air with it.

"Hi, Professor Meyers." I hadn't realized my teeth were chattering until I opened my mouth. We're sneaking past sunset, and the night air bites back.

Kara blinks away her surprise and opens the door the rest of the way, giving me a full view of her Black Friday best: a pilled maroon Weymouth hoodie, black pants with fraying drawstrings, and Christmas-themed slipper socks patterned with little fuzzy ornaments. I've never seen her look so human. "Come in, come in," she says, waving me inside. "Is your stomach feeling better?"

My right palm floats to my belly as Kara shuts out the cold behind me. Right. The fake stomachache that sent me home early from my fake girlfriend's house. I should've known I'd lose track of my lies. "Uh, much better, thanks," I mutter toward the floor. "I think I just ate too much. It was all so delicious."

Kara's eyes narrow behind her glasses. "Ellie wasn't feeling too hot last night either. I'm worried Otto might not have cooked that turkey all the way through." Before I can come to Otto's defense, she's onto the next topic. "How was the grand reopening? Carol sent me a few photos." Either she's genuinely interested or faking it well.

"It was a huge success. I'm glad Carol could stop by." I pause to give Kara a chance to mention someone in particular who *didn't* stop by, but instead, she motions for me to follow before turning over her shoulder. "I'm glad you're here, actually," she says. "You might be just the right person to help me."

I open my mouth to redirect the conversation back to the reason I'm here, but Kara is long gone before I can form a sentence, so I step out of my shoes without untying them and follow behind her, lukewarm chaicoffski still firmly in hand and a string of questions about her daughter tucked just beneath my tongue.

In the kitchen, all signs of Thanksgiving have been wiped, cleaned, and Cloroxed away to make room for a new brand of chaos. Dozens of tiny, tented pieces of cardstock are scattered in clumps across the countertop, each one boasting a name in thick black block letters. It's as though someone has been playing a game of RISK with place cards instead of pawns.

"Is this for . . . ?"

"The seating chart for Marcus's wedding," Kara explains.

Ah yes. Marcus the golden boy, or Marcus the tip-stealing know-it-all, depending on who you ask. Either way, he'll be Marcus the groom this summer. It seems a little soon to be working on seating charts, and yet, here we are, overlooking an army of place cards.

"You have events at Sip, right?" Kara asks.

"Yes, but . . ." I scan the counter, trying to picture each of the tiny name cards as a full-size person in the room with us. The kitchen would overflow. "We definitely can't fit this many people, even in the new space."

"Oh goodness, no," Kara laughs, "that's not what I meant. I've just never had to organize this kind of event before. I thought you might have some experience with it at Sip?" A hopeful shimmer dances in her eyes, and for a second, I consider lying about my seating chart expertise just to make her happy. I'm a little lied out, though, so the truth is what comes out.

"Not really, no," I admit. "We mostly do bridal showers and baby showers and things like that. People usually sit wherever they want."

"Oh, well, that's all right," Kara says, but I catch her wilting a little as she swaps two name cards, pauses, then swaps them back again. "It was worth asking. I still have time to get it just right."

"The wedding's not till June, right?"

If I had blinked, I would've missed Kara's sped up eye roll. "Correct. But Marcus wants one completed seating chart with all the invitees, and then as people RSVP . . ." She plucks two tented name cards from one of the little clusters—presumably representing tables—and places them to the side. "We just condense from there and fill in the gaps with guests they add from the B-list."

"Sounds efficient."

A stern breath of air shoots out of Kara's nose as she pinches another card off the counter. "I'd probably choose a different word, but that's Marcus for you. He has the vision but it's everyone else's job to make it happen." It's the first time she has acknowledged her son with anything other than complete adoration, and while we're miles away from the conversation I'd like to be having, I can't help but peel at the edges of her offhand comment.

"Is that usually how things go?"

Kara sets down the place card and nudges it back into place. "Oh, you know." She looks up at me with a smile that's subtle and polite, in direct contrast to my overt nosiness. "Marcus has always been a planner. He's ten steps ahead of the rest of us most days. But with the wedding, it sometimes feels like twenty or thirty." Her lips pinch for a moment before adding, "He's been sort of a bridezilla."

My laugh comes out louder than I would've hoped. "Sorry."

"No, don't apologize." Kara suppresses a chuckle of her own. "This is our first big family wedding, and everything about it is pretty funny to us. It's exciting, of course, but Otto and I got married at the courthouse, so this"—she slices a hand through the air, overlooking her swarm of name cards—"seems excessive."

"And expensive, I'll bet." I glance toward the staircase and back. Now would be a great time for Ellie to show up. I'm really teeing up the grad school conversation, and I'd prefer if she were here to witness me finally making good on my half of the bargain.

"Well, I don't know if Ellie mentioned it to you," Kara starts, giving me her signature over-the-glasses look, "but we inherited a good sum of money when my parents passed, and we agreed to invest most of it in the kids."

I focus all of my energy into sending telepathic messages to Ellie, then raise my voice a little, hoping she'll hear. "Oh? I think that might've come up on Thanksgiving."

"Riiiight," Kara says. She slowly nods as if to jog her memory. "With the grad school business."

"Yeah, uh. That." My breathing feels shallow, like the airflow is blocked by my heartbeat thumping in my throat. "That's a pretty big deal, right?" C'mon, El. This is your moment. Where are you?

"It was the first I'd heard of it," Kara murmurs, "but it sounds more expensive than a wedding."

"I guess it depends on the wedding?"

Kara floats her pointer finger over her place card congregation. "It's her money to use, but I'd hate for Ellie not to have any of it left for her own wedding someday." Her finger lands on two cards near the center, and she plucks them up and places them on the counter beside me. One card reads "ELLIE" in bold capital letters. The one next to it, "MURPHY." My heart lurches in my chest like a Tilt-a-Whirl, grinding down its rusty gears.

"I . . . I don't think that's anything that would be that soon." My eyes dart from the stairs to the garage door and back again, willing Ellie to walk in and keep this thing from going off the rails. Again.

"Well, what do you think then? You certainly know her better than I do at this point. Is she cut out for a New York grad program? Or . . ."

Kara trails off, but that one little word ricochets off the side of my skull: *or or or*. I can speak up *or* I can stay silent. I can take the lead *or* I can leave this conversation to Ellie. My jaw stings to remind me to stop grinding my teeth. In the end, it's not about me. This is Ellie's future, not mine. "I think Ellie would want to tell you about it herself," I say. "Is she around?"

"Pardon?" A long, quiet stillness falls over the kitchen as Kara's face contorts in a strange mix of concern and confusion, finally settling into a frown that drags her whole face toward the floor. "Murphy." She clears her throat. "Ellie went back to Champaign this morning. Did she not tell you?"

The Tilt-a-Whirl breaks down completely.

eighteen

❄

M y eight-minute drive home is set to the soundtrack of my phone dialing over and over. After a graceless exit from the Meyers house, I've barely taken my foot off the gas or my thumb off the call button below Ellie's contact in my phone.

Hi, you've reached the voicemail of Ellie Meyers. Please leave a—

I smash my thumb against the end call button and try again. It rings for the final few blocks of Ellie's neighborhood and keeps ringing as I turn back onto the main drag. Outside my window, the elementary school smears into the park smears into the houses of my neighborhood, and Ellie's voicemail message starts up again just as the car bumps back into my driveway, launching me a solid three inches off my seat. God, I better slow down. It's a miracle I wasn't pulled over for going 40 in a 25. On any other day, I might call that good luck, but I don't feel particularly lucky at the moment. I'm hurt, but more than that, I feel stupid. If it hurts this bad, I care more than I should.

I throw my car in park, hanging up on Ellie's voicemail greeting for a third and final time. I don't even know what I would say if she picked up, but she doesn't, so it doesn't really matter. She could be away from her phone, but more realistically, she's giving me the silent treatment. We're too old for this shit.

I snatch the tepid chaicoffski out of the cupholder and pop the lid before dumping it on the lawn. The awful sloshing noise it makes as it hits the icy grass is about on par with how I'm feeling. Inside the house, I kick off my shoes and ditch the cup before taking the stairs two at a time up to my room. I resent whatever leftover teenage instinct cues me to slam my door. Mom and Dad are still in Florida; I have no one to keep out.

I don't even bother taking my coat off before crawling into bed, where I pout my way through drafting a text to Ellie. Everything I type reads as too angry or aloof or apologetic. After starting and deleting one too many drafts, I frisbee my phone to the end of the bed. In less than forty-eight hours, Ellie Meyers has gone from distant memory to fake girlfriend and back again. Maybe that was the truest version of her all along. A friend of convenience better left in the past.

I blink up at my ceiling and make a wish on a glow-in-the-dark star: I wish I were much younger or older than I currently am. Young enough for someone else to tell me what's next or old enough to have figured it out already. Not just with Ellie; with all of it. Work and school and what comes next. I'm twenty-one years old and still stuck in the same pattern as sixteen-year-old Murphy, dumb and directionless in the face of shattered plans. Maybe I'm still the same clueless girl with the torn rotator cuff and no next steps. I still have the same decor, that's for sure.

Tie-off blankets, middle school softball trophies, a hedgehog ornament that became a year-round fixture—little testaments to bygone hobbies and interests and a time when you surrounded yourself with the things you liked as evidence that you liked them. I don't even know how I'd replicate that now. I like the Cubs. Coffee. When my direct deposit hits. I like FaceTiming Kat and watching stupid videos that my mom doesn't laugh at when I try to show her.

My breath skids and tumbles down my throat, like the air tripped over its shoelaces. I like Ellie. I'm ready to admit that. By some miracle, she's into me too. If that's all that mattered, we'd be golden. But that doesn't mean our lives line up or that she's ready to think about us instead of just her—and the truth is, I'm not either. We barely know each other. But we don't even have the time to change that, to figure out *us*, especially now that she's icing me out. I draw a breath and hold it there as I picture us back in the garage, throwing pitch after pitch, inching closer and closer to something warm and magnetic and real. Being with Ellie felt like being back on the softball team: I had a place and a role and a future that made sense. Without it, what do I have? A job, I guess. A best friend I see sometimes. And . . . weed. At least I'll always have weed.

I roll out of bed and straight to my dresser to dig my stash bag out of my sock drawer. It's a shitty black fanny pack with a bank logo on the front, a freebie I snagged at Pride a few years back. It's ugly as hell and the frayed strap could fall off at any second, but it does what it needs to. I dump it out on my desk-turned-rolling-station and assess the usual lineup: a bright-blue grinder, papers, a Zippo lighter, cut-up pieces of note card for folding into filters, and a Mickey Mouse pencil that's never been used for anything but stuffing weed into joints. I twist the grinder open and inspect what's left. It's a pretty pitiful amount, but it's enough to get by until I can stop at the dispensary for pre-rolls tomorrow. No more rolling joints inside once Mom and Dad are back, unless I'm interested in an evening of stern looks set to the tune of "we're not mad, we're just disappointed." They know I smoke, but at some point, we all silently agreed that "don't ask, don't tell" still flies as a good policy when it comes to drugs, even legalized ones.

I fold my crutch tight and pinch it against the paper, dismissing the thought that this might actually be the thing I'm best at. Kat's refusal to learn how to roll a joint has given me years of practice. I wonder if Daniel can roll them or if she's back to smoking bowls or, worse yet, not smoking at all.

By the time the Mickey Mouse pencil has been put to use, I've half forgotten the day behind me. It feels like any other ordinary day, and I don't care to decide if that's settling or sad. I should be celebrating Sip's successful reopening, not moping over the one person who didn't show up for it, but I don't think there's an ounce of celebration within me right now. There is, however, a deep loneliness, and only one person I want to call who might actually pick up. With Daniel still in town and dinner plans on their agenda . . . it's a long shot, but it's not zero. I dig my phone out of the comforter and hit dial on Kat's number. *Come on. Pick up pick up pick up.*

"Heyyyyyyyyy!" Just the sound of her voice is stronger and more fast acting than a Xanax. "Heads up, you're on speaker! Daniel's here. We got ice cream."

"Hi Murphy!" Daniel's voice is faint, but enthusiastic.

"Hi Daniel." I mindlessly flip open the lighter, then close it again. Open. Close. Open. Close. "Did you end up grabbing dinner downtown?"

"If ice cream from 7-Eleven counts as dinner, then yes. We were going to see if there were any tables at . . . Wait, turn left here! No, not the parking lot, the next one." The squeal of tires on pavement is just as rattling through the phone as in real life. "Sorry." Kat clicks her tongue. "Daniel's driving."

"I figured."

"Did you end up swinging by Ellie's?"

"Yeah." I sink another inch lower into my comforter. "I'm home now."

"And? How'd it go?"

"Um." I swallow hard. Not a *push back the tears* kind of a swallow, but a *do I really want to have this conversation in front of Daniel* kind of swallow. The words are cramping up in the back of my throat. "Bad. It went bad."

"Fuck, really?" Her tone shifts into sport mode. "What can I do? Do you need me?"

"Um. Kind of? I don't know. Can you just call me back when you're home?"

"No, I'm just gonna have Daniel drop me off. Whip around in the parking lot of this vein clinic, honey."

I set down the Zippo and pick up the joint, something fresh to fidget with. "You really don't have to do that."

"Do you want me to?"

Of course I want her to. That's why I'm calling. But it's also selfish.

"You there, Murph?"

"Yeah," I whisper. "I'm here."

"Do you want me to come over?" Kat asks again, speaking a little slower this time, giving the question room to breathe.

"I, uh. I don't want to take you from Daniel."

"I'll be fine," Daniel says, and it doesn't sound like he's lying either. "Whatever you need to do." It's the best possible thing he could say.

"Um, yeah then, I do. I do want you to come over."

"Cool," Kat says. "See you in five."

We hang up, and exactly five minutes later, the garage door growls open. I smile to myself. Good to know she still remembers the code.

"Murph?" Kat's voice bounces off the vaulted ceilings, along with the sound of her shoes hitting the baseboards as she kicks them off. "You in your room?"

"Yup."

"Coming." Moments later, the shuffle of her socks across the hardwood turns to echoey thuds up the stairs and, finally, the squeal of my door being nudged open. "Knock knock?" Kat walks in, bringing the smell of both Ben and Jerry with her. Some sort of cookies and cream ordeal, if I had to guess.

"Did you bring your ice cream?"

"Nah, I scarfed it in the car," she admits. "I didn't want to be the asshole showing up with only a pint for myself."

"We could've shared," I point out.

"Yeah right. Cool if I borrow shorts?" I'm not sure why she bothers asking, and before I can respond, she's tugging open the bottom-left dresser drawer, digging for her favorite—a worn-down pair of shorts with my parents' alma mater printed across the butt. Luckily, they're clean, and she shimmies out of her jeans and tugs them on before plopping down next to me, my fluffy white comforter giving a puff of air. "It smells like weed in here."

"Are you surprised?" I hold up the joint in one hand and my Zippo in the other. "Wanna smoke this?"

Her shoulders bounce up an inch. "Sure, I'm not driving. Inside or outside?"

"Inside." I throw back the covers and swing my feet over the side. "It's too cold."

"Your parents won't mind?

"They would, but they're not here. We can just blow out the window or whatever."

I flip the lock on the window and muscle it open a few inches, bristling at the cold air leaking in. "We better smoke fast." I crouch down, blocking the wind with one hand and holding the Zippo in the other till the joint drooping from my lips crackles and burns.

"God, I missed the Zippo." Kat shakes her head at half tempo. "I need to buy one. I get so annoyed when the wind keeps blowing it out and you have to . . ." She mimes flicking a lighter again and again, her thumbnail scraping against the bend of her pointer finger. "You know?"

"Yeah, you need a Zippo," I agree through the sides of my mouth, lips rolled in and joint firmly in place. When I exhale, I press my mouth as close to the window screen as I can, release the smoke into the twilight, then pass to Kat. "This shit makes me feel eighteen again."

Her eyes hang low and unimpressed. "You say it like it was so long ago."

"It feels like long ago."

"I guess. Things aren't that different though." Kat looks me up and down, the lit joint dangling between her fingers. "I mean, you're still the same."

"Yeah," I grunt, glaring at my softball trophies. "I've been feeling that a little too much lately."

"No, it's a good thing," Kat reassures me. "And I think I'm the same in most ways too, right? I mean, I think we both changed, like, a little. But in similar ways? And another—"

"You gonna talk or you gonna smoke?"

"Sorry, sorry, sorry." She takes a long drag and practically kisses the screen when she exhales. "Anyway, when we were eighteen, we were already smoking in my basement. So this is more like seventeen."

We're not stoned yet, but we laugh like we are, then smoke like we desperately need to be. In less time than it took for Kat to get here, we've burned this thing down to the filter.

"All right, I think it's done," Kat says, coughing between every two syllables. "All right." *Cough.* "I think." *Cough.* "It's done." *Cough.*

I make the gimme motion, tapping four fingers against my open palm until Kat passes it back.

"Yeah, that's pretty roachy." I grind the barely lit end into the only spot in the house my mother won't notice ash: the little gap of space between the sill and the screen. "Don't tell Susan."

"Oh, I'm calling her immediately," Kat jokes, pressing

buttons on an invisible phone and holding it to her ear. "Hello, 911? Your daughter put a joint out in your window."

"Wait." I choke back a laugh. "You called 911, not my mom."

Her eyes stretch to their limit, bouncing between me and her invisible phone. "Uhhhh. Sorry, wrong number."

A unison THC-fueled cackle explodes out of both of us, loud enough that neighbors several doors down would be within their rights to actually call 911. I don't care. Not right now, not with Kat.

"Oh my God, close it." She bats a limp wrist at the open window. "We're so loud. Plus I'm freezing."

"You're the one who put on shorts!"

"They're the best shorts!" she shrieks and slaps her palms against her thighs, standing up and model-twirling to show off the letters on the butt. When she whips back around, there's an exaggerated amount of sternness on her face. "Murphy, dear," she says in her best RuPaul head voice, "your collegiate shorts made the grade. Con*drag*ulations, you are the winner of this week's challenge."

I topple to my side, wheezing out laugh after laugh. I'm stoned. She's stoned. We're stoned.

"Okay, seriously, I'm closing this." She pushes down on the window till it seals shut with a soft, almost squishy *thunk*, hiding our sins. "I'll go grab snacks, and then you're filling me in, 'kay?"

"I bet you wish you still had that ice cream now."

"Yeah, yeah," she scoffs. "I still wouldn't share if I did."

While Kat runs to the kitchen to scrounge up something to curb the munchies, I crawl back into bed, tugging the comforter up to my chin. She returns with a box of fiber cereal tucked under one arm and a container of blueberries in her hand. "I'm remembering why we started smoking at my house."

She passes me the blueberries, which are without a doubt the better snack, and settles onto the bed. We've spent a decade and a half of friendship in nearly this exact spot—me, propped up by too many throw pillows, snuggled beneath the covers; her, lying on her belly, chin propped up in her hands. This is how we were when I came out to her, and when she told me about her first kiss with her only high school boyfriend, the guy she dated almost exclusively so she'd have a date to senior prom. It's where we first plotted our college experience: two years at community college to get our gen eds out of the way, then U of I, then an apartment in a cool neighborhood on the outskirts of Chicago so we could commute downtown together for work: her at some swanky hotel and me at one of the hundreds of ad agencies in the city. All our most important moments have happened just like this, parallel to each other on my unmade bed, only with varying amounts of acne and bangs and stuffed animals piled next to us.

"So." She sets aside her box of cereal and claps the crumbs off her hands. Goofy Kat has stepped out, taking her RuPaul impression with her. What's left is a quieter, gentler Kat with a squint of concern in her eyes. "What's going on? What happened with Ellie?"

My shoulders deflate. Where do I even begin? The timeline is short, but there are so many points on it, and I want to pause on every single one, to paint each scene with the sort of detail that only Kat would care about. I want to relive every stroke of

Ellie's thumb against my hand, every laugh and uncomfortable dinner table silence. I want to tell her how I started dreaming, the way I never do, about months down the line with Ellie. About next semester. About next year. But I know I have to start with the end.

"She left, Kat," I mumble, unwilling to even hear myself say it. I tug at a loose bit of comforter stitching and the fabric around it puckers. "Ellie left."

Kat's nose scrunches. "What do you mean *left*?"

"I swung by her house, but Ellie had gone back to U of I already, and now she's not picking up or texting me back."

Kat chews her lip. "Okay, go back. We still haven't talked through Thanksgiving."

"Thanksgiving was mostly fine," I say. "I think Professor Meyers actually likes me now. She invited me back for Christmas."

"Nice."

"But Ellie and I got in this big fight after I talked to you on the phone yesterday." I scrape my pointer finger against the side of my thumb, peeling back a strip of dry skin. Talking about it makes it more real, and I feel a little stupid for being this shaken up by a fight with my fake girlfriend of less than a day, especially after calling Kat's two-month relationship the equivalent of twelve seconds. She graciously hears me out anyway.

"What was the fight about?" Kat asks.

What *was* the fight about? "Priorities, I guess?"

"Okay? Say more."

I mine my memory for more concrete details. "Well, she was really weird about me and you."

Kat flinches. "Weird how?"

I place a blueberry between my front teeth, biting it in half as evenly as possible. "She, like, accused me of being in love with you."

"Oh." Kat blinks off toward the window for a moment, then cocks her head back toward me. "Are you?"

I lob a pillow at her head, and she doesn't even try to dodge it.

"I'll take that as a soft maybe," she laughs.

"Do you want to talk about this or not?"

"Sorry, sorry," Kat resituates, wedging the pillow beneath her forearms to prop herself up. "I may also be a little stoned."

"A little? You're stoney baloney."

"Stogna bologna," she whispers, pronouncing the silent *g*'s and ushering us both into another laughing fit. "Fuck," she wheezes as we both catch our breath. "I'm sorry. I suck. Please keep going."

"I would if I remembered what we were talking about . . ."

"Ellie. The fight."

"Right, thank you." I shuffle my mental note cards and pick up where I left off. "I don't know. Ellie thinks we're, like, weirdly close."

"Me and you?"

"Yeah."

Kat hums in thought. "I mean, yeah, we're close. But I wouldn't say it's weird."

"Maybe it's weird by some people's standards," I say.

"But I bet Ellie wouldn't think it was weird if we were sisters," Kat points out.

A warm, easy feeling settles through me like honey. "Exactly," I say. "You get it."

In a brief bit of silence, I almost convince myself this conversation is done and we can go back to being stogna bologna, but when Kat speaks up, the warm honey feeling crusts over. "So that was the fight?" she asks. "It was about me?"

"It wasn't *really* about you," I say, mostly just to make her feel better, but once it's out there, it feels truer than I realized. "It was more about . . . how I put you first. Like, above myself, even." I swallow hard, then in a smaller voice add, "That's what Ellie thinks, anyway."

Kat's lips part on a breath. "Huh. Like when?"

"Like . . . when I stayed back from the family Florida trip to see you, I guess."

"You didn't have to," Kat says. "I didn't like . . . force you." She glances away, but not quickly enough to block me from seeing the guilt in her eyes.

"Of course you didn't force me. We planned that together," I say. "And it worked out with the Sip reopening anyway." I'm hesitant to say anything else. We could sweep all the hard stuff away and just smoke and laugh till we both doze off, like we've done a hundred weekends before. It's tempting, but that's not why I called her. That's not why she's here. So I keep going. "She also mentioned, y'know, how I wanted to go to the same college as you," I say with a little less confidence than before.

"But that's just how it worked out, right?" Kat says. "That we both wanted to do the community college and state school thing?"

I'm not brave enough to tell her that's not quite true, that the primary appeal of my college plan was that it was the same as hers. I can't admit that, when she transferred and left me behind, I couldn't bear to think that maybe I needed her more than she needed me. It hurts too much to say out loud, but my face crumples, and Kat's knowing gaze says it all. I don't have to say a word.

"I miss you at U of I you know," she whispers, reaching over to give my hand a little squeeze.

"You don't have to say that."

"I'm not just saying it," she insists. "It's true."

"Yeah, but you've got so much other stuff going on." My voice cracks, and I wish it wouldn't.

"You have stuff going on too," Kat says. "The Sip stuff is your stuff."

"Yeah, I guess so."

"What do you mean you guess so?" There's a playful shimmer to her voice that scares off the threat of tears. "You saw the place today. It was packed. You did all the marketing for that. That was you."

"It wasn't all me," I admit.

"That's not the point. You've got stuff going on in your life outside of me, and I've got stuff outside of you too. Stuff with Daniel, with school . . . we're just on different paths right now."

I blink up at my glow-in-the-dark stars, allowing myself to remember the magic of how things used to be, back when Kat and I were building a shared path. Middle school, high school, community college—anywhere I went, Kat and I were in lockstep, and nothing was too scary when I knew we were in it together. I never wanted to build a path of my own so long as I could stay on hers.

"I guess I'm still figuring out my path," I say.

"You were on your own path yesterday, right? When you opted to go to Ellie's instead of doing Thanksgiving with us?"

My stomach sinks. "I know, and I'm sor—"

"Nope," Kat interrupts, giving her head one stern shake. "No apologies. Sure, I wish you'd told me sooner that you were going, but I get it. We're both gonna have other things—other *people*—who take priority too." She pauses, smirks, then adds, "Unless this is all part of your long con to turn me gay and live happily ever after."

I know she's only joking this much to keep me from crying, but it's working, so I play along. "Be for real," I tease, giving her and those worn-out sleep shorts a once-over. "You know you're not my type."

"I know who is, though."

There's a tingle in my chest, like rain falling on the roof of my shaky heart. "I know," I say. "It was supposed to be fake."

"But you seemed genuinely happy," Kat says.

I press my tongue to the roof of my mouth, trapping my breath behind it. I heard somewhere that it's supposed to stop you from crying. In my whirlwind twenty-four hours with Ellie Meyers, there were so few moments where it was just us, no lying or schemes being hatched. Whether we were sneaking into Sip or stumbling through a pitching lesson, those moments—rare as they were—absolutely shimmered. I was happier than I remembered I could be.

"Kat," I finally sigh, "she's . . . *wow*."

Kat's eyes glisten, then cloud over with a dreamy look. I recognize that look. It's the same one I saw from her on Wednesday night when she was staring across the bar at Daniel. "Murph," Kat says, "you *deserve* someone who's *wow*."

"I know. You do too. And I'm glad you have Daniel. It's just . . ." A sigh leaks between the gaps in my teeth as I shift upright and meet her gaze. "I miss you, Kat."

She wiggles her fingers in a tiny wave. "I'm right here."

"I mean all the time. I feel like we've hardly talked the last three months."

I watch Kat's eyes wander from the comforter to the Wall of Fame, stopping on pictures of us in Girl Scouts, at homecoming, at Six Flags just last year. "I know," she says. "I'm sorry. But we'll be together again next semester, right?"

My stomach plummets. I guess we have to have this conversation eventually, and now is as good a time as any. I take a deep breath and blow a raspberry into the air. "I, uh. No," I choke out. "No, we won't."

Kat's attention snaps back toward me, her eyebrows scrunched together in suspicion. "I thought you said Thanksgiving went well. You don't think Professor Meyers will pass you?"

"She might," I say, "but it won't matter. I missed the deadline for the transfer application."

Kat looks down at the sheets in front of her for a moment, presumably doing some light mental math. "That can't be right." She shoves off the bed and digs her phone out of the pocket of her jeans. Whether she's referencing the U of I website or just her calendar app, her thumb scrolls with purpose. "Those aren't due until . . ."

"October." I wish I could stabilize the wobble in my voice. "I was so bogged down with everything at Sip and I thought I'd need my final accounting grade to send in my application."

It's quiet again, but I'm too stoned to know if it's an awkward silence or not. They rarely are with Kat. "Well, fuck," she finally says, and I'm sort of relieved to hear her voice wobble too. "That . . . that really sucks."

"Yeah," I agree. "It does." I hold my breath in anticipation of more follow-up questions about my backup plan or whatever, but Kat's mind isn't there yet. She tosses her phone back on the floor with her jeans and perches on the edge of the bed. Another few seconds pass, and she scrapes the last bit of air from her lungs with a final shaky sigh.

"God, I'm so sorry." There's heartbreak in her eyes, but I barely see it before her gaze falls back to the floor. "That, like, really, really sucks. Like, I don't even want to go back now."

"Shut up. You don't mean that."

"I mean, no," she admits without looking up. "Of course I'm going back. I love U of I, but I would love it a lot more if you were there."

"You'll be fine," I say. "You have Daniel."

"Daniel's the best," she admits, "but he's my boyfriend. It's different."

"Better, even. Because you get to make out with him."

Kat's chin doesn't budge from her chest, but her eyes lift up to mine. She looks unimpressed. "Different."

"You just said he's the best," I point out.

"It's not a contest, Murph. I'm not choosing Daniel over you."

"You sure? Because you did this weekend." The words tumble out before I realize I've said them, and they're too heavy to hang in the silence for long. "I'm sorry, I shouldn't have—"

"No, no, you're right." Kat's voice is small, but honest. "I know I sprung the Daniel thing on you last minute and brought him to the bar without running it past you. That was uncool of me."

My shoulders relax an inch. "Why didn't you just tell me?"

She's quiet for a moment, either unsure of her answer or unwilling to share it. "I was scared." Her voice pitches up, like it always has when she's talking but doesn't want to be. "Because, um. Because I didn't want you to be sad."

"I wouldn't have been sad to meet him at Thanksgiving, but Wednesday was supposed to be about us."

"I know, I know." She's staring down at the floor again. "I should've just had him drive out on Thursday instead of bringing him to the bar."

"Why didn't you?"

"Because . . ." I watch her lips open and close, searching for the shape of the right answer. She settles on the truth. "Because I think he's *wow*," Kat says. "He's my boyfriend, Murph. I want him around. Not all the time, but most of the time. That's kind of how it goes."

I swallow twice. The truth didn't sound as good as I had hoped.

When I don't speak up, Kat does. "If you and Ellie were together, like actually together, wouldn't you want her around too?"

I picture a table with Kat and me next to two empty

barstools. When Daniel is seated at one of them, it makes sense that Ellie is there too. When Daniel gets erased, Ellie goes with him, and it's just me and Kat again. Like it used to be.

"Sometimes," I say quietly. "But not all the time. I like when it's just us."

Kat reaches across the bed and gives my arm a squeeze. "Like right now?"

"Yeah," I say, "like right now." I try to bottle up the moment in all its quiet joy. Who knows when it'll happen again. "Where is Daniel, by the way?"

Kat smirks, and her gaze bounces to the window and back. "He's, uh. He's in the driveway."

"What?"

"Yeah, I didn't know how long we'd be, and it's not like he wants to go home and hang out with my parents. He swore he didn't mind."

I shove back the comforter and head for the window facing our driveway. Sure enough, there's Kat's Honda Civic idling with the lights turned off. If I squint, I can just barely catch the outline of an enormous man shoved into a tiny car, his face lit up blue by the light of his phone.

"Oh my God, I feel so bad."

"He's got games on his phone," Kat says with the sort of nonchalance of a mom talking about her iPad child. Meanwhile, someone's going to have to hire a crane to lift my jaw off the floor. To be blunt, I've never seen this kind of selflessness from a straight man. I scrape the last bit of air from my lungs with a sigh.

"I think you're right," I admit. "I think he's *wow*."

Kat's smile is almost too big for her face. "You're the best for saying that, you know that?"

"I mean it. I'm glad you brought him home."

She frowns. "Okay, now I know you're lying."

"I mean, yeah. But not about him being great. Way better than I thought he'd be."

She squints at me, suspicious. "What did you think he'd be?"

"I don't know, he's a straight guy! My expectations were low!"

Kat's laugh must be loud enough for Daniel to hear, or else he just sees us in the window. Either way, the lights in the car flip on, and Daniel gives us a big goofy smile and a wave. We laugh and wave back, and once we do, he kills the lights again and goes back to his phone.

"I like him," I say.

Kat stares out the window with a familiar warmth in her eyes. "Yeah," she sighs, "I like him too."

A question takes shape in my chest, and I'm barely brave enough to ask it. "Do you think you might . . . love him?"

Kat's head snaps to face me, those two vertical lines between her eyebrows back out in full force. "It's only been two months."

"Do you think that matters?"

"I . . . I don't know." She heads back to the bed, hugging a pillow against her chest. "Maybe I love him already. But like, I wouldn't tell him I love him yet, you know? Because that'd be too much too soon, and I don't even know how to know. You know?" She pauses, looks at me, and asks, "Do you know?"

The only thing I know is that she's speaking in riddles. I guess we're both still a little high. I sit next to her on the edge of the bed and match her question with another question. "How do you know you love me?"

Her eyes slip from mine and drift back toward the Wall of Fame. I can't tell what picture she's looking at, but she steadies her gaze there as the words start to come. "I know I love you because I want to be around you even when we're not doing anything. Because just having you around makes everything better. And I'd drop everything and make my boyfriend wait in the car when you need me. No matter what happens between you and me, I know we're gonna work it out."

I squeeze Kat's hand, and when she squeezes back, there's a prickle at the end of my nose, threatening tears. "Do you feel that way about Daniel?"

She looks back toward the window, back toward the dark that's swallowed our view of the car. "Almost," she whispers, then clears her throat and speaks a bit louder. "Do you think it's the same?"

"What do you mean?"

"Friend love and love love," she specifies.

I blink back at her. An answer doesn't come to me. "Do *you* think it's the same? You're closer to knowing than I am."

Kat lifts a shoulder. "I always assumed love love would be just a little bit better. But maybe it's not. Maybe it's just . . . different."

"Different," I agree, "but definitely related. Otherwise we couldn't have stayed friends this long." I trace back my gaze to me and Kat as Girl Scouts. I can't help but think of Ellie, whose longest running friendship isn't half as old as Kat and I are in that picture. "We're lucky," I say. "Most people don't get to have a Kat in their life."

"And hardly anyone gets to have a Murph," Kat says. "Which sucks for them because one of the coolest things about my life is having you in it."

"Me too." I barely smile. "About you, though." I pull her tight against my hip and lean my head onto her shoulder. "I love you, Kat."

"I love you too." She rests her head on top of mine. "And anyone else I love, I'll know how to love them because you taught me first."

"I think you're right," I say, and Kat's shoulder shakes with a laugh.

"Of course I'm right," she says. "Can't remember a time I've been wrong."

I don't remember Kat leaving, I don't remember falling asleep, and I don't remember which happened first. What I do know is when I wake up, squinty-eyed and searching for her, all that's left are the shorts, folded neatly on the dresser for the next time she comes by.

nineteen

❋

ell-OOOO!"

If not for the constant buffering of this episode of *RuPaul's Drag Race*, I may not have heard my parents come home. Lucky or unlucky for me, the living room TV has been still for the last fifteen minutes aside from a spinning loading wheel over the panel of judges, and the low grumble of suitcase wheels rolling across the hardwood comes over loud and clear in the silence. I hip check the dishwasher, sealing off the last of four days' worth of dirty dishes, and hit start while dragging a rag across the counter. To say the house is spotless would be downplaying it; after a hectic Sunday morning barista shift, I've spent the rest of the afternoon erasing all evidence that anyone has ever set foot in this house. Not me, not Kat, and certainly not Ellie. Any hints of her have been bleached away, returning the house to its usual state—tidy to the point of looking practically uninhabited.

"Anyone home?" Mom's voice bounces off the vaulted ceilings

and lands right in the middle of the kitchen floor, where I spot and immediately snatch up a clump of dust and hair. How I manage to shed this much and still have a single strand on my head, I may never know. I pocket the dust bunny, silently cursing the traffic from O'Hare for not being worse. I was planning to wrap up an afternoon of cleaning with a second sweep and a third round of vacuuming, but I was also planning on at least another hour before Mom and Dad got home. Instead, a leathery, middle-aged Barbie and Ken waltz into the kitchen, dragging identical black suitcases behind them.

"Well, don't rush to greet us or anything," Mom teases, tucking a stray strand of silver hair back into her airplane-friendly ponytail.

"Sorry, sorry. Welcome home."

Mom gathers me up in a hug that feels straight out of one of those soldier-comes-home videos. When she grants me full use of my airways again, she doesn't let go altogether; instead, she holds me at an arm's length, like she's searching for evidence that I've changed or grown up at all over the course of less than a week.

"Florida wasn't the same without you." Her eyes are welling up a little, but her subtle yet tragic sunglasses-shaped tan line keeps me from slipping into feeling sentimental. And of course, if the sunglasses tan didn't do it, Dad sure would. He's just a few steps behind her, his winter coat zipped over an unseasonable pair of khaki shorts.

"Hey, Toto, I don't think we're in Florida anymore!" He flashes me the sort of big, eager smile and bouncy eyebrow maneuver that tells me he tried this joke out on Mom already.

"I guess not." I scare up a fake laugh, which I always do, even for Dad's worst jokes.

"See?" He jabs a thumb in my direction, giving Mom a look. "*She* thought it was funny."

While Dad and I riff on *Wizard of Oz* and Thanksgiving crossover jokes (*green beans and corn bread and yams, oh pie!*), Mom goes full real estate appraisal on the house. She twists one of the blue pillar candles in the center of the countertop, examining the wick to be sure I didn't forget these are for decoration, never for lighting. "It doesn't look too bad in here," she finally admits.

"Yeah, you can hardly tell I had a huge rager here last night." I look to Dad, hoping he'll hop on my joke, but the sheer sense of panic emanating from Mom keeps him from saying a word. She freezes in place, only her head pivoting toward me for a quick sarcasm scan.

"You didn't."

"Literally who would I invite?"

"Kat? And Kat's boyfriend?" She's white-knuckling the handle of her suitcase, but I'm not ready to drop the joke yet.

"I don't think Kat and Kat's boyfriend qualifies as a party," I point out.

Dad interrupts with a guttural laugh. "Tell that to Kat and Kat's boyfriend!" When Mom shoots him dagger eyes, he puts up his hands in defense and backs away, returning to the safety of keeping his mouth shut.

"There was no party," I reassure her. "I'm joking. I had Kat over one night, but Daniel didn't even come in."

"Daniel and Kat. Kat and Daniel." Mom releases her grip on her suitcase and turns their names over and over, practicing emphasizing one name and then the other. "What's the verdict on him?"

"I like him. He's . . . patient."

She raises an eyebrow at my choice of descriptors, but we breeze past it and into the other details of my weekend, although they're few and far between. I focus on the success of the reopening, which impresses them enough to ward off any questions about how I spent my Thanksgiving. I'm halfway through recounting Brooklyn's nicknames for our regulars when RuPaul's voice interrupts, unleashing some harsh but fair criticism onto a queen who, from the sound of it, stands little chance at becoming America's Next Drag Superstar.

"Jesus." Mom fans her fingers across her chest while I fumble for the remote and hit mute. "I thought somebody broke in."

"Nah, just RuPaul." I smile sheepishly, feeling embarrassed for no reason I can pinpoint. "Tell me more about Florida."

Mom blinks at me, then at Dad, then back at me. "Actually, we do have something kind of fun to share." Her off-putting, ultrasaccharine smile must be contagious, because seconds later, Dad is giving me the same one.

"We did a little shopping," Dad explains.

"Yeah?" I take a backward grip on the counter behind me, bracing myself for a retelling of the discount golf shirt story. Were they really so drunk on Thanksgiving that they don't remember telling me?

"Some big shopping." Dad loops an arm around Mom's waist, creating a united front. "We put an offer in on a condo."

My eyebrows hop up my forehead and back. "Yeah?" I knew

my family had *Thanksgiving in Florida* money, but having *second property in Florida* money is news to me.

"It's the cutest little spot, right on Sanibel Island. A two-bedroom, but it's only got the one bath." Mom digs into her purse while she talks, fishing out her phone. "We had to make a few compromises to get the location we wanted. Let me pull up the listing. Wait no, better yet." She pulls her readers out of her purse and situates them on her nose, mouth stretching open as she punches her finger against her phone screen. "We took some video during our showing. Look, here's your father standing in the shower."

I shield my eyes with my hands. "Ew, I don't want to see that."

Mom is unimpressed, if not a little annoyed. "He's clothed, Murphy. He's just showing off how spacious it is."

"I got a full wingspan in every direction in that thing!" Dad chimes in with a toothy grin, stretching his arms out airplane style to demonstrate.

Mom cozies up beside me and flips her phone horizontal, and I watch the wobbly footage of her walking past coral walls and bright white cabinets. "We're going to paint, of course," she says. "The previous owners really made it like you're living inside a seashell."

"Did they, uh." I bite my cheek, searching for the right terminology and realizing that, for a realtor's daughter, I know shockingly little about real estate. "Like, do you own it yet or?"

"They accepted the offer," Dad says, putting me out of my misery. "We close on it in a month, so long as everything goes well with the appraisal and there aren't any hang-ups with the HOA. We'll just need to liquidate a few assets first."

I nod along, trying out a smile that suggests I understand even 50 percent of this lingo. Better to fake it than to turn this conversation into a real estate lesson. On Mom's phone, a sky-blue bathroom comes into view, and, as promised, Dad is standing in the shower with arms spread wide and an even bigger smile than the one he has on now. He looks happier than I've seen him in a long time, and while I have dozens of questions—most of them about how much this will cost and whether or not they'll still have room in the budget to contribute to my college fund—none of that feels relevant right now. Mom and Dad are excited. The least I can do is be excited too.

"This is awesome. We'll actually be able to actually have a real Thanksgiving in this kitchen."

"Exactly! See?" Mom purses her lips at Dad, giving him the *I told you so* eyes. "And I know it'll be tough with the one bathroom when you come down to visit, but I promise we'll make it work."

My chin dips to my chest. "Visit? Wouldn't we fly down together?" No sooner do the words come out than the blanks start to fill in. Mom and Dad didn't buy a vacation home; they bought a—

"Actually." Mom pauses, smushes her lips together, and starts again. "Actually, we were planning to sell the house and move down there."

They bought a new home. Shit.

The pit in my stomach threatens to swallow me whole. "We're . . . moving?"

"Well. Your father and I are moving." Mom doesn't trail off so much as end her sentence right in the middle, holding her breath while I draw my own conclusions.

They're moving, and I'll just need to figure it out.

"Once you're off at U of I, we won't really have a whole lot keeping us here anymore," Mom explains. "All my friends moved away years ago, and Dad and I are both just about ready to retire, and with you gone, we just won't need this kind of space anymore. We're always planning these trips down to Florida and spending all this money, and, well, we just thought . . . it's time."

As she works through her clearly rehearsed explanation, Dad nods along in agreement. I wonder if he helped her practice this little speech, if they first ran through it on the plane or when they were touring the place. Has this always been the plan? Have they looked at condos before? And where—if anywhere—do I fit it in?

"This is all great," I lie. "But . . . what if I don't get into U of I?" I try to steady my voice, hoping I come off more nonchalant than I feel.

Mom and Dad share a quick look, thinking I won't notice. "Then we'd help you find an apartment here," Dad says.

If there's a deep breath to be found in this house, in this town, my lungs can't find it. From the root of my tongue to the base of my stomach, nothing will move. Not a word, not a breath, not a scream.

"You could get something closer to school or closer to Sip," Mom offers, tucking her phone away. "Your own place with your own stuff. And so long as you're still in school, we can still help out here and there." She rattles off something about an apartment complex she's shown to a few younger clients of hers, selling me on the faux luxury of having my own shitty apartment in the suburbs. None of it sticks.

"So how soon are we selling the house?" I ask.

"Well, it'll take a week or two to stage it," Mom says. "Make it look all neat and spiffy for the listing photos."

I stretch my arms wide, an unintended imitation of Dad in the shower of their new condo. Their new *home*. "This"—I look left to right, regretting my excellent cleanup job—"this isn't neat and spiffy enough?"

Mom's mouth puckers at the sides, panicked eyes turning toward Dad, silently begging him to intervene.

"Your room, Murph," Dad explains. "We'll just need to stage your room."

If I didn't know better, I'd think God swatted the earth and rocked its orbit backward. Of course. My room. The only room that shows any signs of someone living here. I want to push back, to remind them that I have a final coming up. I need more time. I'm not ready. But all I can croak out is "Oh."

"Oh honey." Mom squeezes me into an uncomfortable side hug. I'm no longer a soldier coming home. I'm a twenty-one-year-old mooch being kicked out of her parents' house. "We know it's not a fun conversation to have, Murph. We were planning to take you out to dinner and tell you, show you all the apartments we've already picked out for you. We thought you'd be excited not to be stuck in your *parents' house* anymore."

Her delivery on *parents' house* is that of someone saying *spoiled milk* or *athlete's foot*. She's doing the realtor thing, the thing I've seen her do with her clients dozens of times when they lose out on listings and she suddenly wants to make a perfectly good house seems like the completely wrong fit. *You didn't want a place with only two bedrooms, did you? It's a shame you got outbid, but did you really want to live with an unfinished basement?* She normally pairs it with a slow shake of her head, subconsciously getting her buyers to agree. *You're so right, that's not what we wanted at all.* Predictably, the next words out of Mom's mouth are accented by her head shaking side to side. "You didn't want to live with us for the rest of college, right?"

My cheeks overheat, and I wouldn't be shocked to see steam come out of my ears. Of course I didn't want to live with them for the rest of college. I didn't even want to be here this semester. But I'm not going to let Mom use her goddamn real estate tactics on me. I'm not her client. I'm her daughter. "Why were you already picking out apartments around here?" I ask. "Because you didn't think I'd get into U of I, right?"

Mom winces, and her mouth opens, but no words come out. Fuckin' figures. Dad steps in with a "Well, Murph, you gotta understand—"

"Well, you're right," I interrupt, then press my tongue to the roof of my mouth. The tears come anyway. My parents have the exact right amount of confidence in me, which is to say, none at all.

"Honey . . ." Dad starts, taking a cautious step forward. I cut him off with a flat palm held up like a traffic guard. It's the sort of thing Mom would usually chew me out for, reminding me to be respectful of my father. Right now, she doesn't say a word.

"No, I mean it," I choke out. "I missed the transfer deadline because I was so busy with the Sip renovations. So congratulations, you called it. Your daughter is exactly the deadbeat you always knew she was."

"Oh sweetie, I'm so sorry." Mom's voice is thick with heart-break, but not an ounce of surprise.

"Yeah. I think I'm just gonna head to . . ." I arrive at the end of the sentence before I can decide how it's going to end. Where am I supposed to go? Work? School? Kat drove back to U of I this morning, so it's not like I can go to her house. "I'm gonna head up to my room, is that okay?"

I feel simultaneously too young and too old for this moment, asking for permission in a house that is entirely mine and entirely not mine, all at once. This is the only home I've ever lived in, the only place the maps app has ever put the little house icon. My house, except not my house at all. At some point, the house you grew up in is supposed to turn a corner from "my house" to "my parents' house," but that never happens if you never leave it. Until now, I guess.

"We love you," Dad says, and I snatch my phone off the counter and head for the staircase, leaving behind fragments of a conversation that will remain unfinished.

Upstairs, I slide into the home base of my bed, breathing in the mix of coffee and detergent that everything I own takes on. It's a comforting smell. A home smell. *This* home. I remember how my pillowcase always smelled just a little different after a sleepover at Kat's. It's the only frame of reference I have to tell me that, even with the same job and the same fabric softener, this smell will eventually tune itself to wherever I live next. I'll probably forget this smell altogether.

I know I'm being dramatic. People move all the time. I just always thought that, when I left this house, it'd be onward and upward and of my own accord, and it would always be mine to come back to.

I roll onto my back, resisting the instinct to reach for my phone and dissociate until the feeling passes, squeezing my eyes tight enough for neon shapes to appear behind my eyelids. I'm going to have to move. I don't know where, and I don't know how soon, but I asked for this. I said I wanted out of Geneva, I just didn't expect some real "Monkey's Paw" bullshit.

The neon shapes linger even when I peel my eyes open again. They flicker and shift across the high school tchotchkes around my room. The trophies, the books—all of it simultaneously sacred and stupid, a three-dimensional scrapbook of a Murphy who no longer exists. Kat and Ellie are both wrong. I have changed. At least a little. Haven't I?

I have to believe I've moved on from who I used to be. Otherwise, I'm no better than those college kids who wander back into their high school classes the first time they come back home. We used to make fun of those kids back in high school—each one had a visitor's pass around their neck and looked a little worse for wear as they talked about the good old days, which were all of two or three years prior. We'd cringe and nod and give them a thumbs-up, wondering why they felt the need to revisit the high school memories they'd hardly left behind. God, don't tell me I've grown up to be like them.

I pat myself down, searching for my phone, and knock out the only instantly urgent item on my to-do list: delete Ellie's number, our chat history, and our photos. I'm done hanging on to things from high school, especially things that were never really mine in the first place.

twenty

*

The right amount of time to spend on a community college campus is exactly the duration that a class requires. Not a second more, but often, a minute or two less. In two and a half years, I've never once stepped foot onto the Weymouth campus for anything that wasn't required—not for a speaker series, not for a sporting event, and certainly not for tutoring (although maybe it would've helped). But on this fully frozen Monday morning, when my calendar app buzzed thirty minutes before an optional study session, I rolled out of bed and started defrosting my car.

Desperate times, as they say, call for desperate last-minute cram sessions.

"Are we ready for the next slide?" Professor Meyers scans the half-filled classroom of C-and-below students and, receiving zero response, clacks her space bar. The projected image shifts to a new page of study guide answers, a fresh crop of buzzwords that I understand even less than the first set.

Maybe desperate is too generous to describe my situation. Doomed might be a little more accurate.

The class marks their wrong answers in silence, and I drum my pen against the gray laminate table, gradually picking up speed until someone has the audacity to shush me. It's me versus this study guide in a battle for a 98 on this final. A losing battle, sure, but with the "schmooze your way to an A" plan off the table, it's my only hope. At least it's better than the 124 I needed last semester. I check off the last wrong answer on my study guide and calculate my score: a triumphant 68. That leaves me four days left to get 30 points better before Friday's final, or else I'll be left with two miserable options: take this class a third time or give up on college altogether. I'm not sure which would be worse.

"Are there any specific questions anyone would like to review?" Professor Meyers's gaze flickers toward me with hopeful skepticism. "Anyone?"

I blink into the fluorescent lights, comparing the correct answers on the screen to the chicken scratch on my packet. Before I can decide if I'm too proud to actively participate in a study session, my seat partner raises his hand.

"Samuel?"

The frail-looking boy next to me offers up a question that I left blank. Much like I would've done with the question "What is your seat partner's name?" had it been asked ten seconds ago.

Professor Meyers uncaps her dry-erase marker and draws a big, red diagram that takes up most of the white board. If she had a feedback box, I'd suggest any color marker but red. I already see enough of it all over my tests. "So there's Company A and Company B." She barely glances at the study guide, reciting the question by heart. "If Company A signs a contract to provide services to Company B for one hundred thousand dollars, and payment is complete before any work has been started, what journal entry does Company A record on this date?"

I flip through my notebook in search of anything about journal entries. Would you believe that I've taken the same notes two semesters in a row and still can't retain this garbage? Maybe accounting is just something I'm not meant to know.

"Murphy?"

Fuck.

I look up from my notes and directly into the expectant eyes of Kara Meyers. Fuck it, here's my best shot. "Um, debit cash credit revenue?"

Her smile wavers. "Close. It's debit cash credit *deferred* revenue. Let's look at the timeline."

I sink into my seat, the base of my head knocking against the back of my chair. I don't want to look at the timeline. I want to look at the inside of my eyelids or the WCC parking lot as I'm pulling away. But I guess if I wanted to avoid stuff I already learned, maybe I should've passed the class on the first go-round.

My left leg bounces in time with the low tick of the wall clock, each passing second introducing a new reason why I should get up and give up.

Tick. My chair has no lumbar support.

Tick. My pen is dying.

Tick. Professor Kara Meyers can't go more than a few minutes without staring me down.

The next time she looks in my direction, I force a smile, and she studies me with the same concentration I should be putting into this review session. Is she waiting for me to speak up? To leave? Last we interacted, I was fleeing her house like it was on fire, muttering some unconvincing excuse as to why her daughter— my alleged girlfriend—might have skipped town without telling me. If the two of them talk as infrequently as Ellie let on, Professor Meyers probably has some questions beyond the ones on the study guide.

An hour of review questions slips away like a good summer, and with five minutes left of class, Professor Meyers opens the floor for one last question. Half a dozen hands shoot into the air, but mine isn't one of them. If my seat were closer to the front, I might just slip out the door and pretend none of this ever happened, that I never fooled myself into thinking a ninety-minute study session or an elaborate lie to a professor would save my grade. Sadly, I'm stuck in the second to last row, and if I tried to sneak out early, it'd be a whole thing. Instead, I endure the last question of the day: what are all of the elements in a basic financial statement? I actually know this one, which should make me feel marginally better. It doesn't.

The session ends with the usual shuffling of papers and zipping of backpacks, but my low-scoring study guide has long since been packed away. I sling my backpack over my shoulder and, although I'm in the back of the classroom, make a serious go at being one of the first out.

"As a reminder, the study guide is also available on the Weymouth Student Portal, in case you've finished yours and want a fresh copy," Professor Meyers shouts over the horrible, squeaky rumble of chairs scooting along tile flooring. Oh, to be the kind of person who does the optional study guide not only once, but multiple times. "Number-two pencils only to the final and one note card with equations written on it . . . Oh, Murphy, would you mind hanging back for a minute?"

My feet freeze to the tile beneath them. I *would* mind, actually. I need to be anywhere but here. I try to invent a convincing excuse to leave—a doctor's appointment, a barista shift, a life-saving medical procedure. What comes out instead is, "Yeah, sure." I guess my lying abilities have officially run dry.

While the rest of the class files out, Professor Meyers steadies herself against the edge of her desk, waiting until it's just the two of us. Something in the silence feels like the earliest stages of a future recurring nightmare. When the last student leaves, she looks me square in the eye, and I'm shocked that I don't instantly turn to stone, ice, or an anxious mess.

"How are you doing, Murphy?"

How am I doing? With regards to what? Her hopelessly vague question garners a hopelessly vague response. "I'm all right, I guess."

"You guess?" she prods. "How are you feeling about the exam?"

My nerves settle a little. We're talking about school. Good.

"I feel . . . all right." I'm repeating myself, but I don't have a better word. "Not bad, not good."

"How'd the study guide go?"

"Better than last semester."

The pitying look on her face says what we both know. *It's not hard to do better than last semester.*

"I, uh. I did the math on my grade, and I think I might pass if

I can somehow manage to pull off a ninety-eight on the exam," I say.

Kara lifts one brow, reaching behind her for her laptop. "I think that's backward. It should be eighty-nine." She clicks her trackpad a few times, all of her frown lines making an appearance as she scrolls, then puts the laptop back in its place and punches a few numbers into her phone calculator. It's reassuring to know that even an accounting professor doesn't trust her mental math. After a few more audibly heavy-handed taps, she rotates her phone toward me, showing off the giant white number on the screen: 0.891. I may suck at math, but even I know that's eighty-nine percent. "That's what you need."

My gaze bounces from the calculator up to her face, checking for any tells. The flat line of her mouth doesn't budge an inch. Why did she know the score I needed already? Did she bump my grade up out of mercy since I last checked it, or did I really do the math wrong? The second seems more likely, but neither are impossible. Either way, the difference between an A and a B+ may not be much, but it's the jump between "almost perfect score" and "normal grade that normal people get." I could be normal people, if I study really hard. Maybe.

"You've taken this final before," Professor Meyers says, as if I need the reminder. "I haven't changed it. Really focus on the study guide and the back half of the textbook."

"Got it. I will. I mean I have been." I straighten a little, collecting myself. "Thanks, Professor Meyers."

"Just Kara is fine."

"Thanks, Kara." Her name feels as clunky on my tongue as it did last week.

"That wasn't the reason I asked you to hang back though." She shuffles behind her desk, her eyes darting around in search of . . . what? A letter from Ellie? A secret advance copy of the final exam with the answers all filled in? She reaches under her desk and pulls out a big pink bowl with a matching pink lid. Ah, right. My Tupperware. Of course.

"I hope it's all right that we finished the puppy chow." When she hands the container off, something jostles inside. If not puppy chow, then what?

"Is there something in here?"

Kara shrugs, but her lips hint at a smile. "Something from Ellie."

I slip a thumb beneath the lid, preparing to pop it open, then stop myself at the last second. Given the events of the last few days, I think keeping Kara in the dark is for the best. "Great," I say. "Well, I'll see you on Friday." I don't even bother putting on my coat; I grab it with one hand and hold the Tupperware clamped to my torso with the other. Not that it's heavy, but that if anything happened that might cause me not to find out what's in here, I'd lose sleep.

"One last question," Professor Meyers says, catching me just before I slip out the door. "I know Ellie is busy with final projects, but we keep missing each other. Have you heard from her lately?"

"Um, not very much." I guess I had one last lie in me after all.

"All right," she says. "Thanks, dear."

"No problem, Professor Kara," I say, losing my brain entirely.

Outside, the wind is wicked, but the sun is shining, giving me that "frozen turkey under a heat lamp" feeling that Illinois winters always seem to deliver on. I grip my Tupperware tight to keep it from blowing out of my arms. When I reach my car, I toss my backpack in the back seat next to my stash bag and a half dozen empty coffee cups, a small shrine to my vices and a reminder I should clean my car. The Tupperware, however, comes with me to the front seat, and my hands shake just the tiniest bit as I pop the lid off. Inside, the rough edge of a sheet of watercolor paper curls up the side of the bowl, warping a painting of a small brick building with a pine-green awning and a big, white baseball on the front. With a felt tip pen, Ellie has written the name of the bar in crisp black lines: Murphy's Bleachers. Beneath the awning, there are two tiny figures: a blonde in Yankee navy and a brunette in Cubby blue.

It's not until I'm home and remove it from the bowl that I realize the painting isn't all—taped to the back is a page ripped out of a notebook with four short sentences scribbled in black ink.

Kara is thankful for company.

Otto is thankful for the guy who let him borrow the smoker.

Carol is thankful for leftover mashed potatoes.

Ellie is thankful for Murphy.

twenty-one

❄

"You deleted her number?"

Kat's voice rings through the phone with so much bewilderment, you'd think I'd insulted her personally. Whether it's luck or perfect timing, she picked up without even a predial "can I call you" text, and I got her up to speed as quickly as possible on the happenings of the thirty-six hours since she left Geneva—most notably, the moving meltdown and the mass destruction of any and all Ellie evidence on my phone. I can't believe the amount that's happened in the few days since I've seen her, and as I sit cross-legged in the center of my bed, it all tumbles out like a verbal rockslide, leaving Kat to sort through the debris.

"God, what a shit show," she mutters. "Are you okay? What can I do to help?"

"Hang on. I haven't even gotten to the real reason I called yet."

"Oh God," Kat groans. "How could there possibly be more?"

"Well, at the study session—"

"You went to the study session?" she interrupts. "Great job!"

A smile creeps over my lips. Not what I was getting at, but the recognition feels nice.

"Yes, but after, Professor Meyers gave me back the Tupperware that I left at her house, and she gave me, like, this little pep talk about my grade and how to study better. More on that later. But inside the Tupperware, there's this painting." I've been thumbing the edge of the watercolor paper our entire call, but I only now realize it. "I'll send you a pic, hang on."

I position the painting right between two sunbeams spilling across my bed, then snap two photos—one of the painting itself and one of the note on the back—and hit send, chomping on my cuticles as I wait for Kat to review the source material. After a brief pause, she squeals.

"Oh my god, Murph. This is gorgeous."

"Gorgeous," I echo. "Do you see the tiny Ellie and Murphy out front?"

She squeals. "Oh my God, I missed that! Murphy!"

"But you have to read the stuff on the back. It's from this Thanksgiving tradition they have where they write down what they're thankful for."

Another pause. "She gave this to you?"

"Yeah, that's what Professor Meyers told me."

"So this has to be an apology," Kat says.

"I think so. At the very least, it's a message. She's going to New York after U of I, and I told her I want to live in Chicago after I graduate, so I think she painted that? Like, what that could be?" I suck the blood off the bleeding edge of my thumb. "I have to talk to her."

"And say what?" Kat's voice is so giddy and cutesy, I almost forget there's a big, nasty truth we need to circle back to.

"It doesn't matter," I groan. "Because my dumb ass has no way to reach her."

"Because you deleted her number," Kat says, verbally tying the loose ends together.

"Yes," I sigh. "Yes I did."

"Fuck."

Someone in the background shushes her, and I use the temporary silence to resituate so I'm facing away from the Wall of Fame. Staring at all the pictures I'm going to have to take down bums me out.

"Quick question," Kat finally says. "Are you dumb?"

I snort. "Obviously yes."

"Why did you have to delete her number? Why didn't you just, like, block her or change her contact name to Spam Likely? Like a normal person?"

"Because I'm *dumb*," I remind her. "But chewing me out for deleting her number isn't going to bring it back."

"Sorry, sorry. You're right." She pauses, then lets out one last exasperated, "Fuck!"

Again, an aggressive *shh* in the background. Louder this time, even.

"Why are you getting shushed?"

"Because I'm at the library," Kat says.

"Oh my God, then leave the library, we're being loud."

"I'm not on the quiet floor!" She sounds defensive, and it's definitely directed more toward her shusher than toward me. "Can you DM her anywhere?"

"What, from the Sip Instagram account?"

"Right, I keep forgetting that you're not chronically online like the rest of us. Hang on, let me find her." Kat does me the favor of muting herself before tapping away at her phone in search of Ellie's digital footprint. When she comes back, she sounds defeated. "Elbell underscore underscore underscore . . . her Insta is private. I requested her, but like . . . we'll see."

I collapse back onto the bed with a sigh, letting the pillow swallow my head on either side. Square one is a shitty place to be.

"You could ask Professor Meyers for her number," Kat suggests, but the upspeak in her voice assures me that we're on the same page there: I'm definitely not going to do that. "I don't know, Murph," Kat says, deflated. "You clearly like this girl. She clearly likes you. You could just wait until she comes home for Christmas?"

"Hate that."

"What's the alternative? Sending me to hunt her down on campus?"

I don't respond.

"Nuh-uh. No chance." Kat shuts me down before I can even offer a solid argument in favor of Operation: Find Ellie. "Do you know how many people go to this school? I'm not just going to bump into her."

"Then what am I supposed to do?" I whine. "Send a carrier pigeon? Smoke signals?"

"Okay, maybe we keep brainstorming. Singing telegram? Message in a bottle? Snail mail?"

Something lights up inside me. "Wait, what about email?"

"You have her email?"

"No," I admit, "but I have a best friend who goes to the same school and knows how they format their student emails."

"First name last name at Illinois dot e-d-u!" She shrieks her answer like it's the winning response on a game show, and her background shusher comes back full force. Kat doesn't seem to mind. "Type it in! Type it in!"

I wedge my phone between my ear and my shoulder, opening my laptop. "So Ellie Meyers at . . ."

"Is that her full name? Ellie?"

My stomach nosedives. "Fuck. Probably not."

"Yearbook," Kat snaps. "Check our high school yearbook."

"Do I still have a yearbook?"

"You have so much shit in that room, there's no way you don't have a yearbook."

"But I might've packed it up already," I point out. "Or thrown it out. I'm throwing out so much."

"Just look," Kat says. "It can't hurt."

I put my phone on speaker and set it on the edge of the bed, keeping within shouting distance while I search. I've already hauled a few bins of books off to Goodwill and tossed a significant amount of junk with a particular emphasis on anything that reeked of High School Murphy. A yearbook would, by definition, be the first to go, but I don't remember seeing one. I open and close my nearly empty corner cabinet and do a quick scan of my bookshelf. Nothing.

"Try your desk," Kat suggests.

"I never use my desk."

"Exactly."

241

As I haul the pile of clothes off my desk chair and onto my bed, I imagine a different version of me, one who sat at this desk twice a week to study for accounting and work on her transfer application instead of using it exclusively to roll joints. A studious Murphy. A more organized Murphy. One who could definitely pull off a passing grade on Friday's final. If I clear a place for her, maybe it's not too late to *be* her, just for this last stretch of days before the exam. I tug on the desk drawer and it tugs back. Too much shit wedged in there. I jiggle the handle, barely fitting my fingers in to prod anything that might come loose.

"What's going on?" Kat asks from where I left her on the bed.

"My desk is jammed." Just as the words come out, I give one last tug and the drawer releases. There, buried between outdated teen magazines and travel softball paperwork, I spot the royal-blue binding of a Geneva High School yearbook. There's quite literally a quarter inch of dust on the top, and I cough a little as I crack the spine. "Found it," I say. "Or found one. From . . ." I do the mental math, subtracting from the current year. "Sophomore year, I think?"

I flip to the junior portraits, thumbing toward the *M*s at a speed that threatens paper cuts. There she is, with long brown hair and a face like an Accutane before picture. Eliana Meyers. Eliana. What a perfect name. I whisper it to myself, enjoying how it pirouettes off my tongue.

"You find it?"

"It's Eliana. Eliana Meyers."

"WOO! ELIANA!" Kat shouts, then pauses and adds. "Wow, that's really pretty."

I run my finger along her name as though it were braille.

Eliana. I wonder why she shortens it. Flipping back a few pages, I find my own picture among the sophomores, looking every bit as sixteen as I'd love to forget I ever was. My pixie cut phase never did me any favors, and the oversize gray sweatshirt I'm wearing stands as evidence that I never put picture day in my planner. I flip back from Ellie to me then back to Ellie. Eliana. I wonder if I fold down the pages in between, I could line our pictures up, our teenage selves permanently kissing so long as the yearbook is closed.

"So what are you saying in the email?" Kat presses, and I re-center myself on the goal at hand.

"I don't know. I have to think about it. But I'll let you know if I need a proofread."

"Or a ghostwriter!" she offers. "Whatever you need. I'm gonna jump, though, if that's okay. I've gotta study."

"Of course, love you."

"Love you back!"

The line goes quiet, leaving me alone in the company of Geneva High School's finest. Across the two-page spread from me, Kat's not-yet-tamed brown curls and precontacts wire frames take me back to a hundred and one high school memories. Given the chance, what would I say to little high school Kat? Or Ellie? I don't bother thinking of what I'd say to my high school self. She wouldn't have listened anyway. I close the cover and slip the yearbook into a slot in one of my packing bins. Maybe I was wrong about memory lane. It doesn't have to be a one-way street. Maybe it's just somewhere you only plan to visit when you're ready.

I climb back into bed, digging my laptop out from under

the covers and clicking into my email again. ElianaMeyers @Illinois.edu. When I hit enter, a tiny headshot-style picture of her appears next to her contact. I'd expect a freshman ID photo, if anything, but the picture is recent—blonde hair, bangs and all. Junior year of high school Ellie wouldn't recognize herself now.

My fingers stall on the keyboard, the cursor pulsing in the subject line box. I could take this a hundred different ways, only one of which is short enough that she may actually read it.

Reminder: IOU one chaicoffski

I hit send, praying the U of I spam filter goes easy on me.

twenty-two

❊

"Keep or toss?"

Without looking up from my dresser drawer, Mom dangles a pair of Captain America pajama pants from her grip.

"Keep," I vote. "I still wear those."

"Fine." She folds them over her arm and adds them to the *keep* pile, which is quickly overflowing into the almost nonexistent *donate* pile.

This is the game of packing, as I've learned it: Mom holds up a piece of my childhood, I vote to keep it, and Mom gives me a skeptical look before adding it to the keep pile with some commentary on how everything can't stay. Rinse and repeat for the entirety of an afternoon. It's excruciating, but Lord knows I wouldn't get it done if she left me to do it on my own.

"Murphy? Keep or toss?" Mom reaches back into the drawer and pulls out the next lucky contestant: the threadbare red pajama shorts with my parents' alma mater printed across the butt.

"Absolutely keep. Those are Kat's favorite."

Mom raises a brow. "Then why don't you just give them to Kat?"

"Because." I pull my heels toward my butt, hugging my knees to my chest. "Then she couldn't wear them when she's here."

Mom rolls her eyes, but folds the shorts and places them on the pile. "You can't keep everything, you know."

"I'm not." My head tips toward the toss pile, a mass grave of softball trophies and seventh-grade diaries. "I'm getting rid of a ton." Mom is really the one to thank for that. If not for her, that toss pile would be less than half its size. But also, if not for her, I wouldn't be cleaning out in the first place. Would it have killed them to wait a week and put the house on the market after my accounting final? When I suggested it, Mom gave me a very calm, apologetic explanation that boiled down to "not a goddamn chance." Something about closings overlapping and needing liquid funds from the house. The second she started using terms I didn't recognize, I dropped the subject. With the photographer coming to take listing photos tomorrow night, I have just over twenty-four hours to box away any evidence that someone, god forbid a twenty-one-year-old community college student, lives here.

"Okay, only half a dresser to go." Mom tugs open a bottom drawer and pinches out a royal-blue softball jersey, holding it up like she's a human clothesline. "When's the last time you wore this?"

My stomach bottoms out. "When I played softball."

"So . . . four years ago? More?"

"I didn't keep it to *wear*."

Mom frowns, waiting on an explanation that I don't have. Why did I keep it? Because throwing it away felt like defeat, and donating it would feel wrong unless I could somehow pass it down to the current number nine for the Geneva High School softball team. The damn thing's probably cursed, though, and that poor girl would end up injured, just like me.

Mom spins the jersey around, giving me a 360-degree view. "So what are we doing with it?"

I chew my lip and think. What would High School Murph say? "Keep."

She arches one brow toward her hairline, like a cat stretching its back. "Really?"

I hug my knees a little tighter. I guess I'm overdue to officially close that chapter. "Fine. Toss."

Mom's other eyebrow joins the one at the top of her forehead. "Really?"

"Is there a right answer here?"

"No, no, that's just fine. We can toss it." With all the tender care of throwing out a used napkin of unknown origin, Mom pinches the jersey and drops it beside the toss pile. The nylon fabric wrinkles and pools, forming a royal-blue puddle on the carpet. No sooner has she dropped it than she's holding up a new shirt, a new memory and version of myself to hold tight to or altogether abandon. "What's this one from?" She inspects the graphics closer. "Key Club? You weren't even *in* Key Club."

We work our way to the bottom of each remaining drawer in

the same way—Mom holding up high school memories while I delegate where they should be dropped. Each goodbye gets a little easier, and I get a little lighter. The toss pile has at least doubled in size, my stash bag has been safely and discreetly placed in the keep pile, and the thud of the last hollow drawer closing sounds like something close to a fresh start.

Mom struggles to her feet, patting the top of the dresser twice with her palm. "Chess said to leave this for staging, so that's a wrap on that."

This is about the thousandth time I've heard Chess's name since they broke the moving news. I'm not sure how someone finds themselves in the business of staging houses, but with the way my parents talk about her, you'd think she was the Jesus Christ of Interior Design. Every suggestion is immediately logged as gospel, and every critique is met with a look of bewilderment and shame, as if there were no greater humiliation than realizing you painted your bathroom in the shade Eggshell instead of opting for the ever-popular Water Chestnut.

"How are they going to stage this room, you think?"

"Chess wants to make it into a kids room," Mom says.

I frown. "Isn't it already kind of a kid's room?"

"A *little* kid's room. To appeal to younger parents."

I stare at the room as though I'm playing *The Sims*, deleting my double bed and rotating a bunk bed until it's flat up against the wall. "Is she going to get rid of my bed?"

"No, you still have to sleep here. Chess agreed that the bed can stay."

Chess this and Chess that and Chess thinks we ought to

repaint the trim to dress the place up a bit. I wonder if Chess has a degree in being a picky bitch.

"So what's next, you think?" Mom asks. "The closet? The Wall of Fame?"

I'm a little bit pleased that she remembers what I call that wall, but a lot bit discouraged that it all has to come down. If anyone is going to undo the years of collaging, it has to be me. "You take the closet, I'll take the Wall of Fame?"

She nods twice and drags over a Sterilite bin, already half full of old birthday cards and notes passed in middle school that I don't have time or emotional energy to sift through yet. It doesn't have to be all packed until they actually do the move. For now, it just has to be clean.

When Mom half disappears behind the rolling closet door, I sneak a quick look at my email inbox for the umpteenth time today, pulling down at the top until the whole screen bounces and refreshes. No new emails, not even a promotional one for a sale or something. It's only been a day, but how long could it take for Ellie to reply to an email that's only a few words long? Maybe I should've been more straightforward. I could've made an actual case for myself instead of being cheeky.

"You know, if you spent a little less time on your phone, this might go by faster."

I snap my head toward the closet, where Mom is still mostly buried among the ghosts of prom dresses past. Maybe she really does have eyes in the back of her head.

"Sorry, I'm waiting on an email."

She turns over her shoulder, craning a brow at me. "From who?"

"It's a school thing," I say. It's not a complete lie. It'll be coming from an email with .edu at the end.

"When is it supposed to come?"

I wrestle the lump in my throat back down to my gut, where it belongs, cementing me to my bed like a paperweight. "I'm not sure if it ever will."

"Oh." For an uncomfortably long moment, she searches for the right words, but finding none, lands on, "Do you want to talk about it?"

"Not any more than this, no." I slap my thighs, hoping it reads as a hard return at the end of this conversation, then roll off the bed and toward the Wall of Fame. How does one begin tearing down twenty-one years of memories? Well, closer to fifteen, I suppose. Back in first grade, it was mostly coloring pages or bulletin-board crafts we made in school. I must've taken a lot of them down at some point, although I only seem to remember putting things on the wall, never taking them off. It's proof that I've done this before. I can take things down. I can start over.

I begin with the small pieces—a theater ticket from a Broadway-in-Chicago production of *Rent*, then a Polaroid from one of my last softball games. I squint at the Murphy in the picture, sunburn creeping along the bridge of her nose, smiling the way you would if you didn't know that sting in your shoulder was more than a pinched nerve, and a life-altering injury was waiting a few weeks down the line. I place the first two memories on the top of the Sterilite bin, not that I know what I'll do with any of them, just that I know I'm not ready to throw them away. I dig a nail under a curling edge of the HANDS OFF OUR BODIES sticker that a younger version of me stuck directly to the wall, cringing as I peel off a circular layer of paint with it.

"Are we going to repaint?"

Mom's eyes narrow. "Do we *need* to repaint?"

"Probably?"

"Just get it all down," she says, then dives back into the closet, tossing clothes over her shoulder like a girl getting ready in an early 2000s teen rom-com. My vest from Girl Scouts, patches still not sewn on. A nightgown that matched my American Girl doll that now would sooner fit the doll than me. A black-and-teal floral-print dress we got on clearance at Kohl's for Kat's Bat Mitzvah. Why didn't we clean any of this out sooner? Or rather, why didn't *I* clean any of this out sooner? I guess because I didn't really have to.

"You can just donate all of that." I gesture to the heap of clothes Mom has piled behind her. "I'm not wearing any of it, obviously."

The emotions on Mom's face pass through her so quickly, it's as if I'm watching them sped up. Sad, then surprised, then relieved. "Sure thing," Mom says finally, then moves it all to the donation pile, hangers and all. "We're making good progress, Murph."

"Yeah, not bad." I pull a ticket stub off the wall for a matinee showing of one of the X-Men movies, and a whole slew of memories comes with it, figuratively and literally. It's like peeling wallpaper—one movie ticket is taped to a photo is taped to a colored pencil drawing of Kat and me as Disney princesses.

Trying to take just one thing down proves almost impossible. You tug a little and you get a lot. "When does this need to be done again?"

"Yesterday."

"No, seriously. 'Cause I'm thinking I might do, like, another thirty minutes of work and then switch to studying."

"Could I quiz you while you work?" Mom offers. "Chess is coming by to stage the house tomorrow morning at ten."

I squeeze my eyes closed, trying to mental math my way into more available hours in the day. It's almost three o'clock now, and I need a full eight hours of sleep before working a double tomorrow. According to my incredibly lackluster math skills, that's not enough hours to get this all done.

"Murph?" Mom says. "Do you have flash cards or something?"

I shake my head. "Not yet. Just a study guide. I guess you could quiz me from that."

Among the half-packed plastic bins and piles of junk destined for Goodwill, finding my backpack is a game of I Spy on expert mode. After shifting some things, the little red Fjällräven fox winks at me from under my newly cleared desk. I dig through my backpack, smoothing down the curled edges of the packet before handing it off to Mom. "Most of the answers should be right."

She frowns. "How are you supposed to study with answers that might not be right?"

"I don't know, Mom! How am I supposed to correct all my answers if I have to spend the whole day packing?"

She speaks to me in a calm, unaffected voice that brings my

blood to a boil. "I told you, you don't have to make decisions on all of it now."

"I know, I know." Inhale, exhale. I focus on the things I can control, like the way I arrange my memories within the Sterilite bin. "A little more warning just would've been nice. I could've gotten this all done on Thanksgiving or something. I could've planned around it."

"I'm sorry, Murphy. This isn't entirely in our control."

"It could've been," I grumble. "You didn't have to randomly buy a condo and decide to move."

Mom's face puckers, and the ground suddenly feels like it's shifting beneath my feet. "I'm sorry," she says, her tone razor-sharp in the way that means whatever she's going to say next she's 100 percent not sorry about. "Do you think this was a spur-of-the-moment purchase? Do you think I've been keeping the house in ready-to-sell shape for the last four years just because I want to? That we looked through the house listings in Florida just for fun? We never planned on retiring in Geneva. But when you opted to do your first two years at community college, we adjusted our plan, because that's what good parents do. They adjust and they make sacrifices for their kids. We worked around what you wanted."

Her voice breaks in the middle of a word, and I watch her eyes plead with mine, only I don't know what for. I hate seeing her like this. Vulnerable and hurt and human.

"I'm sorry," she says again. "We didn't do any of this to hurt you. We thought you were going to be at U of I this year and I'm sorry you're not, I'm sorry you're stuck here, I'm sorry your plan didn't work out how you wanted it to. But you're not the only one with plans, Murphy, and your father and I have always built ours around yours. It didn't work out this time, and I'm sorry, but that's how life goes. You'll just have to make a new plan."

I wish she would stop apologizing and I would start, but before I can come up with anything good to say, she lets out a long, tired sigh, and for the first time, it occurs to me that my parents might be old. The pepper-gray hair spraying up from Mom's roots, the way her skin creases and droops from the corners of her lips like a marionette. Who knows if she'll even renew her real estate license in Florida. I haven't even thought to ask. A day will come when her bad knee catches up to her and the elevator in their new condo building will be a necessity, not a luxury. Dad will retire from his IT job. They'll live the life they should've started already. One where they're people first, parents second. They deserve that.

"I didn't realize that was your plan," I whisper. "The whole moving to Florida thing."

"And maybe we should've told you sooner." Mom's voice wavers just a bit more with each word. "But we never wanted you to feel pushed out before you were ready or like you were the last thing tying us here, but . . ."

"But I was," I finish for her. "I get it."

I sit on the edge of the bed and stare down at the carpet, waiting for her to excuse herself, to hide away in her bedroom for the cry she's dancing on the brink of. But she doesn't. When I look up, her throat bobs, then she forces a smile and returns to the closet and gets back to work. Because that's what the Konowitz women do. They feel something and they keep moving.

I guess there's nothing left to do but pack.

After a painful ten minutes of working in silence, I finally drum up something to say. "I could pass accounting, I think."

"Really?" Mom says through a sniffle.

"Maybe. If I get an eighty-nine on the final."

"Can you do that?"

"I'm gonna try."

"Good for you."

It's a flat, lifeless exchange, but it's better than silence. I peel back picture after poster from the Wall of Fame, choosing to toss more than I'd originally imagined, while Mom slowly removes the last evidence of my childhood from the back corners of the closet. The more we strip away at the old Murphy, the more room there is for a new one, built in the blank, empty space where I'm no longer a kid, not quite an adult. I'm still adjusting to the in-between. Old enough to drink but not old enough to fear the consequences. Old enough to worry about where I'm going but not old enough to know. Hovering in the sort of intermission between one life and another, one Murphy and the next. But I'm ready to move forward.

When I pull back the ring of tape on the last Polaroid, the Wall of Fame is officially just a wall, completely blank besides the few dozen places where the tape stripped up the paint. A clear canvas. I decide I'll print a fresh copy of the study guide tomorrow. I'll focus on the back half of the textbook and give it another go. Pass or fail, I'm not sure what's next for me, but I do know I'm ready to move on. Step one: Pass this class and get out of community college. Step two: TBD.

twenty-three

❋

The back office at Sip is a micro museum to the way things used to be. Emphasis on micro—it's about the size of three cubicles pushed together, or at least that's what my manager said when we were first setting up the space. I've never had the pleasure of spending time in a cubicle, but if my days in the back office are any indication, I don't think I'd mind it too much.

To call it cozy would be generous; there's just enough space for a diner-size table, a coatrack, and two desks—one for me and one for the Sip desktop, which serves exactly two purposes: clocking in and clocking out. The walls are a mismatched gallery of decor from the old shop that didn't fit the new aesthetic. Highlights include several old tin coffee signs, framed pictures from storewide Christmas parties, and a poorly designed poster from our first open mic, hosted shortly after my one-year work anniversary. The poster has since yellowed with time, a subtle reminder that, among my sixteen-year-old coworkers, the real relic here is me. Only in my own hometown would I feel practically prehistoric at twenty-one. At least I feel at home here in the office, surrounded by antiques.

A notification dings in the bottom-right corner of my laptop screen: all 3,099 photos and videos from the reopening are officially uploaded. It'll take hours to sort through them, and I'll probably need to take some work home with me tonight, but I'd still choose this over a barista shift any day. I eject my SD card and the computer whirs to remind me how hard it's working. Nice try, bud, but you can't impress me. I'm working hard too.

Time slips away as I click through the gallery, dragging and dropping my favorite video clips into my editing software. I don't realize I've fallen into a flow state until the buzz of my phone extracts me from it—one text from Mom. It's an apartment listing, the third one she's sent me today. I suffocate my urge to thumbs-down react to it, then click the link and swipe through the photos: plain white countertops, gray paneled flooring, angular faucets on the bathroom sinks. Same as nearly every other suburban apartment that labels itself "affordable luxury housing." The balcony is a nice touch, but the complex is two towns over, which would double my commute to Sip. I send a generic "nice!" and connect my earbuds to Bluetooth before switching on Do Not Disturb. She's trying to be helpful, but I can't think that far ahead right now. I need to stay focused. Popping in my earbuds, I press play on a voice memo I recorded while studying last night.

"What are the tax differences between a Roth IRA and a traditional IRA?" my recorded self asks, and I whisper the right answer along with her. The low-budget audiobook of the study guide was my idea, but listening to it at work was Brooklyn's suggestion. She's a first year at Weymouth, it turns out, which explains why we get along better than I do with my high school coworkers. She and I essentially cohosted a roast of WCC over our lunch break yesterday, followed by an extensive bitch session about the pains of still living with our parents. Us post–high school hires have to stick together, even if it's just for the holiday months.

"When's the group upstairs clearing out?"

This time, it's not my own voice asking the question. I pluck out an earbud and swivel toward the door, where Brooklyn leans against the doorframe, rotating one of the half dozen gold rings stacked on her fingers. We've worked enough shifts together for her to know I'm the person to come to with questions, but not enough shifts to recognize that I'm rarely enthusiastic about answering them. If someone is going to interrupt, I'm at least glad it's her.

"The book club?" I ask. "Are they not out yet?"

Brooklyn shakes her head. "And I can't remember if there's a group after them."

"It's super not your job to remember that," I assure her. "You're doing great."

I swivel my chair back toward my laptop, clicking into today's reservations. Looks like the women's Christian book club is running a little over, and while there's no reservation after them, we'll need the extra seating once school lets out for the day. "Go ahead and clear them out," I say, double-clicking on the reservation and sending the rental receipt to the email on file. "They're a monthly reservation. They'll understand. And remind them to tag us if they took any photos."

Brooklyn makes a clicking sound with the side of her mouth, but instead of turning back around, she leans to the side, catching a peek at my computer screen. "Whatcha workin' on?"

"A highlight reel of the reopening. Wanna see?"

"Duh."

I press play on the rough cut, and although it'll be another hour of editing before I have a presentable draft, Brooklyn seems mesmerized. "That's sick," she says when the screen dips to black. "How'd you get so good at that?"

"Practice, mostly," I say with a shrug. "I didn't learn it at Weymouth, that's for sure."

We share a laugh before Brooklyn disappears to shoo away the Christian book club, and I settle back into work and into an unfamiliar feeling. I feel...content? Hopeful? Like I'm doing what I'm meant to be doing, even if I'm not where I want to be? Maybe it's that I finally have a coworker I can connect with, or maybe it's the rush of editing video, knowing it's something I'm actually good at. There must've been a time when editing didn't come so naturally to me, but now, I'm like a painter with 3,099 different colors on her palette and no instruction other than "paint." Videos, graphics, social media posts—so long as I make the plan and execute on it, there's wiggle room for me to try and fail and experiment along the way. Maybe that's allowed for studying too. Maybe that's allowed for life in general. If I try and I fail, I'm allowed to try again—to retake the class or transfer next year—or experiment with something different, like doing marketing for Monarch.

I can hear Ellie's voice in the back of my head, calling me a small business marketing consultant. If that involves doing more of this type of work, I could be into that. I open a new tab on my laptop, type "small business marketing consultant" into Google, and scroll through the results. Past the ads, I land on the suggested questions. *What does a small business marketing consultant do? How much should a marketing consultant charge?* I click on the second one and try not to tumble backward out of my chair. About $100 to $175 an hour. A few more minutes of browsing Google tells me I'm just about qualified—although a degree might make a big difference.

An email notification hits the events@sipgeneva.com inbox, and I close out of my corporate daydreaming and return to today's tasks. I pop my earbuds back in, testing whether typing emails and studying can happen simultaneously, or if I'll start replying to wedding shower requests with details about accounts payable and revenue projections.

"What are the tax implications of a sole proprietorship versus an LLC?"

I say the answer out loud, and there's a "Huh?" in response from a voice behind me. I flip around—it's Brooklyn again, looking bewildered. "Were you talking to me?"

I hit pause on my phone. "No, I'm studying."

"Ohhh. The recorded question thing." She nods, tossing her long braids over her shoulder. "Got it. And sorry to interrupt. There's just this customer . . ."

I almost laugh at how genuinely sorry she sounds, as if interrupting me at work and asking me to do my job were completely out of bounds. "It's cool. What's up?"

"Someone's trying to use this coupon but"—her nose crinkles—"it doesn't look legit."

"Is it a punch card?" We phased out our classic *Buy nine drinks, get the tenth drink free* model when we closed for renovations, but we'll be dealing with stragglers for the next year, I'm sure.

"I don't think so? It's on their phone."

I push away from my desk and onto my feet. If it was one of the other baristas, I might tell them I'm busy and to figure it out on their own. But I like Brooklyn.

"I've got it," I say. "Lead the way."

I follow Brooklyn down the hall, chatting about finals while inspecting the back of what appears to be an intramural softball T-shirt. Just as I work up the courage to ask her if she has a team for this spring, we pass through the swinging door into the space behind the bar, and my heart bangs against the base of my throat. Standing in front of the register in a MUNA T-shirt and an ultraoversize denim jacket is the coupon user in question, Miss Ellie Meyers. Fuck, I should've pieced that together.

Brooklyn steps up to the register with a winning customer service smile and a bubbly tone to match. "Murphy can help you," she says, stepping out of the way and placing me in full view. While Ellie had at least a three-hour drive to think about what to say to me, the three seconds I've had to prepare don't quite cut it.

"Hi," I squeak out, just to fill the silence as I try to compute how the hell she's here, three hours from campus, in the middle of the day on a Thursday.

"Hi back," she says.

I want to say something poignant, something friendly or romantic or at the very least worthy of a reaction. Instead, all that comes out is, "Trying to redeem a coupon?"

Not my finest work.

"I am." Playful recognition shimmers in Ellie's eyes as she hands her phone to me without breaking our gaze. From the corner of my eye, a screenshot of my email stares up at me. "I don't think I was meant to redeem it so soon, but I'm hoping you can make an exception."

"You drove all the way from Champaign for me?" I blurt out, hoping Brooklyn has lost interest and wandered off. I can't check. I can't take my eyes off Ellie. I'm certain the second I look away, she'll be gone, disappearing like a fine dust into the air. Or else I'll blink twice and she'll turn into a forty-year-old man with a long-expired gift certificate, asking if we sell coffee here.

"No," she says, drawing out the *o* sound. "I drove all the way from Champaign for a free chaicoffski." She leans over the register and taps her phone screen with one blue fingernail. "Lucky coincidence that you happen to be working."

"What would you have done if I wasn't working?"

She breathes a laugh. "I honestly didn't think that through. Is that bad?"

"No." I match her laugh. "But only because it worked out."

Beside me, Brooklyn pops her tongue, startling me out of this hushed conversation and back into my workday. "So does this happen a lot, or . . ." She trails off into a suspicious little smirk.

"Hardly ever," I assure her, punching in my employee ID to comp the drink. "I'm gonna take my lunch break, 'kay? Right after I make this." Without looking at Brooklyn, I head for the back cabinets where we keep the ceramics and pull down a pale yellow mug and its corresponding saucer. "One chaicoffski, coming right up."

I insert myself into the fold of the bar, unapologetically giving myself priority over the existing drinks in the queue. If the other baristas mind, they don't say anything about it.

"Shit, should I have been using for-here mugs?" Brooklyn asks, peering into the back cabinet for what I assume is the first time.

"Nah, we only use them if someone asks," I explain. "But I know this customer. I know she wants to stay awhile." Only the first half of the sentence is true, and even then, just barely. But I know I'm in no rush to get rid of Ellie, and I'll do what I can to keep her here for at least the length of a conversation. I pull two perfect ristretto shots into the mug and top it with our housemade chai and juniper syrup, half a pump of vanilla, a frothy blanket of oat milk, and a delicate sprinkle of cinnamon and nutmeg. A perfectly made, original recipe chaicoffski.

"One chaicoffski for . . ." Brooklyn lifts a brow toward me as I place the mug on the bar. "For?"

"For El Bell," I finish for her.

"Uh, one chaicoffski for El Bell," she repeats with a laugh. Across the shop, Ellie unfolds her legs and presses out of the green velvet bucket chair, the same one she sat in the night we snuck in. Her hair sways against her cheeks, perfectly framing her dimple as she sashays up to the bar and delicately wraps one hand around the mug, guiding the saucer with the other. She moves her drink off the ledge quarter inch by quarter inch, thanking us twice without taking her eyes off the mug, as though she's thanking the chaicoffski just for being itself.

"Mind if I clock out and sit with you for a bit?" I ask. When she doesn't answer, I tack on, "Totally fine if not."

"No, no, I was hoping you would," Ellie says. "Sorry, I'm just so worried I'm going to spill this." At long last, she looks up at me with a sheepish smile. "Don't be offended if I drop your art and ruin it, okay?"

"You're not going to drop it," I promise her. "But if you do, I'll send you another coupon."

I hurry to the back office to clock out for what I'm sure will be a longer than usual lunch break, then step back into the shop to find Ellie almost 90 percent of the way back to her table, which miraculously has gone unclaimed during her long journey back to her seat. She's shuffling across the floor like a little kid trying to pick up static from the carpet. I block her path, holding my hands out and taking the mug and saucer from her. "Please," I say. "Let me."

The saucer clinks against the table, the mug clinks against the saucer, and I sit down on the very edge of the seat across from Ellie's, staying ready to run. "Did you not have class today or something?"

"No, I did." Ellie tucks one leg beneath her, then the other, the heft of her Docs tucked under her thighs giving her a solid three-inch boost. "I skipped."

"For me?"

"No, for a free chaicoffski." She reaches forward and slowly lifts the mug from its saucer, then purses her lips, blowing a ripple of cool air over the surface. "I told you that already, remember?"

"Right, right." I loop a thumb through the scrunchie around my wrist, gathering my hair into a low bun, just like hers. Anything to keep my hands busy while she closes her eyes and takes her first sip.

"Mmm," she hums, mushing her lips together. "Incredible." Her eyes flicker open. They're warm and sweet, like the first sip of chai. "Thanks for this."

"It's the least I can do in exchange for that painting," I say, waving her off.

Ellie's satisfied smirk falls to a flat line. "What painting?"

"The Murphy's Bleachers painting?"

Her eyes narrow behind her mug. "How do you know about that?"

"What do you . . ." I trap my breath behind my teeth, trying to tease apart what I know from what I think I know. If Ellie didn't ask Kara to give me the painting, then . . . "Oh my God," I groan. "Your mom."

"What about my mom?" She sets her mug down with a clatter.

"Your mom gave that painting to me," I explain. "She said it was a gift from you."

As the pieces click together, all of the warmth surrounding our conversation dims to a tepid, room-temperature disappointment. "I started painting that after you left Thursday night," Ellie says. "Mom must've found it, and . . ."

"And when I stopped by on Friday and didn't know you had left . . ."

"And when she texted me to ask about you and I ignored it . . ."

"Yup. She must've known something was up." I make a sound through my lips like a fast-deflating balloon. "So I'm guessing you didn't know about the list either."

"What list?" She asks.

"The list of things your family was thankful for." I bite a hangnail off my thumb. "Your mom taped it to the back of the painting."

Ellie frowns. "Why would she . . ."

"Think about it. What did you say you were thankful for?"

I lean back in my chair and watch as Ellie's face tightens, then slowly releases into a soft smile, her dimple just barely peeking through. "Ahh," she whispers. "Very clever, Mom." She tucks a loose strand of hair into her bun, aiming her smile at the floor. "That's sweet."

"Yeah, it really got me good." I press my tongue against the back of my teeth, then cautiously add, "It felt like . . . an apology?"

Ellie's eyes flutter closed, and she nods as she processes. "Right. Which is why you emailed me. Because you thought I apologized."

"Right."

We sit there, blinking at each other until I break the silence with a strangled sigh. "So are you . . . not apologizing, then?"

"Of course I'm apologizing," she says. "I'm sorry I left like that. I was thinking about what you said about all relationships needing a little space. I thought it'd be best for both of us."

"So you ditched the opening and left town without saying goodbye?"

"You walked away first," she points out. "I didn't think you wanted me showing up on your big day like nothing happened."

"And when I called you afterward?"

She looks down at her nails, which have been painted a fresh shade of blue. "I needed space too. What you said about me being just like Mary . . . that really hurt."

"I'm sorry. I shouldn't have said that. It wasn't fair."

"It wasn't wrong either," Ellie mumbles. "Not entirely." Moving on from her nails, she picks up her mug. A fresh distraction. "I knew you liked me, and it was so easy to pretend we were together that I just . . . I got carried away. But I never meant to give you mixed signals. I was really into you."

My stomach twists. "Was? Past tense?"

She rolls her eyes and takes a sip. "What do you think? I drove three hours to see you, didn't I?"

"I thought you drove three hours for a chaicoffski," I say.

Her cheeks burn red. "Among other things."

"And . . . only because your mom pulled the strings."

Ellie rubs her lips together, her septum ring twitching in response. "You know what that means though, right?"

"No?"

"It means my mom likes you enough to try to smooth things over between us," Ellie says. There's a tiny bit of mischief dancing in her voice. "The plan worked."

"The plan worked," I repeat under my breath, but my mind is still snagged on the word *us*. There was never really an *us* in the first place, but the way it sounds falling off Ellie's tongue feels familiar in an *un*familiar way. Like the feeling I had sitting in the office earlier. Content. Hopeful. Like I'm on the right track.

We're both quiet for a moment, letting the din of the shop take over—the clack of laptop keys, the growl of the espresso machine, the soft indie song I could probably identify if my mind weren't otherwise occupied. I jiggle my leg, trying to shake up the courage to say what I know I need to. Ellie could walk out the front door and never come back again. I could fail my accounting exam and stay stuck in Geneva, and she could graduate and move straight to New York. Our paths might never cross again. I know there's a possibility I'll never even think about last weekend again, that it could be some stupid thing that happened when I was twenty-one that I'll look back on and roll my eyes . . . but if there's even a chance that I could've had something great here if I'd only said something, I'd never forgive myself. I need to speak up.

"I'm . . ." I stop, sigh, start again. "I'm not in love with Kat, okay?"

Ellie startles, finding her place on the other side of an abrupt conversation shift. Her mouth falls open, and for a moment I think she's going to defend herself. I'm ready for another fight, but instead, Ellie's voice hovers beneath her breath, like she doesn't even want to hear herself speak. "I know," she says. "It was never about that, really."

I lift a brow. "No?"

"Of course not." She practically hides behind her mug. "You were right," she admits. "I was jealous."

"You don't have to be jealous of Kat."

"I'm jealous of both of you," she corrects me, then shifts in her seat like she can't quite get comfortable. "I know you don't remember much of high school," she says, "but I do, and it mostly sucked. People think they have good memories from high school, but they don't. They mostly have bad memories, but with good people. That's the only thing that makes it fun, laughing through the bullshit with your best friends that you get to see every day. Without that, most things are just . . . bullshit."

"Kinda dark," I tease.

She glares back at me. "I'm serious. When things are bad, Kat will always have your back, and you'll always have hers. I've only ever had that from Mary." She pauses, then adds, "And some of my boyfriends, I guess."

"And I didn't have your back with your Mom after bringing up grad school," I say, wishing I, too, had a mug to hide behind.

"Right. And then I heard you on the phone with Kat and . . ." Ellie leaves the rest of the thought behind her. "I shouldn't have snapped at you though."

"And I shouldn't have left the table in the first place," I say. "I promised to back you up on the grad school conversation and I didn't. The transfer app deadline thing really sent me into a spiral, and suddenly it was like . . . why am I even keeping up this dating charade, you know?"

"How are you doing with that, by the way?" she asks. "With the transfer stuff?"

If only that were my only concern. Between missing the transfer deadline, Ellie no-showing the reopening, and my parents' upcoming move, I've been striking out left and right. "Honestly, I've been on a losing streak."

Ellie breathes a laugh through her nose, but there isn't an ounce of humor in her sad, sunken eyes. "Me too. I, uh." She swallows hard. "I got rejected from NYU."

My heart drops to my kneecaps. "Shit, really?"

"And my backup school. I got both letters yesterday." She slowly drags her gaze up to meet mine, and when our eyes lock, her eyelids are heavy, like they pulled the weight of the world up with them. "So I guess I'm not moving to New York," she says.

There's a teeny, tiny happy dance brewing inside me, but it drowns in a flood of sympathy. Between this and getting dumped, that's more rejection than anyone could take. And this isn't just anyone. This is Ellie. "How are you feeling?" I ask.

"Sad," she says plainly. "I cried for, like, three hours yesterday. But only one hour today, so that's an improvement."

"Baby steps," I say, realizing I haven't cried at all about U of I. What does that say about me?

"It sucks, but it's not like those were the only two art therapy programs in the country," Ellie goes on. "And living in New York was my dream with Mary. Maybe there's a new dream without her."

"You'll find it."

"Soon, I hope," she grumbles into her mug. "That stable, convincing plan we tried to sell Mom on made me realize how much I need that."

"A plan?"

"Stability," she corrects me. "Like Marcus with his salary and his fiancée and his fixed-rate mortgage. Bringing you home was like . . ." Ellie's eyes glaze over momentarily, but she blinks it away, letting a shudder roll through her. "I felt like that kind of girl, you know? The girl who brings her girlfriend home on holidays and contributes to a retirement fund. Like someone with her life together."

I swivel my chair a little, leaning in with a secret I've been dying to share. "You know, Marcus hasn't always had his life together," I say. "Did you know he got fired from Sip?"

Ellie bristles. "Really? He told us he quit."

I shake my head. "He got caught stealing from the tip jar."

"Seriously?" Ellie's eyes go wide. "Says who?"

"Says my manager."

Her mouth falls open a full two inches. "Shit, that's bad."

"I'm just saying, your brother didn't always have his life together as much as you thought. Maybe we don't have to either."

Ellie's eyes crinkle with the start of a smile. "Thanks for that," she says.

"Of course."

"And for what it's worth, I meant what I wrote on Thanksgiving. I *am* thankful for you. You made me feel like that kind of girl."

A prickle of warmth climbs up my neck. "I'm thankful for you too. If I would have been at the table, that's what I would've said."

"Really?" Her dimple winks at me.

"Obviously." I pause for a breath, enjoying the little bit of space where things between us are easy before my next question makes them hard again. "So what comes next?"

Her laugh is amused, if not a little smug. "Well, next you can admit that you're reaaallly into me."

My eye roll comes with a groan. "Do you have to be so cocky about it?"

"I have every right to be cocky," she says. "I heard it for myself." Ellie flashes me a wicked smile, slowly shaking her head. "Kat really shouldn't have been talking so loud in the library."

I can't confirm whether or not my eyes actually bulge out of my head, but just the mention of Kat in the library instantly converts my brain into a wave pool and my mouth into a leaky inner tube, sputtering out air. And that smile—that devilish smile with that stupid little dimple—could put me in a watery grave.

"Hey, Murphy?" A worried Brooklyn interrupts from behind the bar, stalling my pending short circuit. "I thought the baby shower was booked for tomorrow."

I swallow hard, breathe for the first time in too many seconds, and turn to ask Brooklyn what she's talking about. Before I can get a word out, a woman with armfuls of light-blue gift bags and pacifier-shaped Mylar balloons answers my question.

I turn back toward Ellie with a wobbly smile and panic-stricken eyes. "I can't believe I'm saying this but . . . I have to get back to work," I choke out, pressing my palms against the table and helping myself to my feet. "Are you driving back to school now?"

Ellie lifts a shoulder, that self-satisfied smile still lingering on her lips. "I don't have to. I'm free up until a meeting tomorrow at four, and I already turned in my final projects. You know, in case there was a reason I should stay tonight."

My belly button sucks in toward my spine. "I have to study tonight," I say. "But if you really wanted to, you could come over and quiz me." I'm embarrassed to even offer.

"Of course, what time?" Ellie's eagerness throws me off-balance, and it takes me a second to recalibrate.

"Wait, really? Are you sure?" I can hear the balloon woman's voice getting louder and louder, and Brooklyn's desperate stare is hot on my temple, but I'm not walking away from Ellie until I know I can reach her again. "I've gotta go, but . . . text me?"

"Wait, hang on." Ellie extends one arm, blocking me from the bar. "I, um. I actually deleted your contact." She sheepishly holds out her phone. "Do you mind?"

twenty-four

❄

All along the white quartz countertop, black plastic take-out containers drip with brown sauces and yellow curries, and greasy white to-go bags spill over with packets of soy sauce and crab rangoon. It's not lost on me that the night before showings Mom got delivery from my favorite Thai restaurant, the authentic one she normally vetoes for being too spicy. Call it a peace offering after our blowup earlier this week, or call it an edible apology for selling my childhood home. Either way, as we load up our plates with heaping spoonfuls of comfort food, I'm the first to grab a paper towel and a bottle of all-purpose cleaner to erase any drips and drops. We're nothing if not a household of silent apologies.

With full plates and extra napkins, we each claim our spot at the table, Mom and Dad at either end with me facing the living room. My mind instantly wanders to a sad place. How many family dinners like this do we have left? Less than a dozen at this table, but altogether, maybe less than a hundred? How often will I fly down to Florida? And will we opt to eat at restaurants when I do, the way you take visitors out to eat when they come to your city? I lift another bite of panang curry into my mouth, letting the spice burn against my tongue for a few extra moments before washing it down with water. The burn lingers, and so does the churning in my stomach.

"What time are we planning to be out of here tomorrow?" Dad asks, slicing a rice noodle with the side of his fork.

"Nine thirty should be okay," Mom says. "Tom is getting here at nine, but showings don't start till ten."

Tom is another agent at Mom's brokerage who volunteered to run showings. Having Mom show this particular listing felt, quite literally, too close to home.

"So we'll do one last walk through with him and then . . ."

I tune out the real estate talk, just like I have all week. There's no point in listening when I absorb so little of it, especially when what I do understand just gets me worked up. Picturing generic couples voting on whether my room should be the nursery or the office feels wrong, like strangers playing dress-up with my house and choosing all the wrong outfits.

"Are you good to be out by nine thirty, Murph?" Mom asks, and I jump back in at the sound of my own name.

"What? Tomorrow? No problem. My final's at ten."

My breath cements to the inside of my lungs at the reminder. I check the time on the stove clock—6:55. Just over fifteen hours until the test and only five minutes until Ellie said she'd be stopping by. The dense wall of real estate talk has allowed me to avoid the topic of tonight's visitor, but I better have an explanation by the time she gets here.

Which, the doorbell announces, is right now.

Mom and Dad turn toward each other, each silently waiting for an explanation from the other. Meanwhile, my stomach threatens to reintroduce every bite of curry I've swallowed in reverse order.

"Grubhub guy again?" Dad speculates. "Or is Chess coming over for a final check before the showings?"

"Actually," I say, pushing back from the table and onto my feet, "that's for me."

Mom and Dad perform a synchronized flinch routine.

"A friend," I explain. "To help me study."

"From class?" Mom asks, and I want to say yes. That would make the most logical sense and save me an explanation I don't care to shape. But I haven't rehearsed this lie.

"No, someone from high school." I try to keep a casual *this happens all the time* air about me, but everyone at this table knows better. It's not even that they're leaping to romantic assumptions, although who's to say that they're not. The truth is that I haven't brought over someone new, romantic or otherwise, since the spaghetti night before what turned out to be my last high school softball tournament. Back then, Mom made a point of shaking everyone's hand and repeating their name to be sure she wouldn't forget. *Hi, Lauren. Nice to meet you, Lauren. There's pop in the fridge if you want it, and let me introduce you to my husband. Honey, this is Lauren, she's an outfielder.* Hopefully we won't see that same behavior tonight.

The long melody of the doorbell buys me a little bit of time, but it's not enough for me to decide exactly how I'm going to play this. Maybe I should've thought this through earlier, but I was too happily distracted by the easy pace of texting that Ellie and I had fallen into, exchanging jokes and light teasing and flirty little comments that made me feel like I was floating an inch above the floor. Before I can explain any further, there's a knock at the door, the quintessential fallback for an unanswered doorbell.

"Have they had dinner?" Mom asks the back of my head as I hurry toward the door. Points to her for the neutral pronoun. Maybe she's woke or maybe she's giving me the benefit of the doubt on the gender of tonight's guest. I had male friends in high school. Not many, but a few.

"I'll ask," I call over my shoulder, then unlock the door.

Outside, Ellie is dressed just the same as she was at Sip this afternoon, plus a few familiar layers for warmth. In her camel-colored coat and heather gray Carhartt beanie, she looks a lot like she did the first time she came over, only much more sober. Her hands are a worrying shade of blue, though—the color of a ripe vein. The cold sure has set in early this year.

"Hey." Ellie twirls her keyring around one blue-painted pointer finger, and when she steps inside, I stop short of kissing her. Our halfhearted side hug is deeply unsatisfying, but also deeply parent friendly. Just like last time, Ellie steps out of her Doc Martens and pairs them neatly by the door, revealing a pair of those fuzzy socks that grandmas and great-aunts always get you for Christmas, the same kind Kara was wearing when I swung by after the reopening. Like mother, like daughter.

"My parents are here." I tilt my head back toward the kitchen.

"If you don't mind saying hi. And there's plenty of Thai food, if you want some."

"Of course." She slips off her coat, draping it over one arm. "I'm not super hungry, but thanks. If you have tea or something, that'd be good."

She follows close behind me into the kitchen, where Mom and Dad are openly demonstrating the horrible acting genes they passed on to me. They've very loudly and obviously picked up in the middle of a forced conversation, playing the role of "definitely not eavesdroppers."

"Mom, Dad, this is Ellie. Ellie, this is my mom and dad." I box up my leftover curry and stow it in the fridge, exchanging it for a can of lime LaCroix. "We're just going to study up in my room, if that's okay."

"You have a lovely home," Ellie says, and I realize she's slipped back into actor mode, pretending this is her first time standing in this ready-to-sell kitchen. To *her* parents, we're a couple; to mine, near strangers. The truth is somewhere in the middle.

"Nice to meet you, Ellie. Murph, remember, showings start tomorrow." Mom tries to cover her nerves with an extra dose of excitement in her voice. "I'm not sure if Murphy mentioned that we're selling the place."

Ellie nods, jutting a thumb back toward the door. "I saw the FOR SALE sign in the yard but . . ."

"It's fine, Mom," I interrupt. "We're just studying, not finger painting."

I pull one of a dozen identical light-pink mugs from the cabinet, fill it with water, and pop it into the microwave, prepping Ellie's tea. Maybe it'd be classier to get the teapot out, but I don't see a need to spend more time in the kitchen than we absolutely have to. We can discuss the whole moving fiasco upstairs, I guess. I can't wait until I don't have any more urgent, dramatic news to fill anyone in on.

In the drawer beside the coffee maker, I find a small collection of tea bags organized alphabetically. "Caffeinated or decaf?"

"Decaf," Ellie says. "But I don't care what kind. Thanks."

"So you're in Murphy's accounting class? Or no?" Mom asks, propping her chin in her hand with feigned curiosity. She already knows she's not in my class. She's just digging for dirt.

"No, but my mom . . ." Ellie's eyes widen and dart toward me.

"Her mom is my professor," I explain. No more lying, if I can avoid it. Only exclusion of specific details from here on out.

"Oh?" Dad sets his fork down with a clatter, suddenly intrigued. "So you've got the inside scoop, huh?"

"I wouldn't say that," Ellie admits, adjusting her septum ring. "I'm just trying to help."

When the microwave beeps, I take out the mug, tear open the little paper packet housing the tea bag, and drop a pouch of lemon ginger tea into the steam. I set it on the counter next to Ellie's hands, which are slowly returning to a normal color. "We'll be upstairs studying if you need us."

With beverages of choice in hand, I tip my head toward the stairs, urging Ellie to follow.

"Nice to meet you both," Ellie says, waving to my parents with a tiny wiggle of her fingers.

"You too," Mom says with a genuine smile, then turns to me with that same smile, plus a hint of warning in her eyes. "Don't mess up the staging, please."

I lead Ellie up the stairs and to my room, which doesn't look much like mine anymore. Chess pushed my bed to the opposite wall and dressed it up in an ultrabright white comforter quilted with small olive-colored pom-poms. An old teddy bear from the depths of my closet sits in the center of the bed, cozied between two slate and pale-green throw pillows. I move one of the pillow tassels out of Teddy's face. I wouldn't want to block his view of Ellie, who is trailing her fingers along my desk. It's one of the few elements of the room that still truly feels like mine, and a shudder rolls through me just watching Ellie's fingers trace the width of it. "This is so bizarre," Ellie murmurs, barely choking back her judgment. She lingers on the faux-watercolor print above the bed. It's a baby elephant spraying water into the air from its trunk. Adorable, but hardly my style. "Are you sure this is the same room I saw the other day?"

"They had it staged for showings," I explain.

"Right." She nods slowly. "And since when are you moving?"

"Since my parents came back from Florida with a new condo and a mission to complicate my life."

Her brows knit together. "You're moving to Florida?"

"*They* are moving to Florida," I correct her. "I'm moving . . . somewhere else."

"Around here? Or around Champaign? Or are you gonna just jump straight to Chicago?"

"Try option D: not yet known," I say. "I'm focused on the test and not regressing back to third-grade Murphy while living in this eight-year-old's room."

"It could be worse," she says. "They could've staged it with bunk beds."

"That would've been fine," I say, "because I'd have dibs on top bunk."

Ellie sits on the edge of the bed, and I'm a little fonder of the unfamiliar comforter just by its proximity to her. "Green. Gender neutral. Love it." She pinches and flicks one of the pom-poms in a way that probably isn't supposed to be sexual. Probably. Every bone in my body is begging me to sit down next to her and pick up where we left off in her father's garage. The days of buildup between then and now make having her here—*in my bed*—feel all the more intense. I want to know how it feels to lie beside her—on a real bed, not an air mattress—without liquor or second-guessing in the way. But as bizarrely turned on as I am by the way she's rolling that pom-pom between her fingers, I'm equally turned off by the thought of failing this class two semesters in a row. I shake my head to clear it and focus my energy on organizing my flash cards. "Are you down to quiz me?"

Ellie's brows pinch together momentarily before settling into a look of sheer disbelief. "Oh, we're actually going to study?" she asks. "I thought that was like . . . code."

I swallow. "For?"

"You know." She smirks and flicks a pom-pom again. Of course I know, and she's not helping me shake the thought.

"Tempting," I admit, "but my parents are downstairs."

"We can be quiet."

I can *feel* myself go red. "I *believe* your end of the deal was to help me pass this class." I shuffle my note cards like a classic fifty-two-card deck. They snap and thwack against one another in that satisfying way that as a kid I practiced forever to achieve.

"Buzzkill," Ellie grumbles.

"I'm no happier about this than you are. Now pick your poison: flash cards or study guide?"

I join her on the edge of the bed, keeping a healthy distance for both of our sakes, but I can still feel my heartbeat in the arches of my feet. I run her through all of my study methods—mind mapping, online quizzes, the audio recording on my phone. Each has brought me varying levels of success. "You're working really hard on this, huh?" Ellie says, sounding impressed. "Did you do all this stuff last semester?"

I shake my head. "None of it."

"Why not?"

"Because I would've needed over a hundred on the final to pass," I explain. "There was no point."

"You could've done it and asked for extra credit," she points out.

"Which is what Kat did," I remind her. "But as you may remember, your mother plays favorites, and she isn't a fan of mine."

"*Wasn't* a fan of yours," she corrects me, scooting farther back on the bed and lying down so she's ear to ear with the teddy bear.

"Right." I scoot up next to her, simultaneously wishing for more and less space between us. I pass off the stack of note cards. "I actually think she might've bumped my grade."

"Yeah?" Ellie lifts a brow. "Why do you think that?"

"I thought I needed a ninety-eight on the final, but then I talked to her and she said I needed an eighty-nine. So either she likes me and she changed it, or I miscalculated and I'm bad at math."

"The second one," Ellie says flatly. "You're definitely bad at math."

I'd push her off the bed if it wouldn't mean cleaning up all my note cards. At least it'd be an excuse to touch her. My fingertips go hot, begging me to thread them into her hair and pull her close. But I shouldn't. "I'm still not sure I'll pass," I say, clearing the stubborn, needy feeling from the base of my throat. "Eighty-nine is still tough."

"But you can do it," Ellie waves the stack of note cards in the air like a cheerleader rooting for Team Murphy. "You're going to pass, and everything's going to be fine."

"No, everything's not going to be fine," I argue. "Even if I pass, I can't transfer till next fall, remember?"

Ellie rolls onto her side, propping her head up in her hand. It's very *Draw me like one of your French girls*, and it's not helping my focus. "So you transfer next fall," she says plainly. "You'll still get a whole year with Kat. That's good, right?"

"Well, yeah." I chomp down on my thumb, getting a good taste of hangnail. "But I'm not going to have a home in a month or two, so long as tomorrow's showings go according to plan, and I'll be staring down the barrel of a twelve-month lease here in Geneva that I'll have to buy my way out of just to transfer to U of I." The words pour out like water, a river of worry flowing between us. I thought I knew how much anxiety was bottled inside me, but now that it's spilled out, I feel like I might drown in it. Quietly and with as much steadiness as I can muster, I tack on one additional thought. "Plus you won't be there next year. Which sucks."

"What if we just focused on one thing at a time?" Ellie suggests with a calmness I instantly tether myself to. "One flash card." She plucks a card off the stack and holds it up. *Diversification* is scrawled across it in black ink. An easy one.

"Diversification. That's when you spread your assets around into different investments to lower risk," I rattle off.

Her mouth ticks up. "See? One down." She sets it facedown on the bed, then holds up another card. This one I get wrong, along with the next three. My fingernails dig tiny little crescent moons into my palms.

"One at a time," she reminds me, straightening the small stack of cards I've gotten wrong. "You can manage that, right?"

"Right," I say. After all, I'm talking to the woman who convinced me I could pull off an elaborate lie in front of her entire family. If anyone can fool me into believing in myself, it's her.

We work our way through the stack of flash cards, gradually shifting closer together as we do. If my answer isn't letter-perfect to the definition on the note card, the whole thing goes in the "wrong" pile. I swallow my arguments and keep going. Ellie is slow and deliberate and committed to the details, just like she was while making puppy chow. One card at a time. One vocab word. One practice question. One inch closer to her on the bed as I resituate, shifting a pillow beneath my head or reaching to move the teddy bear out of the way of the expanding "right" stack, not so subtly brushing my hand against hers as I do. Maybe no one is flicking each other's pom-poms, but just being close to her like this is magic in its own right. Whether or not we're close next year, whether or not we're living in the same state or on the same wavelength as to what we are—friends, girlfriends, somewhere blurred in between—I like taking it one thing at a time with her.

Somewhere between midnight and morning, I blink out of a sleepy haze to the sound of gentle snores and all the lights still on. I don't remember drifting off or whether we got through the full stack of flash cards before I slipped away to dreamland, but beside me, Ellie sleeps soundly, her mouth hanging open an inch and a flash card still pinched between her thumb and forefinger. I breathe the smallest laugh through my nose. Not even in my dreams could I imagine something as perfect and downright wholesome as the two of us studying until we both fell asleep. Slowly, I peel myself off the bed, but I pause before my feet hit the floor. I don't want to risk waking Ellie up before I get a chance to fully soak in this moment—the flutter of her lashes while her eyes stay closed, the pinch of pink on her cheeks that shades in the space between her freckles, and most of all, the warmth of knowing that, of all the places she could choose to be, she's right here by my side tonight. I press every detail between the pages of my memory, then tuck this moment away for safekeeping. I'm not sure when—or if—she and I will have another one like it.

I clean up the flash cards, then tiptoe across the bedroom to flip off the lights. Feeling my way through the dark is a lot harder now that the furniture has been rearranged, but by the time I'm back in bed, my eyes have adjusted enough to make out the outline of the woman beside me. I can't resist pressing a kiss against her cheek—one small, delicate kiss, but it's enough to stir her. Ellie groans and drapes one sleepy arm over me, pulling me against her until I'm nested in the curve of her hips. She's the smallest big spoon there ever was, but we fit like this. My breath hitches for a moment; then I align the rhythm of my breathing with hers, each inhale and exhale in perfect synchronicity. I'm certain she's drifted back to sleep until I feel her lips brush against my neck, and my heartbeat quickens. I can feel hers speed up, too, knocking against my back like a visitor asking to be let in. I answer with a tilt of my hips, rocking back into her in time with our breaths.

"Mm." Her low, sweet hum of approval vibrates through me. "Mm-hmm."

"Mm-hmm?" I ask. A question posed wordlessly.

"Mm-hmm," she replies, and her fingertips find the button of my jeans just as I misplace my breath. It crosses my mind that I should stop falling asleep in all of my clothes, but the thought evaporates the moment my button gives way to her fingers. There is no should. Not now. There's just me and Ellie and the warmth of her touch sweeping against the sensitive skin above where I want her most. I rock into her again, hoping the tilt of my hips will guide her hand lower. Her throaty laugh hums against my shoulder. "Yeah?" She whisper-asks. "Can I?'

"Yes." My voice flutters. "Please."

When her hand slips behind my zipper, I close my eyes, and all I can see is blue. Blue like her eyes and the nail polish on her fingertips, stroking and circling and exploring how to best make me tremble. Blue like the first sign of morning in the sky, which creeps up the horizon with the promise of a damp new day. It's blue when she touches me, but what color am I for her? There'll be time to find out later; for now, Ellie asks the questions.

"Can these come off?" She tugs on my belt loop like she's

done a dozen times, but this is different. More eager. My heart tugs back as I jolt upright and start working my jeans over my hips. Midshimmy, I catch the early glow of sun warming the edges of the curtains, and for a moment, I hesitate. The responsible thing to do would be to cut this short and go back to sleep so I'm well rested for my test tomorrow—or rather, my test today—but I've been responsible all week, and I've got a dozen different study methods to prove it. I bite my cheek and bargain with a better version of myself: a few more hours of sleep won't make or break my grade, and my grade won't change the transfer deadline or keep my parents from selling the house. I can feel my priorities shifting like tectonic plates migrating toward a certain earthquake. As they collide, I yank my jeans over my feet and fling them somewhere into the dark.

Ellie giggles, then pulls me by the forearm back onto the pillows and into a long, dizzying kiss, the kind that makes me shudder and confirms I chose correctly. We're not in her father's garage anymore, sneaking victory lap kisses before dinner. This is fervent and frantic, open-mouthed and honest. Ellie kisses me like she needs to, and thank God, because I need it too. I need her palm on my jaw and the cool bump of her septum ring against my upper lip. I need her soft hair tickling my cheeks, even when I have to pull away to pinch a stray blonde strand off my tongue. We laugh and pick up where we left off, just the way I need us to. As long as Ellie is touching me, I have proof she's here with me, and that's what I need the most.

Ellie's fingers wander between my thighs again, and she falls into a gentle rhythm, tracing slow, sleepy circles that pick up speed each time I gasp. She touches me so sweetly, so expertly, that I almost forget my body is new to her. A moan spills like warm honey from my mouth into hers.

"Shh." I feel her smile spread over my lips as her fingers drift back north, cuing my hips to buck without my permission. I'm not choosing anymore, only reacting. My body tenses and rolls against hers in waves that match the rhythm of her fingers, and I don't notice I'm approaching the edge until I'm gazing out over it, trembling and triumphant as I dive into the blue.

A good amount of time elapses before I can find a normal breathing pattern, but Ellie's still holding me when I do. She kisses my nose and forehead before landing on the top of my head, nuzzling into my hair. "So that's what I had in mind when you invited me over to study," she murmurs.

I trace my lower lip with my tongue. My room isn't quite as dark as when we started, but I'd barely call it morning. My exam is still hours away.

"Take your pants off," I say. "We've got a lot more studying to do."

twenty-five

❄

was right from the start—Ellie and I are not the stuff of Hall-mark movies. No Hallmark executive would've green-lighted what just happened in my childhood bedroom under the su-pervision of a teddy bear and a watercolor elephant. Now, Ellie and I are starfished as much as my full-size bed will allow, both of us entirely spent and baking in the tiny bit of sun that's fought its way through both the cloud cover and the curtains. It's early, and I'm exhausted, but I wouldn't trade a second of this for a full night's sleep.

When my panting slows to nice, even breaths, I break the si-lence with a question. "Are accidental sleepovers our thing now?"

Ellie laughs through closed lips. "Who said this was acci-dental? I fully planned on winding up in your bed. I thought we were on the same page until you brought out the flash cards."

I turn my head to the side and see that Ellie has already done the same; we're nose to nose, bathing in each other's morning breath, but neither of us seems to mind. "So this was all part of your master plan, huh?" I squeeze her side, and Ellie squeals, swatting my hand away. So she's ticklish. Noted.

"I didn't have a plan," she says. "Just a lot of hope." She laces her fingers into mine as a preventative measure against further tickling, but the warmth of her palm feels more like a prize than a punishment. In another life, maybe I'll be the type of person who can bask in this glow without analyzing it to death, but right now, I can't be. Especially not with Ellie heading back to Champaign today. We have so little time, and I'm not wasting any more of it wondering where we stand.

"So," I say, "what do you think?"

Ellie shifts, and the sheets rustle beneath her. "What do you mean?"

"You know. What do you think about . . . this?" I sweep my one free hand through the air, gesturing to our sweaty, bare legs, but also to the events of the last hour. Or several hours. I haven't checked the time. "Was this a one-time thing, or . . . ?"

"I told you that I don't do the casual thing," Ellie reminds me.

"You also told me you weren't looking for anything at all," I say. "And I think this qualifies as something."

"Of course it's something," she says. Her face softens with sincerity. "I told you already. I like you, Murph."

"I like you too, Ellie." It feels like too shallow a word. I'm interested in her. I'm curious about her. About us and what we could be. "But, like, that was all said before . . . this." I sweep my hand through the air again, retracing the same path as before. "What does this mean?"

She sits up, letting go of my hand, and looks up at the ceiling. "I think . . . it means . . . I *really* like you." There must be bad news hovering above us because, when Ellie's eyes come down to meet mine, she looks worried. "There are a lot of moving pieces though. You don't know where you'll be next semester, and I don't know where I'll be next year. Even if we tried to make a plan, we'd probably end up needing to change it."

I nod along as I sit up beside her. I'm no stranger to a changed plan.

"But I like who I am when I'm with you," Ellie goes on. She nuzzles into the crook of my shoulder, and I breathe in the familiar scent of grapefruit. "I liked the Thanksgiving trial run of what we could be. I like thinking about going to Pride and Cubs games with you. I like kissing you." She looks up at me with sultry eyes and a hint of a smirk. "I really, really like kissing you."

"I like kissing you too." I lean over and press my lips against her forehead, just to prove it.

"And my mom likes you. My aunt likes you. My dad is obsessed with your entire existence. There's just so much we don't know." She drums her fingers against the exposed stretch of skin beneath the hem of my T-shirt before sighing and pulling away, taking my hand again with a smile too small to grant me dimple privileges. "I'm excited about you, Murphy, but I feel like we need more time, and I'm not sure if we're going to get it."

There's a whine trapped deep inside me that I'm dying to let out. I'm too old to be feeling like this, like a little kid who won't necessarily get her way. I've been feeling that way a lot lately. Childish, but not wanting to be. Ready to be better. Ready to grow up. "I just can't believe I fucked up the U of I application," I grumble. "If I'd just gotten it in on time, we'd have a semester together to figure it out."

"You can't keep beating yourself up for something you can't change, Murph," Ellie says, squeezing my hand for emphasis. "It would've been amazing to be in the same place, but then what? Maybe I'm not moving to New York, but I'm not staying in Champaign either. If it wasn't this, it'd just be something else down the line."

"Cool, so it's just always gonna be hard," I say. "Gotcha."

"Drama queen." Ellie's smile stretches, and her dimple barely pokes through.

"I love your dimple," I say. "Have I told you that?"

"Yeah? It shows up a lot when you're around."

Our tender moment is squashed flat by the thunk of pounding on the door. "Thirty minutes until we need to be out!" Mom shouts in a voice that I think she thinks is cheerful but comes across in the key of panic. Ellie and I both jolt all the way upright, and my heart high jumps to the base of my throat. Thirty minutes? That can't be right. The sun is barely up. I snatch my phone off its charger just in time to watch the time roll over to 9:01. Shit shit shit. How the fuck did I not hear my alarm? Or did we doze off before I remembered to set one?

"Thirty minutes!" Mom calls again. Twenty-nine minutes, technically, but it hardly feels like the time to mention it. "Are you up and moving?"

"I'm up!" I shout back. "I'm moving!" I leap out of bed so it's not technically a lie. Ellie's right behind me, springing into action. While I dig through my mostly empty dresser and start drafting an apology to my optometrist for yet another night sleeping in my contacts, Ellie gets to work making the bed in a

Chess-approved way, arranging the throw pillows while I put in a fresh set of dailies.

"I'm gonna finish getting ready in the bathroom," I say, checking our time as I bolt toward the door. It's 9:06. Shit. "Do you mind picking up in here while I—"

"I've got it." Ellie dismisses me with two flicks of her wrist. "Just go."

I bolt down the hall, moving so fast I accidentally slam the bathroom door behind me. Brush teeth, wash face, dry shampoo, done. After hitting a PR on my morning routine speed run, I stumble out of the bathroom and into a version of my bedroom that almost looks better than when Chess set it up. Not a pom-pom out of place. "You're a lifesaver," I say, squeezing Ellie's hand extra tight. She squeezes back even tighter.

"What do you need?" Her still-sleepy eyes dart around the room. "Study guide? Phone charger?"

I wave her off between swipes of deodorant. "I've got it. Just hand me my backpack."

She does, and I start clearing away all final, lingering evidence that I have ever lived here. Laptop charger, phone charger, headphones—it all gets swept into my backpack along with my flash cards and laptop. I need to go straight to Sip after my final; they'll just have to deal with the fact that I'm in the same clothes as yesterday. While Ellie grabs her mug and my half-empty LaCroix from last night, I give the room a quick Febreze, just to be extra safe. "All right," I sigh, "good enough. Let's get the hell out of here."

I practically fall down the stairs to the kitchen, where Ellie calmly buses her mug while I pour frantic gulps of cold brew straight out of the bottle and down my throat. Today's breakfast of champions gets scooped right from the cereal box, and I hold my hand beneath my chin like I'm a horse at a trough, munching up Cinnamon Toast Crunch. Over the sink, of course, to avoid risk of my parents disowning me. Naturally, I'm licking cinnamon sugar off my palm when I spot a stranger in a golf shirt staring back at me from the living room. Oh right. The other realtor.

"Good morning," Tom greets me in a singsongy voice, and I try to smile and chew at the same time.

"Morning," I say through a mouthful of cereal. "Just finishing up. We'll be out in a sec."

I'm still rinsing cinnamon sugar from my fingers when Mom and Dad walk in, bringing with them an energy that splits the difference between Ellie's calm and my utter distress.

"Good morning!" Ellie says in the sort of genuinely cheerful voice Mom tried to emulate earlier.

"Good morning, Ellie," Mom says, remembering her name by some miracle.

Dad tips his invisible hat. "Morning."

Neither of them bat an eye at my overnight guest, and in the throes of this nightmare, it feels like a moment of pure grace. That moment ends when I check the time. It's 9:26. We've gotta bounce.

After several apologies for drinking straight from the bottle of cold brew, I shove my arms into my jacket, sling my backpack over one shoulder, and hug Mom and Dad goodbye. We don't usually hug before I leave the house, but today feels different. I tell them each individually that I love them, and when they say it back, they tack on a "good luck."

"It was lovely to meet you!" Ellie shouts from the front door, waving with one hand and pulling her beanie down over her bangs with the other.

"You too, sweetheart!" Mom shouts. "Drive safe!"

Only then does it occur to me that Ellie and I are getting into separate cars, and a new brand of panic spills over my nerves. By the time I'm out of my exam, I'm sure she'll be halfway back to U of I.

"Ellie, wait." I catch her arm just as we step outside. "Can we finish our conversation from earlier real quick?"

"We don't have time," she reminds me. "How far is Weymouth from here? Ten minutes?"

"Fifteen."

"Shit, Murph, you have to go! "

"And if we don't talk about this before my test, I'll be distracted and fail," I say. "So can we just talk?"

Ellie claws her phone out of her pocket and checks the time. "One minute. We have literally one minute. Shoot."

I suck in a wobbly breath, steadying my gaze on her wide blue eyes. They stretch a little more, urging me to say something. Time is going too fast. "What you said earlier about this . . . us . . ." I pause, trying to make sense of what I'm even saying. "I know we need more time and—"

"There's no time," she says, and I nod, because it's true, but God I wish it weren't. I wish we had all day, all month, the rest of the year. I wish we had next semester together at U of I. I wish we had three years together back in high school. Ellie takes both of my hands in hers, her cold little thumbs tracing twin hearts on the space between my thumb and forefinger, grounding me. "Murphy," she says. "Whatever happens next for us—"

"Murphy!" My mother's voice yells from near the garage. "You've got us blocked in, honey!"

Shit. I forgot my parents need to get out of here too.

"TWO SECONDS, MOM!" I yell back. Ellie's grip loosens, but I know she won't let go.

"Listen," Ellie says, "I'm willing to try long distance, no matter what that looks like." She pauses, then adds, "I mean, so long as you want that too."

"I do," I say. "I want that. I want us, even if it's not perfect."

Ellie smiles coyly as her fingers wrap a little tighter around mine. "It doesn't have to be perfect to be good," she reminds me.

When she kisses me, it's both.

epilogue

❄

Daley Plaza twinkles and glistens beneath a light dusting of snow, the honking of holiday traffic putting up a fight against the murmur of tourists, the crooning of carolers, the *ding dong, caution, doors are about to close* of the L train above. It is, as the carol says, Christmastime in the city, and Daniel, Kat, Ellie, and I are just four more windburnt faces in the Christkindlmarket crowd.

"Found a table! Over here!" Kat shouts, waving one gloved hand in the air. During peak market hours, a table where you can set down your mulled wine is a hot commodity, but Kat was determined to snag one, even if it meant throwing elbows in the crowd. Luckily, the bright-red sleeve of her puffer jacket makes her easy to spot when she gets a few steps ahead, which she always does.

I lace my gloved fingers into Ellie's, pulling her behind me as we shoulder through the crowd and toward our friends. When we reach their table, we're just in time to see Kat tossing a candied pecan into Daniel's open mouth. They both throw their arms up in victory as he chews it to a pulp.

"You're going to hit someone," I warn her, snagging a handful of toasted nuts from the overflowing paper cone Kat splurged on. Might as well eat them while they're warm.

"No, it's okay, we practiced this in the music building with grapes," Daniel says. "We're experts. See?" He takes a step back and opens his mouth again, and, as if on cue, I witness a nearby caroler in authentic German garb get hit in the braids by an airborne pecan. Kat blushes and looks away, feigning innocence.

"Rough throw," Ellie laughs. "Maybe Murph can give you pitching lessons." She pinches a sugar-crusted almond from my palm and pops it between her lips.

"I don't know what you're talking about," Kat insists, her wide eyes darting from side to side. "I wasn't throwing anything."

"Don't listen to her, sweetie," Daniel slurs, pulling his girlfriend against him and repeatedly kissing the headband of her earmuffs. "You're a perfect pitcher, just as you are."

We all laugh, Daniel included. Unlike the last time the four of us were together, public transit has him off the hook as designated driver, and tipsy Daniel is more fun than I could've imagined.

"Are we still thinking we'll catch the 6:05 train?" Ellie asks, checking the time on her phone. "I'm trying to decide if I want another drink or not."

"Yes to both," I say. We're destined to be the drunk, irritating tourists every commuter desperately wishes they could push out onto the tracks. I'll feel guilty about it next year, when Ellie is one of those commuters, traveling back and forth from her grad program at the School of the Art Institute of Chicago. As lukewarm as she is about moving back in with her parents, I'm twice as excited to know she'll be nearby for the full duration of her three-year program. I pinch my credit card out of my pocket and rally the troops for another mug of mulled wine. "Who else needs a refill? Daniel?"

He pretends to think on it for a moment. "I guess if everyone's getting another round, I probably should."

"Of course you should!" Kat interrupts. "It's Christmas!" Quite the vote of confidence from someone who doesn't celebrate. Also, it's December 29, but close enough. The week between Christmas and New Year is a blur of booze and baked goods anyway. What's another twelve-dollar mug of wine?

Daniel and Ellie hold down the fort while Kat and I slip off to grab another round. It gives us a chance to catch up on our respective pieces of big news: for her, Christmas with Daniel's family. For me, the new downtown Geneva apartment Brooklyn and I just signed a lease on. Two beds, two baths, and only three blocks from both Sip and Monarch, the first two official clients of Murphy Konowitz Marketing. Or at least they will be official once the LLC filing is done.

"I'll drink to that," Kat says, lifting her fresh mug of wine and sliding her credit card to the woman at the booth. "This round's on me."

I don't bother arguing. Call it reimbursement for Blackout Wednesday.

When we return to the table with refills, I set my mug down and tug the glove off my right hand. I'm risking frostbite just to thumb in my phone password and refresh my email for the tenth time in thirty minutes. Just like the last nine times, there's nothing new. I open a tab and check the Weymouth Student Portal, just in case. Still nothing. Back to my email app. This time, the bold text of a new message stills my heart in my chest for half a second until I realize it's not what I'm looking for. It's a message from Carol, sending feedback on the New Year's content I sent over for Monarch last night. From what I can see of the preview text, it looks like she has mostly positive things to say, as usual. Working with her the past few weeks has been both a fun challenge and a comfortable bump in my bank account for Christmas gifts. If things keep going this well, I'm planning to ask Carol if she'll sponsor our rec league softball team this spring. "The Monarchs" would be a pretty sweet team name.

"Hey, Murphy, would you remind me what time your final grades get posted?" Kat asks.

"Five." I refresh my inbox again to the tune of group laughter. "What?"

"She was kidding, sweetie." Ellie presses a kiss against the apple of my cheek. "You've brought it up a couple of times."

"Sorry, sorry." I stuff my phone back into my coat pocket and slip my hand back into its glove, bending and straightening my fingers to keep them from freezing in place. "I should really get those touch-screen gloves. Or the mittens that fold over into gloves. You know the ones I'm talking about?"

"I bet they sell those here." Ellie cranes her neck, scanning the rows of wooden booths, each one with full shelves glowing beneath a warm, yellow light, filled with German steins, ornaments, and big paper stars I think are meant to be tree toppers.

I'm debating buying one to use as year-round decor in the new apartment. Consider it a housewarming gift to myself.

"Can you get a picture of me and Daniel?" Kat hands her phone off to me, then grabs Daniel by the sleeve of his North Face, dragging him into position next to the Christmas tree. Pressing onto her tiptoes, she plants a kiss onto his windburnt cheek, popping one foot behind her. The stuff of holiday cards. My glove has to come off again, and I do my due diligence as a best friend and snap plenty of photos from all her best angles, high and low. When I hand the phone back to her for approval, she smiles, seemingly satisfied with my work.

"Okay, now you and Ellie." She waves us over to the same spot by the tree. To my surprise, Ellie replicates their pose exactly, taking the same stance Kat did. Tiptoes, cheek kiss, foot pop. Unlike the last photo we took together, I don't risk the candid laughing thing again, but the warmth of her kiss has me smiling like a kid in a yearbook photo. Before she pulls away, my phone buzzes, and Ellie plucks it out of my pocket before I can.

"One new email. Your grade has been updated," she reads in a deep robotic voice.

"Gimme that." I snatch it out of her hands, ditching both gloves this time so my fingers can move twice as fast across the keyboard.

"You really do need those glove mitten things," Kat says. "They're actually a pretty cool invention . . ."

I miss the rest of her explanation on the engineering of convertible mittens because I'm too hypnotized by the loading screen of the Weymouth Student Portal. There has to be a few thousand people at this market, and my service is accordingly shitty. I match my breath to the rhythm of the spinning wheel, and when the page loads fully, my toes go numb beneath multiple layers of wool socks. Here we go. Let's see the damage.

Ellie squeezes my thigh. "We'll make it work no matter what," she says.

I press my tongue against the back of my teeth and pinch the screen, zooming in on my grades for both the final exam and the class as a whole.

Exam grade: 90.1%

Final grade: C

Holy shit, I actually passed.

"SHE PASSED!" Ellie yells directly into my ear. I didn't notice her peeking over my shoulder, but her victory cry is confirmation that I'm not the only one seeing this. I may have snuck through by the skin of my teeth, but I did it. I passed. Ellie grips both my forearms and starts jumping and shrieking in a way I've only seen baseball players do after a World Series win. I jump and shriek right along with her. Because why the fuck not?

"SHE PASSED ACCOUNTING!" Kat shouts over the crowd of market shoppers, who seem ambivalent, if not a little worried. It's embarrassing, but I don't care.

"So, what's next for you?" Daniel asks, and Kat thwacks his arm.

"Would you let her have her moment first?" Kat scolds.

"No, no, it's okay," I say, then squeeze Ellie's arms a little tighter, containing our jumping to more of a bounce so I can catch my breath. The smile on my face, however, is uncontainable. For the first time in years, I'm not afraid to discuss next steps. "What's next is graduation."

Kat flinches. "What do you mean?"

"I'd been waiting to say anything until grades were posted, but I've got enough credits for an associate's degree," I say. "I'm sick of school, and going to U of I would mean more impossible classes on stuff I'll probably never use. So I'm done."

"No shit," Kat says, a flicker of wonder beneath her voice. "And then what?"

I bite my lip to keep my smile from splitting my face clean in half. "And then . . . this. Life. I can just focus on getting more marketing clients and . . . living." I look from Kat to Daniel and finally to Ellie, whose dimple is just barely peeking through.

"You'll still visit next semester, right?" Ellie asks. Her lips twitch with a half smile while I draw in a deep breath, releasing a thick, warm cloud into the bitter December air.

"Of course." I reach for her hand, and my red, frozen fingers perfectly intertwine with hers. "I'll probably visit *too* much. Something has to hold me over till you come back to Geneva." I turn toward Kat with a knowing look. "Plus I've gotta make the trip out for our belated birthday celebration."

"Me and you, kid," Kat says, raising her mug. "Just me and you."

I look from Kat's soft smile to Daniel's tipsy grin, then land back on Ellie. Her big, blue eyes are wet with the threat of tears as she pulls me in, sealing her lips to mine for one long, glorious moment. I'm warm in her arms. I'm safe. I'm home. When she breaks our kiss, my lips fumble around what I want to say. We're still a long way from love, but the early stages are undeniable. How do I tell her how grateful I am that she changed all my plans and made living less lonely? How do I thank her for seeing me not just for who I could be, but for what I already am? What do you say when you can't yet say *I love you*?

"You're my favorite," I say, and a smile blooms across Ellie's face like the first day of spring.

"Yeah?" she says. "You're my favorite too."

ACKNOWLEDGMENTS

No one writes a book alone—except for the acknowledgments. This part is a solo project, so wish me luck out here on my own.

Thank you to Dana Murphy and Nidhi Pugalia, who saw the good in this book and in me. Thanks to the entire team at Viking Penguin, of course. Specifically, thank you to Brianna Lopez, Colin Webber, and Katie Smith for making this book look good; to Jane Cavolina and Nicole Celli for catching my mistakes; and to Rachel Wainz, Chantal Canales, Mary Stone, Julia Rickard, and Kristina Fazzalaro for getting this book out there. Thanks beyond measure to Andrea Schulz. From our very first call, I knew Penguin was home. What a dream to work with you all. Can't wait to do it again.

I cannot waste another second before I thank Laura and Lauren Skaar. I am forever grateful you two came into my life at exactly the right time—after the book was written, but just in time to cheerlead, support, and shape the Gay Geneva Book (GGB). To have met you at all is a hallelujah; to be your friend is an amen.

Thanks to Rachel, Caitlyn, and Ella for being early eyes on this thing, and to my assistant/friend/babysitter (of me, not of any children), Cristina. You are the only reason I have not fallen apart, and no one understands my brain like you. We both know that I would be, in the most literal sense, lost without you.

Many thanks to Mom and Dad, obviously, and to John, without whom the book couldn't have happened. Let me say that again: Thank you, John. Thank you. Your love is the stuff of stories, and I live only to reflect it back to you.

Thanks to Al, who taught me how to read and cracked my brain open so I could write this thing. To K, Gray, C, and Connor, who talked me into quitting my job when I needed to write, but to Connor especially. Forever to Connor. We were so lucky to have each other, and we still do, and we still are. I am forever your better so long as you're my best.

Thank you to Mike Fonk, Molly Fonk, Liz Koskiewicz, Anne Malecki, and Meaghan Pauli, all of whom made writing dynamic characters and convincing dialogue easy. Thank you to Sean Qualls for explaining how to smoke a turkey; to Evan Wiseman for all the inside baseball; to Jeff Bishop and Hershel Bhat for the U of I intel; to Alex and Aubrey, who were good to me during the toughest parts of the revising process; to Dr. Tusken and Mrs. Finatri for sending me to creative writing camp in 2009 when I was technically too young to go; to Renae DeLucia for supporting me in writing romance before anyone else did; and to Victoria—always to Victoria—for constantly reminding me that women can do anything.

Thank you to the city of Geneva, Illinois, for all the inspiration. Special thanks to Harvey's Tales, Graham's 318 (may she rest in peace), and Cocoon, and to Geneva High School, duh. Enormous thanks to TikTok, without which I would not have the career I have.

Finally, thank you to every woman I've kissed and the ones who've turned me down on the grounds of being straight, only to come out of the closet several years later. I love you, I resent you, but mostly, I am proud of you.